DELTANDER

CATHERINE MINTZ

www.copper-publishing.com

Cover design by Catherine Mintz
Copyright 2020 by Catherine Mintz

ISBN 978-0-9839589-6-3

As mist, rain, frost, snow,
Arrivals and departures
In these floating worlds.

Deltander Permund

I am Deltander Permund.

It is very likely that I am about to die.

After I had written that, I sat and rubbed the smudges from the marking stylus off my fingers. That melodramatic statement seemed all there was to say.

What abominable taste.

Andur sits across from me, back against the wall, steadily working some tag ends of cord. He picks and pries with the tip of his knife, pulling the fibers apart, drawing them free, and joining them into a longer strand as if there were no more important thing in the world. Only his inward-looking expression shows how intently he is listening to the muffled sounds outside.

Teyr leans against the wall next to him, so relaxed that Andur may think he is sleeping. But I can see the moving glitter of his eyes under lowered lashes. Teyr, too, is listening. Of the three of us, he has the most to fear. Andur and I may be killed in the first rush of the mob. They will take Teyr alive.

I think I could kill him first.

I won't have to try: Andur and I silently agreed some time ago.

Andur pauses in his fiddling work to check the keenness of his knife; draw its small whet lovingly down it.

And as for myself, I smooth the rough length of packing paper and adjust the sleeve on the tip of the stylus over and over, drawing each letter as if it mattered that this be legible. No one will care. Reading is an antiquarian's skill, and in any case our attackers will burn everything. I am my only critic, and my judgment is suspended for the duration.

I will begin at what I think was the beginning.

It was universal standard year 6239. I was head of a team of negotiators on circuit to settle an accumulation of off-world trade disputes, when we received an emergency request for assistance in resolving a crisis aboard the freighter Aeguit.

The ship was in the vicinity of Ventrubli Corporation's free-fall farm, Holk Station, which reluctantly granted permission to dock, but required the Aeguit *to maintain quarantine. The stipulation was a reasonable one: Holk's crops were susceptible to contamination.*

Once docked, the Aeguit's *crew began to shift cargo into the docking bay. Seeing this on the remotes, station personnel questioned the ship's captain. She said they were making repairs.*

The chief of Holk security, alarmed by the change of story, had a team suit up. When they reached the lock opening on the bay, the Aeguit *broke its moorings and pulled out, rupturing the station hull, damaging station life-support, and abandoning their own on-station personnel. Some of these managed to reach shelter in the cargo warehousing section where they resisted attempts to make them come out and report to Holk authorities.*

When I and my team arrived our ship's life-support systems were parasitized to help stabilize the station's. We were stranded: unskilled and unwanted in the middle of a disaster.

There was a deep rumble through the decking beneath his feet. Deltander braced himself against the cold hull-wall, and waited until the loose cargo stopped shifting. He coughed, then wiped his streaming nose on a once-elegant sleeve. Checking the sensor hung on his belt, he resumed shining his hand light into the docking bay's nooks and crannies. Despite the sharp stench of sealant, the air was fit to breathe.

He shoved a pile of casings aside with his foot and watched them tumble away. He was useless at this, totally ignorant of what to look for, not even knowing what looked normal. His only edge on the situation was the unregulated portable com Beybaken Norrey had pressed on him at the last moment. "Del, if anything looks funny, use it."

Del stroked the pebbled surface of the unit with his thumb. *Everything looks funny, Beyba,* he thought. *I just hope I don't kill us all by missing something.*

He pulled a flagger from the bunch at his waist, ripped the tab, and dropped it on top of a mass of tendrils that was attacking a bale of yellow leaves. *Are the leaves the cargo, or are they fodder for whatever that is?*

Ten strides farther on, Del began moving a crumpled heap of animals with long, sinuous, broken necks, and found a woman, face down, dressed for a party in soft blues and greens. He yanked the tab on another flagger and dumped it next to the body. Then he turned her over, tired of the feel of lifeless flesh.

He unslung the scanner and switched it on, looking at the vista of work-scarred hull and discarded cargo as his fingers tuned the tool's high-pitched whine.

The station contamination seemed intentional; it might be. Competition among the biological consortia was savage. Crippled by the loss of its crops, unable to fulfill its contracts and service its debts, Holk would be an easy takeover target—

The unit gave a steady, shrill tone.

Del positioned the head and activated the scanner, looking away again as it hummed and clicked and made its legal record.

The woman's staring, sightless eyes were a relief. Not all the bodies were cold. Inexperienced, often deceived by his own heartbeat in his fingertips, Del sometimes hoped—until he lifted an eyelid. He let the woman's head back down, absently pillowing it on her arm.

Eyes narrowing in thought, he powered down the scanner.

The situation seemed too chaotic to be a planned maneuver. Perhaps the *Aeguit* really had required negotiators before everything went out of control.

It is possible, thought Del, getting to his feet and considering a pile of scaly carcasses as he reslung the scanner, *it is possible that the* Aeguit *specialized in semi-legal cargoes. Goods legal at the point of origin, but banned at their final destination. There could be a lot of credits in that, and ample reason for a crew to quarrel.*

Abandoning speculation, Del put a shoulder to the pile and shoved. It didn't even sway. The massive bodies formed an impenetrable wall. Instinctively Del distrusted it. Most of the *Aeguit*'s discards had been

9

piled as convenience dictated: higher and deeper near the ship's ports, thinner and more scattered where the work crews had farther to go.

This barrier looked deliberate.

He stood, hands on hips, resting his back a moment, surveying the wall of the docking bay. The distribution of the two types of openings, at first glance irregular, was actually strictly governed by the size of the areas they serviced. The smaller niches for emergency equipment were far more frequent than the deep, high bays for cargo movers. Del counted off the intervals. There should be an emergency niche behind this.

He heaved and heaved again, driving muscles accustomed to the carefully monitored routines of a gym, not the jarring strain of manual labor. Not getting anywhere, he mopped his forehead, shoved back sweat-soaked silver hair. Then he focused his hand light through a gap between two rigid, crooked legs. The vivid orange corner of a loading frame, apparently upright in the niche, was emblazoned on the darkness behind it.

That shouldn't be there.

Del could hear continuous shouting from around the station curve; feel the rumble of cargo movers in the decking beneath his feet. The painfully bright flash of a warning beacon sent blue shadows leaping on the outer hull.

It would take several people to move this pile fast. People were in short supply. Del moved around, shining the light, looking for something to lend credence to his suspicions, anything to justify pulling them off other inspections.

The heap had been created by throwing the bodies against the hull wall while they were still warm and flexible. Everything had sagged anti-spinward, leaving a narrow gap between them and the plating. Del flashed his light into this crevice. It appeared to run all the way through to the blackness of the emergency equipment niche itself.

Del switched off the light to conserve power, hung it on his harness, and began forcing himself between the bodies and the outer wall. Claws extended in death caught and tore at his robe. He slid his head along the cold plates as rough hide scraped his cheek. Inside in the near black he could hear only his own breathing, loud in the enclosed space.

He fumbled the hand light off his harness and turned it on.

The white sole of a bare foot hung in the beam.

Leaning against the wall, Del raised the light.

It was a boy, naked from the waist down, legs streaked with blood and dirt, bound spread-eagle on a loading frame jammed upright between two fire-fighting foamers whose sensors seemed, momentarily, activated, because of reflections from the hand light.

Del raised the light further.

Thick dark hair curtained the profiled face. Del was glad he couldn't see the blank stare of death. The bound hands, purple with congested blood, were still locked around the upper edge of the frame, trying to take the weight off wrists so deeply cut by the binding cords that Del could see only one tag end, ornamented with a drop of blood. As he watched it swelled, broke, and fell into the darkness to hit the decking with a tiny sound.

Hands shaking, Del swept the black fall of hair aside and thrust the hand light almost into the bruised and battered face. He forced an eyelid up with his thumb. The grey iris contracted until the pupil was a pinprick.

Alive.

Del tugged at the upper corner of the frame. The square bar bit into his soft hands. *Slowly*, he told himself, *think it through. Free the ankles first, then the wrists, so you can take his weight—*

He knelt on decking slippery with unknown filth, working with the little knife from his belt pouch, intended for nothing more serious than the colored cords and scented wax of a fashionable gentleman's social correspondence.

The blade snapped.

Del pulled the unfamiliar work laser from its loop, crouched back into the niche. One hand over the boy's face, he aimed, closed his eyes, and fired—through the corner of the frame and into the carcasses beyond. The reek of burned hide made him cough. He threw his entire weight into pivoting the bottom bar.

It cracked at the join and he shoved it out into the shadows clawing wildly at the jagged wall of bodies. Something dead hissed as the hot end pierced it.

He shouldered under the boy, straining to break the upper corner and free the wrists. Del felt a thread of pain snap up his forearm, but

11

the frame gave, and the limp body, heavy for its size, sagged into his arms. He staggered off-balance for an instant.

He shifted his grip, and looked down at the face lit by the reflected glow of the hand light swinging at his belt. High, angled cheekbones and a thin-bridged nose. The mouth was too cut and swollen to see its real shape. Del turned the face into the hollow of his shoulder and leaned against the unyielding bodies, sliding the boy along the outer wall, head and hips protected by Del's arms.

Outside in the glare and clamor, he belatedly crushed the button on the comlink.

"Del?" said Beyba's voice.

"I need a doctor," said Del. He could hear Beyba begin shouting before the connection broke, shut off by the station's emergency override clearing the band for official use. He felt the boy's cheek: far too cool. The damaged docking bay was bitter cold, despite the temporary seals. The chill from the frigid decking cut through his heavy boots. The heat must have failed completely in the insulating ring. Del crouched, balancing the boy's torso across his legs, stripped off his robe awkwardly, and wrapped the boy in it. He staggered to his feet with the solid bundle, shivering in his thin damp shirt and trousers.

Del could hear the sharp clangor of running feet coming down the workway around the curve of the docking bay even over the deep drone of a repair unit. He watched Beyba's foreshortened figure appear.

Feet.

Long, thin legs. Fluttering robe.

The jiggling little potbelly Beyba always developed when he was too long in space.

Thin, straining arms clasping something to the chest—a medkit, the overhead light reflected off the stenciled symbol.

Then the face, worried even at this distance, topped by an unruly mane of blond hair. Seeing Del upright, Beyba paused, chest working, appraised the obstacles and distance, and began running again at a more measured pace.

His anxious, long-fingered hand gripped Del, as Del, watching the upside-down horizon line, saw the blue and white uniformed legs of a doctor, walking. Walking fast, but walking.

"You're all right," decided Beyba, reaching for the boy, feeling the corner of the jaw. The he picked up a discolored hand, looked at the deeply cut wrist with its bracelet of cord, let it go and peeled back the folds of Del's robe. He saw the naked, soiled hips and legs. His thin-lipped mouth pursed with distaste.

Squatting, Beyba opened the medkit, took out a package and yanked a ring, spilling the inflating carrier onto the decking where it writhed like a live thing until it was full-sized and the containment of the reaction made it rigid.

"Fit him in," said Beyba, looking up the curve of the bay. "I guess she could walk slower," he said sourly, tripping the red tab on a cover.

Exothermic, thought Del. *The blue must set off the endothermic.*

Beyba tucked the cover in, and took the limp hand from Del and slid it under a fold.

Legs stiff, clumsy, Del stood pulling on his robe. He scanned the up-curving mounds of debris for the doctor. Nowhere in sight. She rounded a pile of cargo pods. Del waved both arms, wide. Observed, she quickened her pace.

Del bit back a comment when she walked up. Her eyes were tired, and there was a ragged slash down one sleeve of her dirty, outsize tunic. Seeing the boy, she sighed, sat on her haunches, cut off his jacket, and attached the monitor and support unit without bothering to clean the arm.

The unit's lights flashed on, blinking, red, red, red—

She punched the reset. A few of the lights switched to green, then dropped back to red. She sniffed and fished a perfumed tissue from a pocket. "He's in bad shape. We're to reserve supplies for those that will live until the relief lighter arrives." She wiped her nose again.

"You won't treat him," said Del, incredulous.

She sniffed, blew. "No. In fact," she said, turning the boy's exotic face toward her, considering. "I bet he's," she rolled the upper lip over her forefinger, "a gen."

Del stared at the character string tattooed across the inner lip. It slipped from view as she released her grip. "I'm sorry," she said, standing, suddenly brisk, "it's cargo. I can't treat gene-sculptures."

Del found Beyba was in the way, one hand on his right arm, restraining. "Del."

Eyes on the woman, Beyba sorted through his belt pouch. "We appreciate your coming." He clasped her right hand in both of his. When he released it, she looked furtively into her palm. Her eyes widened. She stooped to gather her things and was prevented by Beyba's left foot sliding her kit out of reach.

"Oh," she said.

Don't look, Del told himself, staring at the monitor unit blinking. Red, red, red. At the edge of Del's vision, Beyba's robe swayed slightly as he stood taller.

The woman stepped back a pace.

It's a criminal matter, thought Del. *The station's under emergency law. You should stop him*. He closed his eyes, willing the words. And still saw the desperate hands locked on the upper bar of the loading frame.

When Del looked up, the woman was gone.

"Let's go," said Beyba, sweeping both medkits into the carrier. "Take the other end."

Del did, asking, "Where?"

"My quarters, I think. We'll—"

There was a distant sound. Beyba stood, mouth opened, eyes flicking back and forth, listening.

"Beyba?" said Del.

"Be still." Beyba lowered his end of the carrier—Del was forced to do the same—and moved cautiously around the nearest heap of cargo pods. The sound came again, and Beyba retreated as stealthily as he had gone. "That's anti-personnel fire."

It was. The distant tock-tock-tock of plastic pellets bursting on hull plate in a spray of fragments was distinctive.

Del had never heard it anywhere but on viddrams. Too soft to damage space-hardened equipment, the pellets punched big, ragged holes in people. He bent as Beyba bent and picked up the carrier.

They paused a moment, linked by their burden, while Beybaken thought.

Beyba looked at Del, started to say something. "Shit," he said. "All right, let's go for—"

A thunderous fusillade drummed and splattered off the hull beyond them.

Beyba raised his voice. "— the CORE!"

14

The station's center—filled with life-support, the intra-level transporters, the main administrative offices—was usually safest.

It was awkward running with the carrier, dodging behind piles of cargo, sidestepping bodies waiting for the disposal teams. It would have been difficult anyway: Beyba was so much taller than Del.

Low frequency shudders through the decking damped out and began again. There was a dull concussion overhead. Del looked up and saw one of the man-size couplers part in a cloud of steam that turned into a fall of ice crystals. Tasting the bitter grains on his lips, he blew and spat. They detoured around a puddle of brown lubricant. Del could see the reflection of the light-grid, curved and distorted as the liquid swelled upward.

Losing heat, losing spin, armed aggressors loose in the docking bay. Del ran hard.

And nearly tripped over himself when Beyba skidded off at a sharp angle to his previous course. Following blindly, Del gave everything he had, conscious of his extra fifteen years, his shorter legs, the burning in his chest. They were in a race where seconds counted, and he was slow—

They passed under the guillotine-panel of the emergency seal as its warning beacon flashed red and a wave of sound hit their faces. Deafened by the massive rumble behind them, they sprinted for the safety of the green beacon beyond. In the agony of effort, Del counted the seconds. They weren't going to make it.

He tried to tell Beyba to let go and save himself, and found he couldn't speak, his breath whistling in his lungs.

Beyba jerked left, thrust forward the ball of his shoulder to bang on a door release. Del followed him through, and almost dropped the carrier to the floor in his haste to turn and slam the close bar.

The thick shelter door muted the high shriek of the life-systems failure alarm to almost nothing. They would be safe here, temporarily. There was a self-contained recycler, a bare minimum of water, air, and heat for at least several days.

Del unlatched his tool-weighted harness and sat on the floor by the carrier, watching spots come and go. Beyba pulled him to his feet again.

"You've got to—keep moving." Beyba's chest heaved. He pumped his arms up and down. "Can't stop—all at once."

Leaning against the wall, mechanically following Beyba's example, Del looked around.

Del wondered if they were going to strain the recycler. It was a small shelter, evidently meant for no more than two people. There was a pair of shelf-like beds with folded disposable covers on them, their sleeping pads encased in something slick-looking that was probably waterproof.

Beyba prodded the material expertly. "Looks like a cheap brothel." He slammed back a cabinet door. "Plenty of liquor—" He opened another. "—and no food." He opened another, crushed a crumpled handful of wrappers together, and threw them into the disposer where they made a brief blue flare.

"They should lock Inte into one of these for a few days." Beyba slammed the doors. "Stupid shit." Beyba prowled the circumference of the room. "He didn't have the brains to post guards. Or keep up the emergency supplies on his fucking station."

Beyba glared at the door.

Doubled forward, Del rubbed his chest without comment. He could feel the alarm through the wall but the sound was muted, fading. The corridor must be losing pressure. It had been a near thing. He coughed and felt the sharp pain in his chest ease.

Beyba gave him a sharp look. "You all right?"

Del nodded. "Nerves."

Beyba slammed the flat of his hand against a cabinet.

Del swallowed a metallic taste, knelt, and tried to wipe the dirt from one of the gen's cold cheeks.

Mouth one tight line, Beyba squatted across from him, checking the support unit, sorting through the colored vials in the medkit. "Del," he said quietly, fingers busy, "it's going to die."

Del made an inarticulate protest, rubbing the other cheek. Most of the dirt was bruises.

Beyba raised one long finger for Del's attention. "They ship gens in a closed environment. Once the seal was broken without their being immunized against local diseases, their chances for survival were no better than fifty-fifty. Once this," Beyba shifted the now-cooling emergency cover over the gen's thighs, "happened—they're effectively zero."

Beyba punched reset and watched the relentless red flicker resume.

16

"Why did you think they killed all those others and dumped them? Millions of credits. It beat waiting for half of them to rot and die on shipboard. And they'd lose a lot of air venting that many bodies."

Del ripped open a cleaning pad and began sponging. The clammy skin was almost transparent with shock.

"Del?" Beyba put one hand on his arm; Deltander shook it off. Beyba pulled one warning-labeled vial out of the kit. "We can get it over with—"

Del looked up and Beyba drew back at his expression. "Fucking romantic," he said, and stood up.

Del watched his own hands move.

"It's not feeling anything. It may not be sentient. Let it die."

Del pressed his lips together.

Anti-personnel fire drumming along the corridor wall made the room's air throb. Beyba went to the door, fiddled, and then punched the com call. He seemed unsurprised when the screen remained blank. He moved around, opening all the cabinet doors, shutting them. He went into the adjoining personal and came back out immediately.

"It'd been dead by now if we'd just left it where it was."

Del looked up.

"The only reason I decided to bring it was it was faster than arguing with you." Beyba's tone softened. He put a hand on Del's shoulder and Del shook it away. "Come on, stubborn, leave it alone."

Del worked on in silence, refolding the pad to a clean surface.

"Del?"

Del remembered the desperate hands, "I have to try." He looked up at tall, frowning Beyba.

Beyba never argued pointlessly. He turned away and shook out a cover on one of the beds, then came and crouched by the medkits, fishing. "I'm putting this one," he shifted the larger kit, "away. For us. The instructions," he flipped a fanfold of plastic leaves onto the other bed, "are there. I'm going to sleep."

There was a long cut running around to the back of the head.

Del delicately parted the hair and dabbed at the crusty edges. It started bleeding.

Beyba sat on his bed, pressing his fingers in his shoulder muscles. "I jimmied the door. It won't open from the outside, and it won't show the room's occupied. If the com comes up, wake me before you answer." He swung his long legs onto the bed. He peered at Del, his eyes highlighted by the high intensity hand light Del had switched on. "Don't take it too hard when it dies, all right? Del?"

Del watched the rusty brown turn to red streaks under his cleaning pad.

Beyba blew a puff of annoyance, and rolled himself into the cover. Presently Del heard his breathing drop into a long, slow rhythm. He had sent himself to sleep.

Del started to tuck the now-cold emergency cover in, and noticed the carrier was starting to deflate. He lifted the gen onto the empty bed, feeling a stab of pain in his forearm, and sat beside. He fanned open the instructions.

The printed information, packed with a portable reader, was a deliberate anachronism, a backup for AI systems failure. There were pictures keyed to symbols to help the illiterate find the most useful material quickly. Del flipped the pages, searching. Although he had a modest collection of manuscripts—some actually on carefully preserved paper—it was strange to be reading modern script in hardcopy. But it was faster than using the reader with its optic unit and voice-in-the-ear.

First, check the monitor display.

Del put the fanfold down.

The only steady green lights were those indicating the intravenous supply was adequate and flowing. Del fumbled with the charts to see what the doctor had given. A diagnostic solution. Nothing else. He was entirely on his own.

Del pulled a discolored hand from under the cover and held it, thinking hard. *Beyba might be right. It might be kinder to let it die.*

He thought of the gen clinging to the frame. It must have known when it was walled up, alone in the dark with the stink of death. It had gone on trying.

Del pressed the cold hand between his own. *They didn't kill it. Which meant they intended to come back?*

He looked at the door, put the hand back under the cover, picked up and reopened his instructions. Beyba would have provided their best defense. And as for the gen—

Del let the pages flip shut, looked at the monitor. He turned the exotic face toward him, feeling the faint moist warmth of the skin. The face was slack with unconsciousness, defenseless, beyond pain.

I'm sorry, thought Del. *I have to try.*

The stiff sheets flipped over regularly as Del scanned headings, read subheadings, sections, cross-referenced. Most of the material assumed the user had the assistance of a diagnostic AI and a vast array of drugs.

What could a DAI tell him that he could use?

Basically all he could do was provide support until the station regained control. The relief lighter should be arriving in a shift and a half.

Del felt the less-bruised cheek. It had warmed to an illusion of health. *That might be fever from infection.* He cursed the seconds that had left them trapped here. In the core, Beyba was perfectly capable of getting medical aid as long as Del looked the other way.

At least, he thought, *I've been spared that choice.*

Del laughed soundlessly at himself. *Problems I'd like to have.*

He smoothed tangled hair off the face, and then moved his puzzled fingertips back and forth. Above the ear, hidden among the finer strands, a tuff of stiff, faintly oily hairs had stained Del's skin. He sniffed his fingers. Sweet, musky.

He rubbed his chilly hands together. The room was becoming colder. He sniffed his fingers again, puzzled, then abruptly decided to deal with the immediate problem.

A few minute's search through the cramped, crowded personal produced extra bedding. Del carried back two covers, threw one over Beyba, who was huddled into a ball, and the other over the gen. Then he went back for a third. Wrapping it around himself coat-wise, Del opened the small medkit Beyba had brought.

It contained a brief version of the instructions he had been reading and a cheap reader. A quick flip-through and Del set that aside. Foam, bandages, salves for the treatment of minor bruises, cuts, abrasions. He could use all that. Pills, liquids, powders for minor discomforts. And a sealed section designed to be opened on command from a diagnostic.

Del put the case on the floor and stepped, once, hard, on the lock. It gave with a satisfying crack and he pried the section open.

There was enough amphotrin to give two full shifts at maximum dose. Amphotrin was considered foolproof, and many, like Del, carried it to self-medicate themselves against the inevitable upsets of travel. He jacked a dose into the monitor and turned it on, full.

He sat tented in his cover for a long time before he dared punch the reset button.

Most of the frantic red flickering had slowed.

But there was one giving the short, short, short of extreme urgency. Del shuffled through the pages, nicking his thumb on a sharp edge, and sat reading as he sucked the welling cut. *Section twenty-eight. Dehydration.*

Del hastily felt under the covers. The inner layer was sodden with sweat.

He rubbed his hand down his face. *Of course. Fighting an infection, there is fever, sweating. Perfectly easy to treat with the proper stuff. Which I don't have.*

Which reminded Del he was thirsty, himself.

Rummaging through the liquor cabinet for a cup—he could never drink from folded dispenser cups—Del found a carton of free-fall bulbs. He juggled the package in his hand. *Worth a try*. He filled the bulb in the personal and carried it back cupped in his hands to warm the icy water.

The gen's mouth was sealed with a line of dried blood. Del had to moisten a fingertip and coax the lips apart. He worked the plastic spout between the teeth, and pressed, gently.

Del, astonished, jerked back as the patient coughed convulsively, and fought to free himself, hands tearing into the covers from underneath. Del could hear the fabric rip.

The stiff hairs had risen, lifting the finer mass of hair and increasing the apparent size of the head. Del could smell the musk. The grey eyes, wide-open and alert for a few moments, went blurry.

Del reached forward tentatively.

The head snapped back, teeth bared in pitiful defiance, then slumped back, unable to hold the pose.

Del reached to support it.

The gen's teeth gripped the soft area between Del's thumb and forefinger. Del felt sick agony up to his elbow. He held very still.

They looked at one another.

Del eased his hand slightly.

The grip tightened. Grey eyes studied him.

With extreme care, Del offered his left hand.

With a disdainful sideways jerk of the head his right hand was released.

Del flexed his hand cautiously, rubbing the reddened marks of teeth: the skin wasn't broken but he'd have a painful bruise.

The gen lay, eyes closing then reopening with an obvious effort of will.

Del retrieved the bulb, dripped water into his own mouth, and then offered the bulb.

The gen bit the spout.

Del tried to free it, then responded to the tug by squeezing. It was an awkward business. The bulbs were designed not to release liquid unless the fluid valve was held open, otherwise the partially pressured areas of free-fall stations would be full of drifting globules of fluid. Between them, they managed.

When the bulb was completely collapsed, the teeth released. The gen shivered all over and huddled under the covers. Del moved the face to look at it again.

An elegant, artificial-looking face. The eyes focused. For an instant, the swollen mouth firmed, and Del had an impression of a fierce will. Then the eyes began to wander again.

Del lowered the head to the cold, slick bed and pulled the covers around. He licked his own dry lips, thinking. What had looked at him might not be human. But he was sure it was sentient. Which raised a lot of questions.

Gene-sculptures were biological constructs for specific purposes, never as long-lived or intelligent as similar truforms. They were expensive: tools for specialized purposes, or toys for a luxury market. Del had never seen or heard of a humanoid gen. There were plenty of human beings, and there were plenty of laws prohibiting human genes in gens.

Mind busy with half-formed thoughts, Del began systematically treating the injuries he could see. There was the long cut in the scalp, bruises down the sides of the throat. Something heavy and flexible had been wrapped around the ribs, once, twice, and left welts spiraling around the torso.

He uncovered the patient, section by section, washing off blood and dirt, foaming out embedded grit, tweezing out the glassy shards of some object that had been crushed when the gen was thrown on top and dragged.

The boy's back was relatively unmarred except for minor scrapes, the extension of the welts around the ribs, and, Del sighed, the blood seeping from between the buttocks, each of which was clearly marked with the livid bruises of a five-fingered grip. It took a lot of numbing gel and a large towel secured with bandage clips before Del went on to the legs.

As he worked, Del noted the differences between them. There were the clusters of stiff hairs and their scent glands, hidden in the hair above the ears. The teeth looked narrower and sharper than the human norm, with a distinct gap on each side of the pointed teeth just back of the incisors in the upper jaw.

Del looked at the bite marks on his hand. He could feel how deeply they had pressed; a dot of blood showed where one had pricked him after all.

The gen's nails had a rib down the middle, underneath, and were hard enough to resist bending, despite their being as long as a gentleman's. The cleft between the great toe and the others was deeper than Del's own. He slid a finger into it, wondering if the boy could grip with it.

The tally finished, Del sat, wiping his hands.

None of the differences were decisive. He had seen human beings who were odder, and heard of others odder still. If it were not for the characters tattooed across the inner lip, this would pass for human.

Maybe it is.

Slavery was, as far as Del knew, universally illegal. Those rich enough to indulge in human servants had no reason to risk the confiscation of their property and its award to the enslaved. *If you a taste for unusual services, your man of business writes a tight contract, and you pay the fee.*

There were always those poor enough and desperate enough to do anything. A lifetime spent negotiating and judging disputes had not left Deltander naive about the aberrations of the powerful and wealthy. He had adjudicated one case of a man agreeing to be murdered for the benefit of a third party. It had been an ugly business, but the contract had been held legal.

Brooding, Del jiggled the useless reset button on the monitor. If this were reading correctly, the boy would be dead. Either the unit was broken, or it was not adjusted to deal with this patient. In any case, its only use was to deliver the drug Del hoped was doing some good.

It was a long shift.

The boy drifted in and out of consciousness, cooperative when he was alert, struggling weakly when he wasn't. Del wiped sweat and brought water, jacked ampoules in and out, and dozed, sitting. A dribble of urine soaking the towel sent Del on a hasty search for a container that culminated with a looped-necked decanter's emptying and abrupt decapitation in the personal. The result won a faint nervous smile from the patient.

"No worse than what was in there," said Del. "These station synthetics—" He hesitated.

The boy looked at him, puzzled, not quite frightened.

Can't understand a word you're saying, thought Del. He pulled the covers back up and went to empty the improvised urinal.

He held the stuff up to light. It seemed dark and cloudy.

Del shrugged and poured it away. He couldn't tell. The testing equipment didn't work; he didn't have anything to deal with the results even if it did. He could hope that plenty of fluids, staying still, and the amphotrin would keep the situation in check for, Del pulled out his chrono, another half shift. Maybe longer if they had to retake the station.

He sniffed himself and wrinkled his nose with disgust.

The face that looked back at him from the videoplane was tired, black eyes bloodshot, the lines from nose to mouth graven deep, silver hair lank. The golden tone of his skin was ashy with fatigue. He needed to wash. The water would be recycled.

Halfway through, Del, cringing from the icy spray of the hand-held cleaner, regretted his decision. The emergency shelter was cold enough as it was. Finished, he rubbed his shivering body with the rough towels and put on two layers of paper bath clothing—his own was damp and filthy.

Clean, dry, wrapped in a bedcover, Del sat on the edge of the gen's bed and listened to the boom, thud, thud of some nearby disturbance. Beyba slept on, his breath bubbling through parted lips.

Del's eyes closed and he jerked himself upright. He would just lie down for a moment—it was cold in his thin clothes, he wouldn't sleep—then wake Beybaken and ask him to help. Rest should have cooled Beyba's temper.

It was almost completely dark when Del woke, feeling a warm stirring on his neck. He could hear the whirr of the in-room heating system switching on in the silence. So power was still on. Beyba must have gotten up and switched off the light, leaving only the permanent glow at the edge of the floor.

He craned his neck to look down at the ebbing and flowing pool of warmth trapped by the edge of the cover spread over him. The gen slept, one fist gripping Del's paper shirt—it had parted at the shoulder seam.

Muzzy with sleep, Del shifted slightly, exploring.

He had both arms tight around the gen, whose battered hands and arms were tucked between them. One foot lay between Del's calves, the other, leg doubled up, pressed against Del's upper thigh. Del could feel the hard, rounded corners of the almost-useless monitor against his chest. Cautiously, not to wake the sleeper, he disentangled the weighted arm, checked the drug supply, and reswaddled the arm in the covers.

The boy was warm, breathing slowly. Del could feel the gen's heartbeat where his hand cupped its nape: faster than his own, but steady. No matter what Beyba said, if help came in time, the boy might live.

Del wanted something to survive the *Aeguit* disaster.

He had never seen anything like the wanton slaughter in the docking bay. It was not just the deaths, but also the cruel curiosity. The bellies carved open, spilling their contents. The woman drowned in her own blood. The eyeless—

Tears of frustration and exhaustion overflowed Del's eyes and ran down his cheeks. He lay, angry at himself, biting his lip, trying not to make a sound. It finally escaped through clenched teeth.

"Del?" Beyba unwrapped himself from his covers with a smooth motion that suggested he hadn't been asleep. He began, gently, to try and separate Del and the boy. "You did everything you could—"

The sound the gen made suggested something with a mean temper three or four times his real size.

Beyba leaped back and hit the wall so hard it boomed. "What the FUCK!" Then, carefully, out of the darkness, "Del?"

"What?" Del was busy holding on. The gen was wobbly but combative.

"Are you all right?" Beyba spoke on the light.

"You startled him."

"No shit," said Beyba, standing with his clenched hands well away from his sides.

"Sit down," said Del irritably, trying to pull the covers up over the boy. Getting chilled would do him no good. "He didn't know you were here."

Beyba sat.

Del coaxed the gen to lie down.

Beyba watched the process with a sort of grim fascination. "Tell me that monitor isn't red all the way."

"I don't think it's working," said Del.

"No shit," said Beyba, again. His expression went ugly. "Lazy whore."

Del soothed stiff hairs down. "Maybe it doesn't work for him."

"It would," said Beyba, "properly calibrated. But that's why she was so sure he wasn't human. Not," he added, standing up, "that a court would accept that. You want a drink?"

"No," said Del. "We don't have anything to eat—"

Beyba poured something into a cup, and sniffed. "We're going to have to live on conrats."

Del gagged involuntarily. He'd smelled the concentrated rations when he'd been looking for the decanter.

Beyba grinned. "Better than nothing. Maybe your little friend will settle for some in place of chewing out my throat." And to the gen, "How about it? You like it dead or is it more fun if it's still wiggling?" He leaned forward, talking into the gen's face, one hand clenched.

The gen gave Beyba a blurry, cautious look, then looked to Del.

"Beyba." Del rubbed the fine hairs at the base of the head, thinking, *Don't mind him, he's embarrassed you scared him.*

Beyba offered a cup of the amber syrup to Del.

Del passed it to the gen, who sniffed suspiciously and waited until Del took and drank his own. The boy had a hard time with the inward-rolled rim of the cup, and, by the way he licked his lips, scraped his tongue against his teeth, he didn't like the taste.

Del didn't either.

Beyba drank his in one steady set of swallows. "Ahh! Tastes just like it looks. Stale piss."

"Beyba," said Del, tiredly. He handed Beyba his empty cup. "The lighter'll be here in another quarter shift."

Beyba said sourly. "We hope."

"Fill this," said Del, offering the free-fall bulb. "He's having trouble drinking."

"Why not just nick a vein? He's already bitten your hand."

"Fill it." Del slid upright. "I'm scared too."

"I'm not." Beyba took the crumpled bulb. "This'll leak, where's the rest of the package?"

Del pointed, and then concealed his bruised hand in the covers.

The gen drank the second dose reluctantly and settled back, fingers locked firmly on Del's shoulder.

Beyba sat down on his bed, elbows planted on bony knees. He looked at Del.

"We're stuck," said Del, with only the faintest hint of a question.

Beyba waved a hand in an indeterminate gesture.

The gen was hunting for a position that wasn't painful.

Del felt the tears start sliding down his face again, and looked away, hoping Beyba wouldn't see. It was just nerves.

Beyba, lost in his own dark thoughts, didn't notice until he got up to get himself a drink. "Del?"

"Just tired." He mopped ineffectually. "I'm all right."

Beyba's long hands coaxed and pulled. "Come on, get up, move over here," Beyba sat Del on the other bed. "I'll get you a drink."

Del shook his head.

Beyba covered the drowsy gen. Very cautiously. "He's asleep. Have a drink, lie down, I'll get you if he wakes up." Beyba pressed a liquor-filled bulb into Del's hand. "Enough to relax you: we may be here a while."

The liquor stung a cut on his lip Del hadn't known he'd had.

"I'll handle things for a while, then the lighter will be here, and it'll all be over except the shouting." Beyba laughed a hard little laugh. "Expensive shouting. There'll be legal reps building fortunes for their grandchildren on this one."

Del smiled too. "One for the histories."

Beyba diluted his drink. "Beginning with my suit for personal endangerment—"

The discussion wound on, stopping, starting, with outrageous claims on the property of any company remotely involved.

The gen sighed, woke, peered at them, and slept again.

They were deep in constructing a case against the doctor, when Del gripped Beyba's arm. "Beyba. What if no one will treat him when the lighter gets here?"

Beyba shrugged free. "We'll try credits."

Uncomfortable, Del looked at his hand around his cup.

Beyba poured two fingers of concentrate and added liquor. He tasted it and coughed. "A waste of bad liquor. I could market this stuff to the penal colonies."

Del didn't respond. He swayed.

"Hey." Beyba put his drink down. "You drunk?"

"No," said Del. The floor seemed to have floated to an immense distance. "Yess," he said, uncertainly. "Beyba?" Beyba maneuvered Del out flat on the bed. *I had less than a cupful*, he thought, staring at the bright pinpoint of light.

Beyba didn't sit down. He paced back and forth, into the personal, out again, holding a wet towel against his face.

That water's awfully cold, thought Del, lost somewhere away from himself.

Cloth in hand, Beyba kept walking, swinging his arms from time to time, looking at his chrono, turn, pace, turn, pace.

The rhythmic sound was soothing. Del lay listening to it in the silence.

He sat up.

Beyba turned around. "You might as well rest. One of us should."

"Lissen," said Del, thickly.

Beyba shook his head. "I don't hear anything."

"S'quiet."

Beyba stood, mouth half open, straining to hear. "Nothing." He leaned his head against the wall, frowning. "Nothing at all."

Del did likewise.

The absolute quiet was eerie: every station had its background signature composed of the hum of machinery, the vibrations of people moving, the slow, continuous redistribution of strain on the structure. Holk station was as silent as space.

"Life systems failure or they've dumped this section."

There was an odd, nauseous flutter.

Going into free-fall.

Beyba and Del looked at one another.

They spoke simultaneously.

"I think—"

"Is—"

"Get it into the net," said Beyba, unlatching the crash defense. Del had never seen the mechanism that spun safety netting wall to wall in operation and didn't take the time now. He turned to help the boy. But the gen was already half-awake and swarmed into the cocoon without prompting. He locked his hands into the fibers, and relaxed, breathing hard. Del and Beyba followed suit.

The sickening shudder came again.

Del extended a careful hand and began working his fingers back and forth in the fine, dark hair. He didn't know if it reassured the gen, but he found it soothing.

They could feel it coming, a massive wave of sound and motion. Del sank his hands into the net and gripped as hard as he could, felt his teeth grind, tried to go slack—you were supposed to relax.

Beyba yelled over the approaching swell of sound. "I've been a bad boy all my life! But not—"

"—not bad enough!" Del answered. Stupid punch line of a stupid joke they'd shared for years. Stupid, stupid.

Then all Del could feel was the vibration through him, the stinging blows of small objects that showered from a sprung cabinet. Finally there was nothing but the enormous noise and the sticky netting in his clenched hands.

The sound trailed away to a distant growl.

Del opened his eyes.

It didn't make any difference: the darkness seemed absolute.

"Beyba?" His own voice sounded strange. "Beyba!" His heart accelerated.

There was a soft whisper of motion to his right. Del extended his hand, searching, and it was gripped. The nails, pricking his skin, told him it was the gen. Del pulled gently. The smell of musk and medifoam settled next to him. Del felt blindly: shoulder, hard with muscle, neck, cheek—

He could feel the gen craning to look over him. *He can see,* thought Del, straining his own eyes. Nothing but phantoms of the dark. Nothing from the monitor on the gen's arm.

Broken, thought Del.

A long time went by.

The gen sighed and settled into the net: asleep or unconscious. Del ran his hands over the body. The skin felt moist, warm. Struggling out of one flimsy shirt Del put it over the boy and lay still again. He could smell the sharp scent of his own fear. He could hear nothing but the stutter of his own heart. *It's just nerves,* he told himself. *All you have to do is wait. That's easy enough.*

From somewhere below and to Del's left came a welcome sound. "Sshiit," slurred Beyba. Then, more clearly, "Del?"

"Here."

"Can you see?"

"No." Del shifted slightly in the cocoon. "But I think he can."

"Why?"

Del explained.

"I hope you're right. Unless we're still connected it's probably a one-way trip."

Del pressed his face against the net, glad of the darkness. All he could hear was the presence of the other two, the whisper of fabric and the almost-soundless stirring of breathing.

He had counted to almost one hundred very slowly when he lost his place. Dogged, he started over. One. Pause. Two. Pause—

—four thousand nine hundred and ninety-nine. Pause. Five thousand.

Well, that was boring enough.

He peeled his cheek off the sticky netting. There must be a more interesting way of handling this.

Presently he said, "Beyba? We could name him?"

Beyba made an impatient movement—Del could hear the clinging fibers rip free, and the cocoon jerked—then checked himself. "Sure."

Del rummaged for an idea.

"Well?" said Beyba, and offered a name, obviously at random. "Hendre?"

"I never did like that. Jorelle?"

"Sounds like a girl."

Time went by.

"Kise," suggested Beyba, yawning. "Short, simple, and—"

Del could feel Beyba shift away and the net jitter.

"—you and I would be the only ones to know it's Maren for 'trouble.'"

"No," said Del, soberly into the blackness. Never give an ill-omened name.

"Ahh." By the motion of the net, Beyba had stretched. "Probably *has* a name," he said, drowsily.

Which we may never know, thought Del. He flexed his fingers in the silky mass of hair. The boy was definitely asleep, either undisturbed by their change of fortune or so ill it didn't matter. Del traced the outline of an ear with a fingertip. Somehow the gen felt better, warm, relaxed. He had awakened fast enough when there was need. And known what to do.

You're used to spacing, aren't you, thought Del. *I'd guess*—he sniffed his musky fingers—*you were with somebody. Which means you would have been immunized. So I might have been able to do enough to matter.* He clenched his fists in anger much more comfortable than fear.

It was not only dark: it was getting colder.

Every moment that passed by lowered their chances of being rescued. Deltander did not undervalue himself. The death of Deltander Entaneray Solt Permund on Holk would subject Ventrubli to intense scrutiny from his colleagues—in their own interest if for no other reasons—and cause the company trouble for years to come. If station personnel could save him, they would.

And they hadn't come.

Beyba's breath made a faint purring sound in his throat. He had drifted off. To sleep, Del hoped, thinking of how groggy he had sounded. Beyba might be injured. Or still a little drunk.

Del felt numb and disorientated himself. He sniffed suspiciously. The air still seemed all right. It must be the sensory deprivation.

He dropped into a half-waking state.

The soft clanks and thuds of loose objects hitting the walls, the scrittering sounds of metal sliding around inside a cabinet kept waking him. The boy moved closer, and Del tucked the cold hands into his armpits, wondering if he should try and locate anything. They had blankets, water, drugs. There was an emergency hand light somewhere—

Momentarily forgetful, Del tried to see, then closed his eyes. The dark was less oppressive that way. There was nothing sensible to do: caught out of the net when the station reacquired spin, he would certainly be injured and might be killed. Del felt a chill stab of anxiety. He had to believe the station was going to reacquire spin. One. Two—

A louder than usual noise woke Del fully, heart pounding.

The boy shifted, alert, in his arms, his eyes silvered with reflected light. So dim it was still at the edge of visibility for Del, the nightglow was intensifying.

"Teyr," said Del hoarsely, grateful for the light.

The boy looked at him, inquiring.

Teyr. First light, reflected over the still-dark rim of the world.

There was a poem. "Dawn's pale messenger—" Completely out of fashion, but his grandfather had insisted a gentleman should know even the most obscure periods of Eslean literature: his grandfather was not quite a gentleman and had some odd ideas.

Although, thought Del, giving up the effort to remember more than sunlight creeping across the breakfast table, the green smell of the fresh-watered gardens, and the rumble of his grandfather's labored, over-patient voice, *the world might be a better place if gentlemen were what Grandfather believed them to be.*

He ruffled the dark hair under his hand, thinking. "Teyr" would do very well.

Teyr began a cautious reach toward a shadowy drifting cover. Longer-armed than the gen, Del got two fingertips on the edge, and coaxed it toward them, his breath misting the air.

On a different level, Beyba hung in the net, unconscious or asleep, a semi-circular cut on his forehead.

A cup did that, thought Del, wrapping the blanket around Teyr, pulling a fold into a hood. He looked around for another.

There was a loud clanging.

Del fumbled for a grip on the net.

Teyr made a pleased sound.

Del looked at the sharp line of smile-bared teeth. *That's good, is it? I'm ready for something good.*

The metal walls rang like a gong.

Help was on the way.

I have always felt sorry for Javenor Inte. A competent biologist, a brilliant research director, and completely incapable, by temperament and training, of handling an emergency. Ventrubli's appointing him station authority was an error. That they agreed to his standing trial, rather than paying his fines themselves, was an outrage.

I am ahead of myself.

I had hoped the arrival of the lighter Forrei *with its supplies and reinforcements would be the end of my involvement. But when we reached the core the staff was in disarray and Inte incapable of acting. I did what I could, and it was less than was needed.*

Exhausted, and out of the realm of my own experience, it was frustrating to be able to see what was needed and be unable to respond effectively.

But that was still more comfortable than the endless waiting I had gone through before, trapped, dependent on the efforts of others who would, quite reasonably, put their own interests before mine.

And neither was as bad as this moment, waiting for people who may be merciful only because they are unable to restrain their passions sufficiently to play out my pain.

Bondre died slowly.

The security guards sent to escort Permund, Norrey, and Teyr from the medical section to the Station Master were jumpy, pointing their weapons at every wisp of smoke. Del thought the station was in greater danger from them than from the miserable handful of the *Aeguit*'s personnel still under siege in the storage bays.

The walk from medical to administrative was terrifyingly informative. Here and there the bare struts of structural supports, stripped of their protective covering by laser fire, showed blackened and dented, and their guards jumped as one at unexpected pops and groans from shifting stresses. Security doors hung jammed in their tracks, useless to hold off attack or seal in their environment. There was a sharp smell of smoke and burned composite even where there was no visible damage other than streaks of soot down the white-paneled walls.

In one hall, the yellow and red flare of warning lights sent jagged shadows hurrying out and back across splattered debris, unrecognizable except for one human hand, open, palm up, that protruded from the massive remains of a cargo mover smashed by a fallen beam.

The air smelled of crushed flesh.

Del swallowed hard and began to wonder if there were any layers left between the main hull's external seals and the internal containment. There would have been no point to their trying to clear this hall if there were others in better shape. He stepped around a dark, oozing trickle, trying not to speculate on what it was.

There was an irregular drumming close at hand, and the silent guards looked at one another with white-rimmed eyes. With unspoken consent, they all moved faster, although if the wall failed it would make no difference. Decompression would empty the hall faster than anyone could run.

The three of them had been safer in the shelter than here. Even Teyr, ill as he was. Del hoped he was too feverish to understand what he was seeing. It would frighten him.

It certainly frightened Del.

As they maneuvered around a collapsed wall, its storage cabinets' contents strewn across the buckled flooring, Del glanced at Beyba, then down at the uncertain footing. Beyba's face was grim, moving lips white with anger.

Del made certain his own expression was composed, but said nothing. He couldn't hope to sooth Beyba with a few words, and anything he said would draw attention to Beyba's rage. The wealthy, self-made merchant's temper was legend on the docks and in the offices of a dozen systems. Given that, perhaps it would do little harm if Norrey looked furious.

But Del, a senior official, could not indulge himself in public anger—or fear. He must look confident, in control. Anything else would lead to rumors, and here rumor could swell to panic.

Panic destroyed stations.

The doctor's check-over of them had been perfunctory at best. He had dosed them with stimulant and told them the Station Master wished to see them immediately. At Beyba's hot protest they required more attention, he said, "You can walk," and turned away.

Whatever Beyba is muttering, thought Del, *it is just as well our escort can't understand. It will not be complimentary*. He tried to smile reassurance at Teyr, and met groggy incomprehension. Even if he didn't understand what he was seeing, the boy looked worse than he had earlier.

Much worse.

Del's hand knotted into a fist and relaxed with an effort.

They scrambled into a battered transporter and a guard set it into creaking motion. Del looked at the transporter's crawling indicator, nearly bit his lip, and restrained himself. Six decks to go. The machine dropped erratically, banging against the containing walls, and there was a thrumming in the cables.

Teyr had begun an inarticulate moaning, traitorous plea of his unconscious body. One of the guards, irritated by the sound, shifted away, banged the indicator impatiently. It jumped a floor without apparent motion from the transporter and she cursed. Del gritted his teeth. Once they were on the *Forrei*, Del counted on Beyba to do something for Teyr.

If he didn't lose his temper first.

"Come *on*," snarled one man.

Beyba tapped the indicator with one long forefinger. The lights ran uselessly, and then the cables whined and begin pulling again.

Past the mid-point.

The doors opened on Inte's elegantly false-sunlit reception room: the noise-level was stunning. The room was full of staff in every stage of dress and undress, all talking at once. Del frowned. He knew chaos when he saw it.

Pressed up against one wall, Beyba's orange-clad security came to attention as he got off. Their wedge pushed through the crowd and surrounded Norrey, then regrouped to include the carrier with Teyr.

Del looked around. No one in sight was wearing his own black-and-grey. He lifted his chin a fraction against his sag in spirits. He wanted the comfort of his own people around him. The buzz of stimulant was no substitute.

The stationmaster, Javenor Inte, space-plump figure draped in a robe with slashed and puffed sleeves, bustled through the crowd. "Del. How good to see you—" For all the world like some diplomatic reception, but Inte's damp hands left marks on Deltander's paper sleeve. "Are you all right?"

"Tired," said Del. Finding the moist hand gripping his forearm distasteful, he freed himself by patting Inte on the shoulder and stepping away.

Beyba was deep in conference with his guards.

Del saw the familiar face of Jyse, his body servant, inching his way through the crowd, face stiff with denial. Asen Permund was not facing the stationmaster clad in nothing but rumpled paper.

Del made a courteous, meaningless response to Inte's stream of words, as Beyba and his guards, having regained the transporter, faced front and were cut from view by the closing doors. Beyba's expression was savage. Del hoped he got Teyr aid before he exploded, although Beyba's credits would probably get him what he wanted even if his charm failed.

Jyse, having made his way to Del's side, mutely held up a robe as elaborate and inappropriate as the one Inte was wearing. Del extended his arms and let Jyse put it on him, wondering the while whom he was borrowing it from: it was far too short and he himself was not a tall man.

Listening to Inte's stammered summary, Del sorted through the faces in the crowd. There were too many people here doing nothing, most of them important enough that their faces were vaguely familiar after two and a half days on Holk.

With mounting annoyance Del identified the life support director, the head biologist, the chief of the medical facilities, the com controller, the two women who split directing maintenance and repair with other jobs—

He interrupted Inte's monologue with, "Why are all these people here?"

Inte cringed. "We're gathering information."

"We could end up well-informed and dead." Del kicked off his slippery felted scuffs and stepped up on a seat that sighed beneath his weight.

It was a relief that years of practice made his voice full and strong despite his fatigue. He gave a short, patchwork speech, concluding, "You know your jobs. If it needs doing, do it. If there's a problem, call here. We'll coordinate."

He stepped down and heard, under the swelling babble, the seat hiss in inanimate contempt as it reinflated.

Inte gave one wave of his arm, apparently seconding Del's speech, and headed for his office.

The room emptied abruptly. The station personnel were anxious to protect themselves from the hazards they understood. Let others cope with the rest. Life on a station demanded that kind of tunnel-vision trust.

Del was left in the near-empty room with Jyse, who held a battered-looking stunner—the weapon must be as old as Jyse himself—obviously filling in for Andur, Del's bodyguard.

About to ask where Andur was, Del saw Javenor Inte come to his office door and look around the emptied room. His foolish, cheerful expression was gone; he looked haggard and old. Del stared a moment at the transformation, slow-witted with exhaustion, then went to him.

Jyse turned his back to the closing door, and balanced the stunner in the crook of his arm.

The room, large and cluttered, stank with sweaty fear.

Del cleared a seat and sat down, carefully arranged the particularly hideous fabric of the borrowed robe to cover his bare ankles, leaving Inte to flutter about like something newly-caged, talking.

Half-listening to Inte's flood of words, Del looked around him. The office told as much about the man as anything. There was little of

the apparatus of an administrator. Plastic charts and globular
specimen cases crowded the walls. Heaps of rod-files covered every
flat surface.

Loose, Del noted with annoyance, every one of them a lethal
missile if the station shuddered again. He was looking at the
accumulated trash of a research scientist engrossed in a project.

Del managed not to sigh.

He was so tired.

Inte might not know enough to take charge, if his subordinates
handled the day-today routine. That meant decisions were made by
committee, something workable when there was time and a common
goal, but disastrous in an emergency.

The grinding progress of the nearby transport rattled the charts
continuously. Inte jumped and clapped both hands to his ears at a
harsh mechanical shriek. The cutter sounded like it was coming
through the office wall. A woman yelled a fierce, meaningless
obscenity that met with sullen mutters. The cutter's shrill wail
resumed a short distance away. That the station was in dire straits was
easily apparent to even the not very knowledgeable.

Someone had to do something—Inte wouldn't or couldn't.

Del was an experienced administrator, but he had little to offer
here except commonsense, and that was not enough, since what Inte
really wanted someone to make the decisions. Failing that, he was
perfectly capable of letting everything be settled by default, a
terrifying prospect in the fragile environment of a damaged station.

Del started sweating himself. "Inte," he said stemming the flow of
words, "do you have a set of emergency prioritizations?"

"In the com," said Inte.

In the com, where it was useless if the power failed.

"Would," said Del, hands busy clearing a corner of the desk, "you
print that out for me?"

Inte fumbled with the equipment, tongue-tip between clenched
teeth.

Del took a deep calming breath. Whatever he did, it couldn't be
worse than inaction. "Let's set up a set of emergency procedures. Do
we have life-support data?"

"Some of the sensors are out."

Assume the worst, you fool. Del unclipped the protective cover. His hands began moving on the auxiliary board. He could hear Inte's stumbling voice trying to cue the hardcopy function. Talking with the machine would take far too long. Del punched in the command. The machine sputtered to life.

"There," said Inte. "I wasn't sure that would work."

Del smiled with reflexive courtesy and pulled the slick copy from its slot.

"One," he read.

Inte leaned to look over his shoulder. "I've always meant to—"

The lights flickered ominously. Del looked up. Hardcopy was all very good, but he'd still need light. "Ask if they have a hand light in the outer office," he said.

Inte went.

Del picked up a chart stylus and began scratching across the unnecessary and the irrelevant.

It was going to be a long shift.

"I'll need something to eat," he said to the shaking hands that positioned the hand light. "And make sure that's fastened down." All backup power to be conserved for the core and medical sections, other sections to be evacuated now, with the exception of designated repair crews working in sections—

"How?" said Inte.

Del stared at him. "What?"

"How did you want it fastened?" said Inte.

"So it stays in one place," said Del. "The following people should file situation reports as soon as possible—" The screen sprang to life with symbols as the com translated the mutter of incoming messages.

There was the click of sliding food containers as Jyse maneuvered through the door.

"Good," said Inte, hunting something on the floor. "He wanted something to eat."

Jyse looked down without comment and positioned the tray.

Del squeezed a pak open one-handed, and continued to enter data as he licked the bland paste.

"Can I do anything?" said Inte.

"Check the personnel roster."

Jyse began stacking hardcopy.

Inte's voice, busy muttering corrections to the roster, had acquired an official drone.

Del called another dataset. If he just got Inte started—

His right eye felt as if it was caged in hot wires.

When Del was able to go to the office designated for his use during his stay, its disused smell seemed fresh after the stench in the public areas. He turned off the ventilation that had come on automatically.

Jyse took up a position facing the closed door, weapon in hand. It seemed foolish to Del, but Andur presumably had told Jyse to do it, and Andur was in charge of Del's security.

Del sat, uncapped a tube of stim, inhaled, and began listening to the high whispers of his own accumulated messages on the comnet. The lighter captain was pushing her crew hard to unload supplies, load the medical cases that were being evacuated, and depart. Hearing the schedule, Del could almost hear the clang and rattle of over-driven equipment, distant though he was from the docking bays.

He yawned and took another whiff from the tube in his left hand. The stimulant was not doing much, but the sharp, medical odor was pleasant. Del had reached with quivering fingers to tell the captain to push the departure time back, when Beyba's voice, shrill from the override message speed-up, whispered in his ear, urging him to board the *Forrei*. "Now." Beyba's voice was tense with urgency, as if there were things he wouldn't say on an open circuit.

Del took stock of the situation.

He was tired, emotionally and physically. Holk was in chaos, burdened with tons of rotting material, a situation so dangerous that the *Forrei*'s captain was running everyone through decon before allowing them to board. Beyba, whose assessment Del respected, thought things were critical.

But he had taken a great deal of time getting Inte started. Del still had his own work to do. It was absolutely necessary to establish a system for dealing with the rotting cargo and human bodies in order to be able to make criminal and civil cases in the matter. There was no else here to do it. Those who might have been delegated to the task were busy with more immediate problems, and none of them had any experience. No records, no justice. No justice, no protection for other stations. Del inhaled again, and bent to his work.

In the midst of entering a protocol, Del heard the door open. Jyse must be checking on something. He entered another set of specifications in a bureaucratic murmur, then stopped, alert. There should be the brisk but muted sounds of half a dozen people hard at work in the outer office: but there was nothing.

Del turned around, heart speeding up.

And looked square into Andur's narrow blue eyes, crinkled at the corners with suppressed laughter. "I've told you not to sit with your back to the door," said Andur.

"The console doesn't turn," said Del.

Andur bent, reached under, and pushed. The entire setup rotated one hundred eighty degrees.

Del spread his hands, conceding the point.

Andur would have been a handsome man if his looks had not been marred by the pattern of scars that proclaimed him a Kel: someone whose childhood had been spent learning how to protect and defend. Now in his early thirties, he was second-in-command of Del's security and Del's bodyguard on this trip. If he survived to his late forties he would go home, rich with his accumulated pay, to sire and raise another generation of Kel.

Del found what little he knew of the Kel's neo-primitivism peculiar, but he was honored, as his father and his father's father had been, to be chosen as an acceptable employer by one. Andur was as dangerous as a sane, well-trained human being could be, and frightening to anyone who only knew of the Kel by reputation. It was easy to understand the hush in the outer office.

Del began to ask where Jyse had gone, and closed his mouth. Jyse would be on board the *Forrei*, attending to whatever was necessary, as Andur had been busy before with the security check. All that was left was for him to finish this, and leave the stinking chaos of Holk Station without shame or regret.

He straightened his back—something in there had been strained, and it eased it to lean forward—and sniffed more stim. A wave of dizziness swept over him, and he grabbed for the edge of the console.

"Asen?"

Andur's scarred face seemed too large and was hard to focus.

"Asen?" Andur's fingers fumbled at his neck for a pulse.

Del pushed his hand, away, impatient. His grandfather had died of a massive heart attack. Del had undergone every painful and humiliating test the most reputable doctors of Belsyrtis had been able to devise for the assurance there was nothing wrong with him but his nerves. "Leave me alone. How far to the *Forrei*?"

Andur said, "I'll get—"

The cubical shook with the hollow booming of composite sections taking new stresses. Del looked around, bewildered by the enveloping sound.

Andur turned and ripped open the emergency gear locker.

Del shucked his borrowed robe and donned the baggy one-size suit with shaking hands.

Having sealed the front of his own suit, Andur lifted a helmet over Del's head and sealed it to the old-fashioned, rigid shoulder ring.

The helm liner smelled of old, powdery dirt. Del sneezed.

Andur punched on the whirring air filter. "Can you hear me?" his tinny voice asked in Del's ear, as he opened the door.

"Yes," said Del, and urged his stiff, sore legs to their greatest speed. If they were taking the spin off the station again, then there was serious damage at the core. If they weren't taking off spin, then those sounds were the herald of catastrophic failure.

They were in the corridor to the transporter down to the *Forrei*'s docking bay when its doors sprang open. Five or six of Beyba's orange-uniformed security people poured out and ran toward them.

Andur unfastened his helmet and yelled something to them.

Del reached to undo his own.

Andur pulled his hand away. He put the neck opening of his helmet to his mouth and said, "Leave it on, Asen. They think there's a systems failure."

Unable to hear, Del watched Andur confer with the group leader, Rogany, Beyba's security chief. Rogany shook his head emphatically, sent one man running back to jam the transporter doors, and gestured at Del.

They were coming for me, thought Del. He would rather Beyba had sent somebody else. It was not comfortable being in Rogany's debt.

When Beyba first hired the man, Del, uneasy, asked Andur for his opinion. Andur said, shortly, "He loves his work." Del had known what he meant. Rogany enjoyed violence and might not be above causing a little, should the natural supply run short.

Rogany snapped something. Two of the guards stood on either side of Del and lifted him onto a seat formed of their interlinked arms. Del was surprised: one of them was a woman. She must be very good. Beyba didn't like women close to him.

They trotted down the corridor to the transporter.

Listening to his own shallow breathing inside the helmet, Del watched Rogany and Andur talk as the cab dropped to the outer levels. The indicator jerked and flickered and there was an intermittent grinding under the floor.

The machine made an unrequested stop, and the doors opened. Every member of Rogany's party, except for the two burdened with Del, thrust their weapons at the startled civilian crowd. The foremost struggled to avoid being shoved aboard as the doors were forced shut by two of Rogany's people.

Del closed his eyes, dismayed.

If there hadn't been panic before, there would be now.

There was a squealing as of something stressed to the limit. The transporter jarred back and forth. Del held his breath with the rest, watching the indicator crawl. The spin of the station tended to throw the cab to the outer rim, but if the machinery failed they would be trapped.

One more level.

The cab bounced against the bottom of the shaft. Knees sagged; Del felt the woman holding him slip and tighten her grip. They absorbed a second, then a third, hand's-breadth drop.

Three-quarters open, the doors jammed. They pressed them back and got out. Behind them the futile arrival signal droned over and over.

The illuminated government logo dimmed momentarily as the *Forrei*'s lock opened and the mist of the preceding decon puffed out. Their entire party squeezed in, and there was a hissing inrush of cold, recycled air.

Safe.

No matter how long the decon took, they were now secure in the ship's environment.

Del slid off the arms that supported him, stripped off the suit and the soggy paper bath clothing, and stuffed them into the hopper. There was a flash of blue light around the edges. The suit might be salvageable, but the bath clothing would be nothing but fine ash.

Andur's hard hand braced him, as, dripping with decon fluids, panting from the inhalants, they made their way through the jostling mass of naked people. The stink of chemicals and sweat was sickening. Del pressed the back of his hand to his mouth.

There was a deep metallic groaning and Del felt the jerk of the ship's release from the docking bay. "No," he said, fumbling a towel around himself. "Where's the Captain." His voice was so flat with fatigue it didn't sound like a question.

"Captain Evert is in the control room. If you will follow me to your quarters, Asen." The officer turned one way. Del, familiar with this class of ship from past trips, turned the other. A glare from Andur stopped the officer's protest.

The control room of the *Forrei* was a tight fit for the four officers that ordinarily manned it. With Captain Evert pressed against the back wall it was overcrowded. Standing in the doorway Del felt intimidated even before the Captain slapped at the wall of switches, threw the safety cover, and turned around.

She snarled over her shoulder, "Reduce our cross-section!" Then to Del, "The coupler broke. If the station fails while we're docked the debris will shred us."

"Captain." The senior officer's hands stroked the controls.

Del felt the ship respond. "Holk's in a near-panic situation." he said.

"I'm responsible for my ship!"

"See if you can keep that fat fool from killing everyone," said Beyba, unexpectedly behind Del.

"Beyba." Beyba had been tapped for this tour because of his commercial expertise, not his innate diplomacy. Del looked to the Captain. "If you could provide me with comnet facilities."

The junior officer's cubical was cramped and none-too-clean. Inte's double-chinned face jiggled alarmingly in the screen. Del shoved back his hair with disgust—it was still sticky with decon fluid—and asked, "Javenor, what's your status?"

"I don't know!" Inte's voice had a shrill edge.

"Is the rotation stable?" And the unasked question, will the station hold together?

"I don't know, I don't know—" Inte's face blurred out of existence as he backed out of comcam range.

Del sat back. Took a deep breath. He wasn't responding. Get him working on something, anything. "Javenor? Feed me the status information." Surely the man was capable of punching a few buttons.

"You're safe," accused Inte, an unfocussed ghost.

"We're taking the injured off."

"Safe," said Inte. His eyes showed white all the way around.

"Javenor." Del hoped his face didn't show how appalled he was.

"We're all going to die!" Inte's voice held absolute conviction.

Del tried to infuse his own with the same certainty. "Javenor. Everything can be gotten under control. A coupler broke. We're just standing off until the situation stabilizes."

Wild-eyed Inte wasn't listening.

"You have good people," said Del. "Just let—"

"We're all going to die!" Inte swung blindly at the comcam, which rotated until it stared at the blank ceiling. Del could hear the crash of something knocked over on his progress across the office, the hiss-thump of the door opening and closing, then nothing but the faint hum of the com itself.

"They're going to red-line on oxygen if they don't rig for emergency soon," said Beyba.

"Be still," said Del. He locked his hands together so hard they hurt and thought. Inte might do something foolish, and the station was damaged enough that the fail-safes might not stop him. *He must know all the overrides, anyway*, thought Del as he reached for the com.

He began whispering call numbers.

He got the brurr and static of no connection, once, twice, then a click and a view of an empty office.

Del signaled an emergency call.

"This important?" snapped the grey-haired woman who turned the comcam to face her. "Asen Permund," she added with scant courtesy.

Heffer. Dro Heffer. Head of the biological section. Sharp-tempered, impatient, steady.

Del explained.

Heffer listened, nodded. "We'll find him. Kenth!" She began to speak to her subordinate, then turned back to the pickup. "Stay with this connection, Asen. If you switch we might lose you."

"Yes," said Del. "I'll wait." He hitched the towel across his lap. The stupid government-issue thing was too short.

The hunt was on.

A half shift later, Del, lying in bed safe on the *Forrei*, sighed and pulled the collar of his padded robe closed. There was a barely visible thread of light around the door to the dressing room. He could hear faint sounds as Jyse cleaned and put things away.

It had seemed to take a long time to capture the stationmaster, even though it was only moments before Inte was tentatively identified on an undamaged station security monitor. He eluded the first searchers, got into the maintenance tunnels, and was making his way to the core machinery when he was finally captured. Shuffling along, talking to himself, his appearance had been enough to quash any doubts: he was unfit to exercise authority.

Del, wretched with the hyper-alertness of too much stim, thought it was probably a good thing that the station personnel had to search for Inte. It focused their fear and frustration. And as for Inte himself, quiet under sedation leads in the *Forrei*'s med section, he was safe enough until they landed at Belsyrtis. Del was glad his own involvement in the matter guaranteed he would not be the one to spell out to Inte just how thoroughly his life was destroyed.

The kindest charge would be that he was incompetent. There would be others who would say Inte had faked his way into a secure berth on the *Forrei*, taking a place that should have belonged to one of the injured. It was unlikely he would ever be employed on another station, and Inte's entire career was in free-fall biologicals.

Del rolled onto his side, trying to ease sore muscles.

If he couldn't go to sleep, he might at least think about something pleasant. Another image forced its way into his mind. Teyr.

He had managed to call the *Forrei*'s chief medical officer sometime in the rush and wait of backing up Heffer's decisions. She had told Del Teyr was "stable, sedated, and asleep," and switched off. At the time he had taken her terseness for the impatience of a busy specialist confronted with a layman's interruption.

45

Now, with the ship underway, Del was not so sure. He remembered the station doctor, relieved she didn't have to treat Teyr. Gene-sculptures had no rights. That Teyr looked human did not change the case. In fact, given the *Forrei* was carrying critically injured human beings, it might weigh against him. The officer might not want any questions raised why she had wasted time and supplies on someone's expensive pet.

Del told himself that Beyba was more than capable of dealing with all that. He was tired and he could feel a tentative flutter every so often under his sternum. He tried to settle his head more comfortably. *Relax*, he repeated to himself, *It's just nerves, relax—*

His hand knotted in the bedding. Beyba was also perfectly capable of arousing bleak fury in otherwise placid people. Del sighed, and sat up, feet feeling for his soft boots. The line of light around the dressing room door was out. Jyse was probably asleep.

Del pulled his outer robe from its stand, and sniffed a sleeve as he put it on. Left alone while Del was stranded, Jyse had overhauled Del's entire wardrobe and scented everything. In the stench of death that pervaded Holk Station the strong, sweet fragrance would have been welcome. But on shipboard strong smells of any kind were to be avoided: you had to live with them for the entire trip.

When he opened the outer door to his room, a quick movement in the darkness showed he had awakened Andur. Del spoke on the lights.

"Asen?" Andur sat up, naked except for the fabric-thin chest and groin shields and the contoured strap of his weapons belt. He shoved his fingers through the fuzz of blond hair working its way loose from his wrist-thick manhood braid, blinked hard, and rose in one easy motion.

Deltander stepped back slightly, making room: Andur was a big, heavy-boned man, and an impressive sight even pulling on his uniform one leg at a time. "Where are we going?" he asked.

"I want to check on the gen."

Andur twitched his shoulders to make his shirt settle more comfortably. "I could do that."

"He doesn't know you."

Andur didn't quite smile.

Del raised his eyebrows in a silent question.

"'He,'" quoted Andur, clipping weapons on. "I'm ready."

The air in the med section was thick with the smells of suffering humanity. Del's chest jabbed painfully at the appetizing odor of roast meat: laser burns.

From where he stood, Del could see one man's blackened arm, bagged with gel, obviously awaiting removal for there was nothing left to save. If he were untreated, there must be others worse off. No medical staff was in sight.

Del rubbed the insistent flutter beneath his sternum.

Andur gave him a sideways, worried look.

"It's just nerves," said Del.

Andur looked unconvinced.

Del stopped rubbing.

Andur rolled through the whispering roster. Teyr's flash-startled face rolled up the screen. "They processed him first."

Probably to get rid of Beyba, thought Del.

Andur referenced the location map. Nothing.

Del pressed his hand to his chest.

Andur, uncharacteristically, swore. "Stay here, Asen. I'll find him."

Andur examined the ranks of packed bodies quickly, dismissively, stopping only to check the two smallest figures. Then he moved on to the med staff's private cubicles, ducking in and out. Del could hear the squeak of something being forced, the sharp splatter of something knocked over. When Andur came to one outer door that refused to yield, he braced his shoulder against it, and tore it open. He looked, and beckoned Del. "Asen?"

There was a half-inflated carrier on the floor with a cover lapping from its empty interior.

Del started forward and was blocked by Del's arm.

"What?" said Del.

"Does he know your voice?"

"We didn't talk much," said Del.

Andur nodded, surveying the cubical without moving beyond the jamb. "Keep talking anyway. Anything."

"Trade statistics are not available for the current session, but will be posted in the session following. Legal matters under consideration—"

Andur gave Del an odd look.

Del shrugged. He wasn't going to recite poetry, and he had listened to that message every time he had called his own office for years.

Head inclined, Andur listened intently, then lunged around the edge of the door at floor level. He dragged a thrashing figure out and up and pinned it against the wall.

Andur turned it to face Del and said, "Yours?"

Tumbled black hair obscured the face, but Del nodded and reached.

Andur pulled back. "Asen. Not until I've searched him."

"That's not—"

Andur ran his hands lightly over the boy as if taking his measure. Then he stripped off the towel clipped around his hips. Andur's expression grew hard when he saw the deep, five-fingered bruises on the boy's buttocks. He ran his hand more gently through the tangled hair, and said, "All right."

Del pushed the hair back out of his face. Only then did Teyr recognize him. *What did you think was happening*, wondered Del, looking over the top of the dark head at Andur.

Andur, still holding the towel, winced.

Del gestured and they got the improvised loincloth refastened.

The med staff hadn't wasted much time in caring for him. The rough, discolored foam on his bruises and cuts hadn't been renewed since Del applied it. Someone had replaced the broken monitor unit and refilled it.

Other than that Teyr had been left alone in a locked office for at least one shift. *Maybe almost two*, thought Del, examining the monitor. It was amazing he had ever lifted Teyr: the top of his head came to Del's chin.

Andur moved around the office, restless with suppressed anger. He bumped the desk, and a half-used ampoule rolled off onto the floor. He shoved it out of the way with his foot and watched the orange liquid stain the floor padding. Then, quite deliberately, he stepped on it, ground it in.

Del looked at the mess and went back to the monitor without comment. The blinking red and green lights made him nervous.

"Jyse has some medic's training," said Andur, scars livid in the overhead lighting.

"Yes," said Del. So did Andur.

Pick-a-back, Andur carried Teyr back to their quarters. Del walking alongside, one stim-jittery hand holding a cold, bare foot whose long toes closed about his fingers.

Keying open the outer door, they were confronted by Jyse, grey hair ruffled around his bald pate, who said, perfectly automatically, "Asen, where have you been. You need rest." Then, really seeing them, "What's this?"

"Teyr," said Del.

"His gen," said Andur, sliding Teyr to the floor and supporting him.

"You're *sure*," said Jyse, in the same tone he had used years ago when Del told him his grandfather's formal jewelry, laid out for a ceremony, had fallen, untouched by Del, on the floor.

"He's marked," said Del.

Jyse looked profoundly skeptical, and closed the outer door. "Take him into the dressing room," he said to Andur.

Del followed meekly.

Once there, Jyse took his time. Stripping off the towel, he looked, turned, felt, without a change of expression, and then picked up the hand cleaner. "Put him on the table." Andur boosted Teyr up.

There was a steady slurping from the tool as Jyse moved it over the skin, pumping water against the skin, sucking it off. Clean, the patient was a varicolored pattern of purple, blue, and green on starkly white skin. He was shivering, and there was blood seeping from between his buttocks again.

Jyse opened his kit and began laying things out.

He took his time, rubbing on the foam in long, slow strokes, easing Teyr onto his belly to treat the anal damage. Del supposed it was a reflection of the problems of a sedentary, late middle-aged man that Jyse was so well supplied. Washing his hands, Jyse examined Teyr's mouth, checking the teeth, looking briefly at the tattoo under the upper lip.

"Andur, would you get the recorder from the Asen's desk?"

Jyse flipped the upper lip back again and took a record.

Then he picked up an angled probe and studied the patient's throat. Teyr began to gag. Jyse released him with a pat and began putting the tools away with brisk snaps. "Look at the record, Asen."

Del looked at the tiny screen.

In the dim lighting in the docking bay, Del had not tried to read the saliva-glossy characters under the upper lip. It had not occurred to him that they would be anything other than the standard string of numbers.

"I've never seen that before," said Jyse. "And I would remember a script like that." He pointed, "See how it's accented below the line. Asen?"

Del shook his head.

"Andur?"

Andur craned to look. "No," he said.

"Might mean anything," said Jyse.

"Um," said Del, inadvertently giving a good imitation of his grandfather being noncommittal.

"And," said Jyse, "he may have been muted. Has he made any sound?"

Del described the cry that had sent Beyba leaping back.

"His vocal cords look odd. Nothing articulate?"

"No," said Del, "but he wouldn't speak Beyal in any case."

Jyse, nodded, and, having made his points, waited for orders.

"Well," said Del, watching Teyr's sharp teeth show in a yawn, "— we won't settle it now. Make up a bed for him." Del loosened the collar of his robe. "We need sleep."

"Asen," said Jyse, reaching for one of the cabinets.

"A pleasant night," said Andur, already unfastening his shirt.

Del lay, feeling the smoothness of the sheet against his cheek sooth a friction burn from the crash netting. He was listening to the silence compounded of a hundred small, living noises. The purr of the air system. The distant vibration of a transporter rising to the upper levels. A deep, steady note that might be from the ship's drive—

Sometime later Del woke up enough to know he had been asleep and was going to sleep again.

My grandfather never met Beyba, of course.

His point of view was that one must deal kindly and fairly with the upstart rich, but that their wealth was no reason to admit them to one's social life. A gentleman spent his time among his peers, surrounded by properly trained staff and servants.

I remember holding him as he died. He was appalled to be doing something so unseemly in public. His two servants knelt on either side, open coats spread wide, trying to shield his pain-wracked face from the curious. He put his whole tough, well-trained will into not crying out at the agony in his chest.

I resented his wasting his effort so trivially at the time.

I'm older now, and know that there are times when all one can do is try to keep up appearances and hope.

Andur has joined his cord into one seamless loop, and fitted it over Teyr's outstretched hands. He reaches in, forefingers and thumbs like pincers, and plucks it off. The suddenly slackened string collapses; his fingers spread it into another pattern. Teyr leans forward, intent on the web, looking for his move. Something with more crossings that will force Andur back to a simpler pattern. Intent on their game, they might be sitting in the garden room on a winter evening.

I can hear the mob even through walls of solid stone.

The insistent chiming of the comcall woke Del. He could hear Andur's answering voice, rough with sleep and annoyance. He stretched.

It was amazing how many different kinds of pain the human body could sustain. The bitter after-taste of too much stim coated his tongue. He swallowed, and his empty stomach knotted. A good time to lie in bed and do nothing.

Slowly, he drew himself up.

Standing, it was not so bad if he didn't move too fast, and there was probably time to visit the personal before Beyba—Del was sure it was Beyba on the com—talked Andur into waking him up.

Teyr, bedded down on the heated floor, woke up to take an interest in Del's proceedings that was unsettling, until the boy struggled up and it became plain that his interest was informational.

Sorry, fellow, thought Del, *we didn't think to give you a tour of the facilities*. He drank a second cup of water, and stared into the vidplane. He looked exactly like he felt.

Although he was uncertain on his feet, Teyr, driven by curiosity or caution, was trying every machine in the place. Del reached hastily to stop a flood of shampoo, one ear cocked for Andur's entrance into his bedroom.

"Asen?" The frowsy blond head poked into the personal. "I didn't know you were up."

"I'm not sure I am," said Del. "I look like walking death."

"Better than Asen Norrey."

Del grunted doubt. "Jyse up?"

"No," said Andur.

"Yes," said Jyse, coming in still fastening his robe. Then to Andur, "You weren't to wake him."

Andur shrugged. "I didn't. Norrey's swearing he'll get the Captain to override and let him in if someone doesn't answer."

Jyse looked disgusted. "Asen, let me speak to him. I'll tell him you're resting—"

Del, seated on the tub surround, shook his head. "He's calling because Teyr's not in the med section, and no one saw us leave."

Jyse opened, then closed, his mouth.

Water began pouring into the tub. Del creaked upright in time to escape being coated by the tub's sealant film. Teyr poked at the tough layer and discovered you could force your hands through it, slowly, to the rising water beneath. Andur shut the inflow off.

A heavy-fisted thudding came from the outer door.

Andur left.

"Asen," said Jyse, "you should go back to bed."

Del reseated himself on the massage table. "It will be faster to get it over with."

Jyse's pale brows, so different from Del's thick black ones, drew together.

Del looked down, annoyed. Jyse was a good servant, but not inclined to undervalue his own opinion.

"Asen Norrey forgets you are not as young as he is."

No, he doesn't, thought Del. *I'd probably be dead if he did.* "Leave it."

Jyse's face went stony. "Asen."

"Del! Where is he?" Beyba's voice.

Andur stopped in the door and said, "Asen Norrey would like to speak with you."

"Del!"

Andur stepped out of the way.

Beyba came through the door into the personal without a pause.

Jyse's mouth grew very prim.

Del started to speak.

Beyba held out a hand to stop him. "I've got security looking everywhere, and," he took a deep breath, "I'll pay you his value if anything's been done to him, but your gen is—"

Teyr, who had retreated behind Jyse at all the noise, looked around Jyse's thin, disapproving figure.

"Son of a bitch," said Beyba, and sat down, hard, on the counter. He was sweating at the hairline. "Del," he said reproachfully.

Andur was right. Beyba looked like a man who'd had a bad shock on top of a hangover after being spun in free-fall with a collection of hard, sharp objects.

"Son of a bitch," he said again, shaking his head and wincing as his hair pulled at the swelling around the semi-circular cut on his forehead. "Rogany!"

Del felt his own mouth go thin when Rogany entered. Angry eyes looked them all over. *Beyba's really chewed him out*, thought Del.

Andur moved a shoulder slightly and Rogany tensed just as fractionally.

Warning given, warning taken.

"Asen," said Rogany, giving his attention to his employer.

Beyba gestured at Teyr.

"Will you want the search called off, Asen?"

"Don't play the drooling idiot with me," said Beyba. "Get going." He wiped the sweat from his face with his sleeve.

It took considerable force to slam a sliding door, but Rogany did.

"There wasn't anyone with him," Del said into the silence.

"I know," said Beyba. "And they didn't bother to call security when they noticed he was missing. And when they finally did call security, they didn't bother to do anything. I found out when Rogany went to check and they couldn't produce him. Shit."

Del considered what to say.

Beyba looked at Andur.

Andur walked out.

Beyba wiped his face again. "So how is he?"

"Jyse is treating him."

"Jyse," said Beyba. "I spent all the time getting up here wondering how to liquefy enough assets to cover the value of your," he paused, "*pet.* And your body servant is treating him."

"I don't understand," said Del.

Beyba, having taken charge of Del's property, might feel obliged to reimburse him, but he wasn't a man to grudge a few credits to keep a friendship sweet. Or a business relationship, either.

Beyba looked at him. "That," he pointed, "is worth more than everything you own, or a substantial chunk of everything I own."

Del looked at Teyr. Millions of credits looked back, doubtful about what was going on. *I'll have to hire more security*, thought Del.

"Del?"

"Yes?" said Del, distracted. *Now you know why they hid him. Worth risking a few lives.*

Beyba made a disgusted noise. "You hadn't given it a thought. Aristocrat."

Jyse looked as if he had a pleasant taste in his mouth.

Beyba slumped for a moment. "I need sleep." He called into the next room. "Andur! You want a new job?"

Andur filled the doorway. "No." He pulled a strip of red-brown gevilt from his belt pouch, cut off a sliver, and chewed it.

Beyba watched the whole leisurely process.

Del loosened the collar of his robe. *Avoid*, said his grandfather's voice in his mind, *reprimanding the servants in the presence of others, particularly strangers. It breeds resentment.*

Beyba rose. "I've talked with Evert. The med section's to give your calls priority. Even for that. Particularly for that." He slapped his hands against his thighs. "If they don't, call me."

"Thank you," said Del, dryly. He'd been a negotiator before Beyba was born.

He left, and Andur followed. Del could hear Andur open and reset the outer door. Del went to meet Andur. "Andur," he said.

"Asen." He stared down at Del.

"You could be polite about it."

Andur sat down in the seat next to Del's bed, pulled off a boot, and held the orange-stained sole out. "Left a trail all they way up here." He dropped the boot to the floor. "He pays a fortune for security."

Del sighed.

Andur pulled off the other boot. "He thinks everything's for sale at the right price." The other boot hit the floor with a thump.

"Andur."

"He has no business trying to hire me."

"He was joking."

"No." Andur shoved his boots together and picked at a knotted lace on his weapons belt. He stank with anger.

We're in for a long session of exercises, thought Del, looking around the small space, overcrowded with the four of them.

Andur jerked at the lace, swore, and cut it. "When I saw him to the door he got specific." The sum Andur named made Del blink.

"I can't match that."

"I didn't ask you to." Andur rethreaded the shortened lace and laid the belt aside.

Del considered him judicially. "What, then?"

Andur stripped off his shirt and refastened his belt around his naked waist. "None of you," Andur chin jerked to indicate the two in the room beyond, "is to leave this suite without me."

"Andur," said Del, warningly. "I think—"

"Asen. What do you think Norrey thought happened to Teyr? Who took him? He was locked in. Norrey didn't even think of you."

Del turned the questions over, slowly.

Andur tugged down his trousers. "Some of Norrey's business was," he tilted a hand back and forth, "especially when he was getting started." He rolled his pants into a compact bundle with his shirt. "That's not my concern. Go far enough and any man's outside the law. But he hired a bunch of cutthroats for security then." He tucked his clothes into one of the nets for small objects. "I've listened to the ideas they banter around joking." He looked at Del, estimating the best way to put his thought.

"Under the right circumstances, they might not be jokes," said Del.

Andur nodded, very serious.

Del fingered the empty closing loop at his neck. "Are we safe? Here. Now."

"Safe as Norrey, anyhow." Andur sighted in his stunner—Del could see the three displays overlap and converge—refastened it on his belt.

"And Rogany?" said Del.

"Could be big trouble." Stripped, Andur lay flat on his back and began his routine.

Del went to see what Teyr and Jyse were up to.

Jyse was reapplying the foam to Teyr's bruises and cuts. The unit on Teyr's arm blinked placidly as it pumped amphotrin into him. He looked alert enough, but there was a tense transparency to him that told the real state of affairs. He would collapse almost immediately if support were removed.

Jyse made another slow stroke and considered the effect. The stuff worked best if enough was applied to leave a thin film rather than a spongy layer. Apply too little and it was ineffective.

It would be unfair to say Jyse was a snob, thought Del. But there was no doubt he took pleasure in anything that increased the wealth and standing of the Permund house.

Jyse had been kind to Teyr before. But now his efforts had become distinctly more attentive. "Just a moment, Asen," he said, torn between opposing duties.

"Do a good job." Del settled himself comfortably.

He had thinking to do. Too many things had happened in the last two standard days, and many of them didn't make sense. He sat, puzzling through what he knew. He would never have thought a wealthy person would be traveling on a freighter like the *Aeguit*. Even a relatively minor player like Beyba maintained a small, fast ship for his personal use in-system. Someone traveling with a million-credit asset could afford his own, and would need the security.

Del sat smelling the clean odors, listening to Jyse's half-voiced commentary to Teyr. "Lift your arm, turn a bit, good. This is cold, this is warmer—" Jyse was simply making soothing noises that happened to be words, without much thought for what he was saying. Del straightened up abruptly from a half-nap. He was still too tired for tight reasoning.

And hungry, he realized, suddenly. That vague, wobbly feeling was hunger. He hadn't eaten since the conrats in the shelter.

Jyse rinsed off his tools, twice, then dried them. "Asen."

Del took his place as Jyse bent to work.

Teyr seemed content to lie flat on his belly on the bedding still piled on the floor.

"Make it quick," said Deltander. "I'm hungry."

"Asen."

Presently Andur came in for the hand cleaner, dripping with sweat. Del felt Jyse's supple hands bear down on his reflexive tension. It was hard being cooped in such a small space with three other people. But there was no choice on the *Forrei*. She was loaded to her maximum capacity and beyond.

Beyba might be regretting his lavish security force. They had been assigned no more space than Del and his party. Some of the guards were sleeping in shifts while the others prowled the corridors.

Andur made a meticulous job of it, going over himself twice and cleaning the tool.

It wouldn't be enough, Del knew. No matter how careful you were, an extended trip with several people in tight quarters became steadily less pleasant. You could only delay, not avoid, the assault on your senses. Still, he reflected, he'd rather be trapped with Andur than Rogany. He felt his stomach rumble.

Jyse hands began a series of pats. "Asen," he said. "I'll see what they have."

"I go with you," said Andur.

"I don't need help," said Jyse, finishing with a light tattoo up and down the spine.

"We have a security problem."

Jyse's hands froze. "What," he said.

Andur explained.

"You'd better get my cases," said Jyse.

"I hope you remembered to have them sent to accessible storage." Andur had memories of hunting for Jyse's baggage.

"Of course."

"'Of course'?"

Del rolled over to look at them. "It's going to be a long, crowded trip," he said. They both subsided.

The com scanner signaled.

Del looked at Andur.

Jyse pursed his lips.

They had all been expecting it. That was why the scanner was on. But if it was what Del expected, the comnet had set a new record in simulating news events.

He supposed, he reflected, that the viddrams could never show what spacing was really like. Nothing could capture the grinding monotony. The charming little adventures of the stories never happened. You knew your fellow passengers all too thoroughly. Anyone reclusive enough to escape being boring was also suspect in the tense dynamics of on-board sociability. A long trip was an exercise in one's ability to charm and amuse and be unobtrusive.

So the comnet created dramas from real life events. Truth became distorted. Most people would never make the trip into space. It was too expensive for any but the wealthiest. Those who did go, went on business, or as government employees, worked hard at dull jobs, and came home, glad to be through another tour of duty. But to the general public the cluster was filled with exploding suns, drifting clouds of mutant viruses, beautiful women and handsome men, all of whom were either dashing pirates or stern government officials enforcing enough order that everything would continue to exist for tomorrow's episode.

In real life, any surprises were apt to be terrifying. The air circulation had failed on one of Del's trips, and though they were in no danger—the natural diffusion caused by people moving, doors opening and shutting, and so forth, was more than adequate to maintain health— the passengers had voluntarily manned the hand generators. It was something to relieve the boredom. But the real roots of their effort lay in the unspoken fear of the fragility of the ship they depended upon and most did not understand.

Whenever he got home, Del wanted nothing but absolute solitude and reassuring routine.

And food that hasn't been thawed or rehydrated. Del's stomach rumbled again. Right now, even the preserved food in Jyse's luggage would be welcome.

"I guess I'd better look," said Del.

Jyse flipped on the holobloc.

It had been well established that public officials could not sue successfully if their portrayal was merely unflattering. There had to be malice. Still, Del was relieved to see the com-generated figure on the screen was a reasonable facsimile of himself. A little too heavy, and his eyebrows were not nearly so ferocious, but he could hope that his role would a reasonable approximation of reality.

Del settled himself to watch. If breakfast were going to be from Jyse's supplies, then it would be a while.

In the holobloc, he and Beyba, in full formal dress, were walking down a long stairway to the glittering platform where the assembled notables of Holk Station waited in arranged-by-height rows. Del gave points to the director for imagination, not accuracy, and let his thoughts wander.

He hoped Jyse and Andur kept down the bickering. The thud of Jyse's luggage on the decking was the signal for the start of a battle that lasted through every trip. Bitter complaints from Andur. Asen, I have to search the thing at every stop. And carry it half the time. All countered by Jyse's, these are essentials, Asen. What will we do if—

Cautious by nature, a tendency refined by years of experience in what could go wrong in the course of an official trip, Jyse had assembled a motley collection of things. Tailoring tools. A portable cooker with self-contained power cells. Spare power cells. Concentrated rations. Spices. Salt. Medicines. A pitifully underpowered com comp that had saved the day, twice, and been merely convenient on every other trip. A datapak on official etiquette with Jyse's notes and additions under a tight security code. All compressed into two dark, anonymous carrying cases, either of which could set the unwary staggering with surprise.

Del was watching himself make a particularly pompous speech in an atrocious accent when Andur delivered the cases with a thump, then went to rouse out Teyr.

"Leave him alone," said Jyse. "He needs rest."

"He got beaten," said Andur, "and he has to learn to get up and go on."

Jyse stopped sorting through the contents of the trunk. "Asen."

Teyr retreated back to the tumbled pile of bedding.

Del considered, watching Beyba's tall, thin figure in the bloc. Beyba hadn't worn that half-shaven hairstyle for years, and it looked ridiculous. With luck, Beyba was still too unused to government work to have set his com to capture personal references. It would be a kindness to let him miss this one—

Del refocussed his mind on Andur and Jyse's dispute.

Andur was the only one of them with any experience of children, if you could call the rigorous training he had both undergone and taught something a child should learn.

Jyse had more medical training.

Andur went and pulled back the cover.

Teyr was amazingly discolored. The welts around his torso almost black. But he looked alert and the monitor was reassuring.

"Up," said Andur sternly.

Teyr looked back with incomprehension.

"Up."

What?

Jyse smoothed away a smile at Andur's frustration.

"Andur," said Del.

"Asen."

"What did you have in mind?"

Andur began explaining.

In the holobloc Beyba and Del ran through the legs of an equipment mover, something no one in his right mind would do at any time.

Del forced himself to pay attention to Andur.

"— then we ought—"

A large hunk of hull fell away to reveal an impossibly starry sky and two external (!) foamers battling to save what should have been a completely decompressed station.

Del winced and said, "I think you should let him rest, Andur. Tomorrow will be soon enough."

Andur suppressed a rude gesture.

Del pretended not to have seen. "He's not a warrior," he said.

Andur's expression was—Del pulled his attention from the holobloc.

Whatever it had been, Andur had smoothed it away. "Asen," he said, and leaned against the wall to wait.

The next ten-days passed slowly, if tolerably. Teyr slept, Andur and Jyse bickered, more or less amiably, and Del worked.

The staff-woman's image shivered out of the holobloc as the light signaling his own image was being transmitted went out. Permund rose, face still impassively official, and finished filing the day's business. Then he checked the transmitter was truly off and stripped off his robe. "Jyse!"

A preoccupied Jyse gathered the robe out of his hands, put it away, and returned to Teyr, who stood patiently, arms wide, waist tubby with excess material.

There was a thud as Andur flipped a knife into a floor target: a knife was silent, reusable, and, with practice, accurate and effective even in free-fall. They were at half-gravity now, the ship's energy reserved for cushioning their fall into Syrtis' gravity well. Andur had been honing his skills since he got up. He pulled the knife from the target, backed away, and threw again. Thud.

"Don't," said Jyse, irritably readjusting the drape of the fabric.

Andur walked over, pulled the knife out, and looked at Deltander, who shook his head. Andur sheathed the knife with a click.

Jyse released the waist-tabs and Teyr stepped out of the material. In the low gravity, the stiff pants held their shape for an instant before collapsing.

Deltander dumped his handful of files into the catchall next to his customary seat. He could deal with them later. On ship, there was always plenty of later to fill.

Jyse was making Teyr clothes from Del's green semiformal suit. He had carefully removed all the embroidery, sectioned the motifs to scale them down, then cut completely new clothes from the unmarred fabric. It was almost completely wasted effort, but Jyse was busy and happy.

Del watched him tacking the designs around the collar and cuffs of the shirt. Though the clothes were quite different in style from the ones Del had found Teyr in, he was still uncomfortable with the long, bare legs discolored with bruises. Teyr looked so vulnerable.

Cheeks hollowed by fever and hunger, you could make a guess at Teyr's adult appearance. He was older than Del had first thought. His hands and feet were disproportionately large, there was a barely visible line of dark down on the belly and a shadowy fluff at the armpits and groin. He was going to be a deceptively delicate-looking man for someone so heavy-boned. His fat-free body, roped and corded with musculature as impressive in its way as Andur's, could only have been achieved by prolonged, strenuous exercise—

Del broke off, wondering why anyone would train a child so vigorously and then ship him over so vast a distance, and turned to the file rods. His eyes met Andur's. Andur probably could make some shrewd guesses about that. Del didn't want to hear them. It had already occurred to Del that a child bodyguard had the advantage of being unobtrusive, surprising. A very effective backup if you considered him disposable.

"Give him a break, Jyse," said Andur.

"Just let me finish this," said Jyse, brows knit. "There. You're bored, Andur."

Andur shrugged. He unrolled the film of plastic he used in his exercises. Del could see a ghostly dance of footprints as he set the controls. The object was to follow the not-quite-random motions. Released from the shirt, Teyr placed his feet, and Andur set the thing off, slow.

Jyse began running the seamer up and down the pants legs.

Del began reviewing tomorrow's business, half-listening to the irregular rhythm of bare feet, struggling to visualize the reality behind the whispering words of the official reports.

Presently Andur laughed.

Del and Jyse looked up.

Andur had cut a strip of gevilt and was holding it just out of Teyr's reach. Teyr stretched up. Andur grinned down, chewing his own.

"Andur," said Del.

Teyr leaped and locked his hands on Andur's wrists, dragging him down. They rolled over and over on the floor, legs sliding over thighs, hands over arms, until Andur, breathing hard, pinned Teyr.

Del relaxed his fists.

Andur sat up and split the gevilt with Teyr.

"Should he eat that?" asked Del.

"Good for him," said Andur.

"If he can stand the taste," added Jyse, holding up a sleeve and sighting down the seam. He folded it and began trimming excess material from the waist-darts.

Mouth full, Andur offered a sliver to Del, who sniffed it—musty, fruity—then rolled it between his fingers and tasted it. "Ptah!"

Jyse managed not to laugh.

Andur thumped himself on the chest, coughing.

Teyr's scarlet-stained lips parted in soundless laughter.

Del poured himself a cup of water. "Barbarians," he said, without force, and rinsed his mouth. The end of this trip was three shifts away. But tonight Beyba was giving a dinner that would break the monotony.

He watched the Teyr and Andur resume maneuvers on the exercise film. Del was looking forward to the enforced vacation he would have once they reached Belsyrtis. He sipped the water, ignoring the peculiar aftertaste. Recycled water always hinted at the thousands of times it had been through other bodies. He added a finger's-width of kvess and got a sharp look from Jyse.

Jyse shook out his handiwork. "I hope you haven't gotten him sweating, Andur. I need to check this, then start dressing *him*," Jyse's chin jerked in Del's direction, "for this dinner."

"Maybe Norrey's found something fit to eat," said Andur, waving Teyr in Jyse's direction. "If I see another ration cube, I'll eat the wrapper."

"S'edible," said Jyse through a mouthful of laces.

Andur grimaced.

If Teyr had not been with them, Del would have considered fasting for two meals out of three. All Jyse's efforts barely made the food tolerable, and he *was* a little thick at the waist. But it was hard to get enough calories into Teyr. The high fat rations he needed to speed healing had been reserved for the burn cases on board.

Beyba had made an ugly and unsuccessful scene.

And apparently a more quiet approach that had been effective. One battered box of the greasy stuff had been smuggled out of the sick bay. Andur watched every bite of Teyr's daily ration of it to make sure it actually got swallowed. The smell was awful, Del assumed the taste was worse. Teyr ate it in fits and starts like a starving man gorging on half-spoiled food, then chewed the bitter, greasy wrappers, one by one, desperate for the fat content.

Del frowned and splashed a little more liquor in his cup.

"Asen." Del looked up, about to tell Jyse he could regulate his own drinking. But Jyse was asking approval of Teyr.

Jyse was really very skillful.

"Very nice," said Del, judicially.

"Goes with his bruises," said Andur.

Del laughed. It was true. The suit's green picked up the fading marks.

"I thought," said Jyse, "a little powder—"

"No," said Andur.

"He'll have to wear something when we disembark," said Jyse.

"Try it," said Del.

Jyse was probably right. Only once had Deltander landed in Belsyrtis without makeup stiff on his cheeks and color oozing on his lips. It had taken several ten-days for the rumors of his ill-health to die out of the vidcasts, and much longer to convince some of the plaintiffs in legal cases that he was not going to conveniently drop dead. The high-intensity pin spots on the floating vidcam remotes had bleached all color from his face, making his smooth gold skin look grey as a corpse.

Not to mention, thought Del, sipping his drink as Jyse picked through his array of colored creams and powders, *what the rumors will be if I walk off with an obviously battered Teyr in the company of Beybaken Norrey and Prit. That is going to take some skillful handing.*

You became accustomed, early on, to the outrageous probing of your personal life by the media. Then you either retreated into what privacy you could muster, and defended it with discretion and wealth, or you blatantly advertised everything and let the stories fly.

Del seldom let down his guard, even in the company of his closest friends. His servants, well paid and dedicated, were, perhaps, marginally more trustworthy than his friends.

"Asen?" said Jyse.

Time to get ready.

The one advantage of Rogany's hostility was that Beyba's company had a freshness that it would not have if he and Del had been seeing each other every day throughout the trip.

And—Del sniffed appreciatively—the food looked good. He settled into his place at the table in a rustle of robes. They were informal, which is to say that Prit and Teyr, as well as Rogany and Andur, sat down to eat with them. One of Beyba's body servants and Jyse stood behind them, ostensibly tasting the food and actually eating very well.

Prit, red hair springing from its helmet of braids, sneaked a sweet, and, Del thought, kicked Teyr under the table. His sudden leap back and odd expression suggested he had discovered that, even with both hands in plain sight and his feet shod in the thin, felt soled boots they all wore on board ship, Teyr could pinch.

Andur looked under the table and smiled.

Arriving last as host, Beyba swept in—an explosion of orange and silver robes. Del saw Jyse's face draw slightly with distaste. Beyba's sense of theater often outweighed his interest in aesthetics.

Del, as highest status present, rose. Beyba seated himself. Del reseated himself, and the service began. There was seafood in some sort of broth, a little mushy after being released from cryo, but wonderful after days of rations.

Then a great cut of venison, brown and oozing juices. Del caught Jyse's severe expression, and lifted a warning eyebrow. Jyse smoothed his face. Cut into smaller pieces and mixed with fol-starch, that hunk could have fed five times as many—or made several luxurious meals for everyone present.

Prit, Del noticed, was eating very little, a sure sign he would be performing later. Del hoped not at great length. Beyba's one openly acknowledged cultural passion was for classical dance, and Prit danced all the heroic roles, face gilded, hands and feet rouged, fluttering green or purple eyelids. Del had never found watching a boy's hips gyrate of great interest. He picked at his meat, appetite blunted by the gross quantity.

Teyr, unfamiliar with the various implements, looked around, struggled briefly to imitate, and then reverted to fingers. He rolled the slices and ate them. It was a tidy process, obviously governed by etiquette as well developed as that Del knew, but different.

Prit giggled.

Beyba said, "He has lovely manners."

Prit laughed aloud.

"He's hungry," said Del, "and he hasn't—"

At Del's gesture, Andur intervened to cut the meat into smaller pieces. Teyr lowered his hands and looked around, embarrassed.

"No," said Beyba, "You just spent ten days with a starving young carnivore and there's not a tooth mark on you."

Rogany laughed.

Beyba rolled a piece of his own and bit in. He licked juice from his thumb. "You're too fussy, Del. Besides," he grinned, greasy-chinned, "It's not good manners to show up your host."

Prit and Rogany followed his lead, mocking, until Beyba frowned. Rogany abruptly yielded his plate to the servitors, and Prit's hands scuttled to imitate Teyr with fair accuracy. Rogany could find other, if less profitable, employment, but Beyba had found Prit on the streets and could put him there again.

Beyba prodded a conversation into being, and Del responded with practiced official charm.

Teyr finished the meat self-consciously and barely picked at the rest of the meal. By the time the final tidbits were on the table he was beginning to nod. His head drooped forward and Del could hear a dull clank when the monitor, still fastened to his arm under his sleeve, hit the table's edge. As he straightened with an effort, Andur looked to Del and suggested they leave: in less than two shifts they would be disembarking at Belsyrtis. Teyr still slept three-quarters of the time, and it was hardly worth exhausting him on social niceties.

Beyba genially protested. "Put him on one of the benches, Andur. He can sleep here as well as anywhere."

Andur's eyes queried Del, who shrugged consent. He, too, was enjoying the change of company.

Beyba's staff began folding the table, rearranging the seating to form a stage not much wider than Andur was tall.

Prit positioned himself, fist-harps in hand, center stage, and began to dance.

Del sipped his last, well-watered drink.

Beyba had found Prit somewhere in the swarming underbelly of Belsyrtian nightlife. He was uneducated, had thin, under-nourished features and a bony body, and was, Del suspected, vicious.

Solo, he could dance like nothing Del had ever seen.

If he ever learned to translate the elegant bravado he conveyed on the stage to the rest of his life, he would be dangerously charming. As it was, a few moments' conversation broke the spell, for he shed the ancient, noble characters he danced more quickly than his makeup.

They were well into the liquor, Prit earnestly pursuing some foe around the stage, Teyr sound asleep on his back, the hard, round mound of his stomach crowned by his crossed arms, when Andur left

66

the room. Del assumed he had gone to the personal—he was starting to think that way himself. Rogany, ignoring the stage, was telling an anecdote to another of Beyba's guards. He picked up a carving knife from the service board and made a series of misjudged lunges, getting a loud objection from Beyba.

Teyr awoke to see Rogany, armed with a dripping knife, feint at Del, who jerked back, startled.

Rogany's face as he went over backwards was totally bewildered, but his reflexes were still good. He rolled, knife in hand, to counter-attack. Teyr was protected only by his claw-enhanced grip on Rogany's back and neck: he went with him. Rogany threw himself backwards at the wall, and began battering Teyr, as Del and Beyba, on their feet, yelling, tried to stop the fight.

Andur sprinted through the door and solved the problem by hitting Rogany in the solar plexus, after disarming him with a kick. "What's going on?" he said, tossing the carving knife on the table, and beginning to fasten his clothes.

Rogany, doubled forward on his knees, swore violently. "I'll cut the braid off you!" He held his stomach with one hand and felt the long, ragged scratches where his falling forward had torn him from Teyr's grip with the other.

Andur laughed with real amusement. Rogany's chances in stripping Andur of his manhood emblem in one-to-one combat were nonexistent.

"Fuck you," said Rogany. "May your name be purged from the lists." Adult Kel picked their names from those of the recently, honorably dead. Name-death was the ultimate disgrace. A man without a braid and a name was no longer a Kel.

Andur made his face more sober. "What happened?" he asked again.

"We had a misunderstanding," said Del.

Beyba's eyes were shining as he looked at Teyr.

Teyr began licking blood off his hands.

Andur looked from one to one to one and reached a conclusion he kept to himself.

Rogany lurched to his feet and Teyr snarled, upper lip lifted over sharp, strong teeth. Rogany moved, in, away, testing.

Teyr nearly removed some more skin.

"That's dangerous," said Rogany.

"So am I," said Andur, very pleasantly.

Rogany drew back.

Del was trying to sooth Teyr. The stiff hairs above his ears were erect. Del could smell the musk. The boy still snarled silently. The slightly longer, narrower canine tooth looked formidable, isolated as it was by gaps in front and back and positioned at the front corner of a jaw whose outline was angled rather than arched.

You could drive that into the soft flesh of a throat, or shear through muscle, thought Del. He had watched those teeth cut the thick pieces of roast and never thought they would work as well on live flesh.

Rogany, assessing the scratches on his neck and back, swore again.

"Shut up, you stupid son of a bitch," said Beyba.

"Well," said Del, feeling fatuous in the extreme, "It's been an interesting evening, Beyba, but I think we're all tired."

Beyba ran through the conventional formulas of courtesy at speed.

They all chorused the proper responses, silent Teyr copying Andur's studied gesture of courtesy.

Not even the thick, well-sealed door entirely muffled Beyba's opening remarks.

"What happened?" said Andur.

Del described.

Andur said, "Asen, don't ever give Norrey any cause to believe he can get him," his hand was on Teyr's shoulder, "if anything happens to you. He's worth a lot of credits, Norrey may think he should have spoken for a share. And," Andur paused, "he may be interested in Teyr."

Del, remembering Beyba's excited face, nodded.

Jyse, looking at the bloodstains on Teyr's sleeves, shook his head. "I hope I can clean those—"

"Easier than sewing the Asen's throat up," said Andur. "It's lucky he's fast."

Cold ran down Del's back. It had not occurred to him that the incident was anything but an unfortunate misunderstanding.

"It would have been easy for Rogany to trip and overreach himself," said Andur. "And I think Norrey would eventually have seen his way to forgiving him."

"Beyba wouldn't," said Del.

"Have you killed. No. You're useful, you're safe. But if there'd been an accident, he wouldn't have thrown back the prize, either," said Andur.

"No," said Del, soberly. Beyba could be chillingly pragmatic.

A shift later, the *Forrei* shuddering with atmospheric buffeting, Andur had Teyr by the shoulders at the observation screen. Del came to stand beside them, watching the surface resolve into water, forests, and the tender tint of spring grasslands.

The long lake of the landing path appeared beneath them, a string of beads straight across the landscape, churned to glitter by the ship landing ahead of them. Del studied the scalloped shoreline, counting the explosions that had been used to carve it. When the port was first built it had been easier to blast holes and let their interconnected craters fill with water than to clear and level the rough terrain, and so that was what was done. It was a highly visible navigation mark: no automatic system could mistake it.

Spray exploded against the screen as their field exhausted its force into the water.

Teyr jumped, and Del pulled him upright against him, forearm locked across. He looked across the sleek black head, and took a deep breath as the water fell away and they regained altitude to cross the rocky ridge that guarded the city's millions. Out of control, too fast, too slow, the notch culled them all with extreme prejudice.

The raw scar on the left of the climbing path marked a recent crash: no survivors. There almost never were. If you wanted a safer approach you landed well away from the capital and shuttled in. The approach to Belsyrtis was designed to protect the city first.

The scattered bits of metal left sun streaks down Del's field of vision. He was as tense as Teyr. The *Forrei*'s pilot was showing off, cutting everything very fine. Del took a breath of relief as they topped the ridge and the port and city filled the screen, stretching beyond the horizon.

At some time the two had been separate entities, but they had grown together, then up into multistoried buildings, and even further up into the ground-anchored aerostats that soared above like tiers of clouds.

Del felt Teyr move, alert, curious, and let go. The boy didn't seem surprised. Maybe he had seen a city before. *If so, good*, thought Del.

Although he was wealthy enough to have extensive grounds around his home, Belsyrtis was one of the densest concentrations of humanity in near space. Down in the port transients walked the ways, sat in the restaurants, bars, and drug shops, and slept in one, two, and three person bunks, packed tightly as any ship, all for a price. It was impossible to simply stand somewhere for free. There was a constant nibble of tiny charges for room.

In the city proper, only government buildings made ostentatious display of open spaces, and there were life-long city residents who never crossed them, but went around by the edges. It was an old trick to send some newly-appointed clerk to pick up an authorization chit on the far side of a plaza and tell him sternly to "take the short way, we're in a hurry." His more experienced co-workers would gather to watch his faltering creep or panic-stricken run. In eighteen or twenty ten-days, the panting nervous wreck would be standing jeering the next unfortunate's rite of passage, but at that moment most regretted being successful in the governmental tests.

Del had seen Andur run himself to exhaustion to escape the oppressive sense of being surrounded by humanity. Teyr looked at the wind-borne towers with eager eyes. The upper city was beautiful, like something organic, all rhythmic similarity and subtle difference.

The view screen opaqued, as external sensors were covered to protect them during final maneuvers. Del felt their forward motion slow and stop as the port's field gripped the *Forrei*.

Andur slapped his com to life, watched the coded call flash the verifier. Del's people were waiting. He slid back the door. Out in the hall, Del could hear Beyba, loud and angry. "How did they get in?"

Del settled his robes, tasted the glaze of color on his lips. It sounded like Beyba had lost his bet. The media were out there, hungry for the story.

Jyse gave Andur a tight, brittle smile.

It would have been simplest to leave Teyr under guard in the *Forrei*, to be removed later. But, given the Rogany's ill-feeling toward Teyr and Andur that would not do. Rogany was still sporting med foam on visible areas of his neck, and Teyr watched him with predatory eyes whenever their paths crossed. Andur expressed his contempt by seeming to ignore Rogany utterly.

Del had considered having Teyr smuggled off with the luggage, and abandoned the idea after visualizing Teyr panicking in a small, dark space. Teyr's trust was far too fragile to bear testing.

So Andur would be doing nothing more complicated than walking Teyr off one way to meet some of Del's guards while Deltander met the rest and faced the media with Beyba.

Del suppressed a quiver of nerves. It would be only seconds before Teyr would be safely surrounded.

When the media was satisfied, then they could head for the roof where their skimmers were waiting to take them home.

Jyse flicked his fingers down the folds of Del's robes.

Del stood, square-shouldered, waiting for the lock to open.

Beyba swore inventively.

It is the media that keeps government officials humble—or humbles them in the end. One day the state of your health is urgent news for trillions. The next year you could die in the gutter without comment.

The media was waiting when the Forrei *was towed into the docking bay—a Norrey company bay. Beybaken had persuaded the Captain that his company could provide better facilities and more security for the debarking passengers, particularly the injured, than the government bays overlooked by the public galleries. He was furious the vidders had gotten onto his property.*

I was amazed they let us disembark without sending a remote onto the ship.

They surrounded us, and Beyba broke out in a fine sweat.

It takes experience to know that, while they are eager to wound, they are not eager to kill. Unless, of course, you are one of those unfortunates who spring to fame and must be ruthlessly exploited before your destined fall back into obscurity.

Beyba started to curse.

I gestured him quiet and moved to the fore. It went better than I expected: they were going to play us for heroes. When the first rush of questions slowed, I pleaded tiredness, and retired into the Norrey Company transporter.

Beyba watched a guard signal for the rooftop landing pad, and said, he wouldn't want to face that twice.

I told him it was just beginning.
Beyba combined three obscenities into one improbability; his
employees grinned sycophantically.
It was then I should have noticed Rogany was missing.
But I never gave him a thought.

Del could see the other skimmer being pulled into the shelter as they floated onto his landing pad. For the ten-thousandth time he considered, and rejected, building one down at the end of the estate near his own house. This one, squeezed in to accommodate the main house when his father was a young man, would have to do. It was the only major inconvenience of giving the main house over to his younger brother Hanro and his family.

The low, elegant house in its surround of woods and water was Deltander's much needed refuge from public life. The stately main house did not compare.

The skimmer hit with a bump. The pilot had misjudged again. Del frowned, and saw Jyse take notice.

Teyr, waiting with Andur, looked cold and nervous.

"You should have gone on, Andur."

"I tried."

"Ah."

But Teyr fell in behind readily enough.

The walk downhill under trees shedding for the beginning of spring was too brisk to be truly enjoyable, but the air, whipped across open ocean before hitting the coast was wonderful: free of the thousand odors of humanity.

Del could see a stir at the door of the main house as they passed the low, wide steps that swept back up the hillside to the portico. Riana, pallid and pretty like her mother, was too old to scamper but she was setting a stiff pace for the aging maidservant who accompanied her.

"Uncle!"

Del made his face pleased. He was too tired to stand and talk, but Riana was so painfully shy. He wondered if Riana would have been happier living with the same-sex parent, as was conventional. Living in a male-orientated household had made her very feminine by contrast, but, thought Del, touching his rough cheek to her smooth one, that didn't bode well for her future. She could not spend her life isolated with an indulgent father and uncle and their servants.

But it was out of the question she live with Marel, given her mother's temperament. Hanro was a sociable, easy-going fellow, whatever his faults. He had to be to stay contracted to Marel. "How pretty you look," said Del.

She did.

Marel was an elegant, pale-haired blond, and Riana had inherited that and her father's deep brown eyes. Whoever dressed her—at fourteen standard Del guessed she was old enough to pick her own clothes—took full advantage of the unusual coloring.

"Del." Coming at a more dignified pace, Hanro looked not so much pleased at seeing his older brother as relieved. "Good you're back." Hanro ritually touched cheeks. Then, in a lower voice, "We've had a few problems."

Del saw Jyse and Andur exchange looks.

Hanro's problems had ranged widely over the years with only one common factor: expense.

"Nothing serious," said Del firmly, continuing on his way.

"Well," Hanro pulled his thin robe closer and fell into step. "It seems to be the environmental system this time. The heating cycle switches off for no reason."

"Um," said Del, thinking of Holk's systems failure. His younger brother had never been off world.

Hanro moved a little closer. Del wished he'd use a different scent. "I'm a little short of credits right now—" He looked sideways into Del's face and faltered.

"Carnath will always advance you money for necessary expenses."

Hanro had at least the grace to look embarrassed. "I'm afraid Jasil and I had a difference of opinion—"

I wish you'd finish a sentence, Hanro, thought Del.

Riana had discovered Teyr.

"Uncle?"

"Um?"

"Who's that?"

Andur edged Teyr to his other side.

"I found him," said Del, uninformatively.

73

One of Marel and Hanro's binding similarities was their relentless curiosity about Del's finances, personal life, and habits. Even after he had built his own house, it had taken considerable diplomacy to convince his brother and his family that it was off-limits without some notice.

Hanro looked Teyr over, considered Del, and then returned to his main interest. "So, if you could call Jasil, Del, and explain—"

Del stopped on the path. If Hanro came along Del would be a half-shift getting rid of him. "Hanro. Unless someone's after you tonight—"

Hanro went red.

"—I'm tired. I'll straighten it out in the morning. Jyse. Ask Ikal to see about the heating." He brushed cheeks again with Hanro, bent to be kissed by Riana, and started down the path.

Hanro, left standing, said, a little louder, "Del?"

Del turned. "Yes?"

"We missed you."

Del waved acknowledgement.

At the click of his own gate closing behind him, Del looked at Andur and Jyse.

"Asen?" said the two with straight-faced correctness. Then Andur grinned. "Welcome home," he said.

"Andur," said Jyse.

Del pulled his robe closer. "Let's go in."

The half-frozen rain was stripping the last of the leaves from the trees and tapping at the floor to ceiling windows. Del listened to a particularly wild rush of wind and settled the fur at his neck closer.

Horrible to be out in, it was wonderful early spring weather. The bitter cold snap guaranteed the tolnen and helt would set prolifically even this far south. Even under the city domes they must be able to hear the hiss of ice driven by the wind.

Del yawned and pulled the fur up to his chin again, pleasantly warm in the pleasantly cool room. He avoided looking in the direction of the chrono. The grey, muted light was timeless. It would be a day for doing nothing. The staff would be indoors, noisy with pent-up energy. This time of year, there was little work and many hands.

He stretched, feeling muscles pull against one another. He stood and studied himself in the vidplane. A hint of sag under the chin there, as excess fluid left his face. A little bulge at the waist, probably space-bloat. He hadn't been eating that high on the *Forrei*.

Del paced about, relishing the feeling of being alone for the first time in several ten-days, repossessing his own space: the thick, pale carpets on the patterned stone floor, the ornate furniture from his grandfather's time, the hint of fruit and earth from the potted miniature trees against the window wall. Beyond wide-opened doors his tumbled, unmade bed lay half-open and inviting.

He stopped at a half-slid panel to the next room and checked. Teyr, huddled under the covers, was nothing but a dark shadow of hair and a sweet musk in the air. Del slowly pushed the panel shut.

He moved on to the personal and made himself comfortable, then wandered back into his bedroom, drinking a cup of water that tasted of nothing but itself. Del sat down and switched on the com.

There was a backlog of messages, some of them ten-days old, mostly worthless, that would have to be reviewed. There was always someone with an official complaint who got his private code and left information there, somehow hoping it would get special, discreet attention that would protect them from the angry attentions of whoever they were informing on.

Del flipped to the newest and began working backwards. He was not pleased to see that Hanro's latest message had references going back nearly a ten-days. Which meant Hanro was afraid for Del to find out what was going on when he couldn't beg and plead in person. It would have been easy to call Deltander on the *Forrei*.

Del's good mood evaporated.

He began punching the call for his man of business, Jasil Carnath. If Hanro was in trouble, Jasil was supposed to have put the brakes on.

"Del." Jasil looked pleased. "I just finished telling your steward to have you call me as soon as you were up."

"I haven't rung for anyone yet," said Del. "But Hanro was after me about something as soon as I landed."

Jasil put his fingertips together, mark of his approaching a delicate topic ever since he and Del had interned in Carnath senior's company. "You may remember you gave me authority to oversee Hanro's spending after the last investment episode?"

The one Beyba bailed me out of, thought Del, *or I would have had to file for bankruptcy.* "Yes."

75

"Hanro gave some thought to the matter and has decided where he went wrong—"

Del started rubbing his chest.

"—on to a good thing, and was hoping to surprise you by recouping your losses, and, incidentally, turn a nice profit for his own use."

"I trust you restrained him," said Asen Permund in tones icier than the chill wind outside. "I recall paying four different people to make sure there was absolutely no way I could be held responsible for his debts again."

"At my advice."

"At your advice. What now?"

"Your brother has been informed that, if he files for the payment of his share of the estate inherited jointly from your father, you will settle, in cash, and enable him to make this prime—"

The sound Del made indicated astonished rage.

"—after which he will be able to smooth things over with you by reason of the successful investment. Which he will, generously, share with you."

"I can live on his charity after he destroys my estate. Is that what you're telling me, Jasil?"

Jasil pursed his lips and gave a single, precise nod. "You should have gone into private advice, Del, and made a few credits for yourself. You have a good head for it."

Del rubbed his chest. "What's the final word on this?"

"Your brother, somewhat belatedly—"

Jasil was rather enjoying this.

"—and then decided you might be offended and tried to withdraw the suit. Unfortunately that requires posting a bond not to renew the suit and paying—"

"A fine for wasting the court's time, which is money he doesn't have. How much?"

Jasil named it.

Del sat back and sighed.

Jasil ran a finger along the edge of the comconsole. "I've told you, Del, you're going to have to force him off the estate to stop this." Jasil wiped his finger against his palm. "Buy him something up on the

76

coast. Anything is cheaper than baling him out every six or seven ten-days."

The taste in Del's mouth was bitter. "I will. Look into it."

Jasil's face went slack for an instant.

You never thought I'd do it. Here's another surprise. "And, Jasil, I need to set up a trust for someone with a clouded civil status."

"If," said Jasil carefully, "you're thinking of Riana, I can't imagine there would be any problem with her being a minor."

Del stared into the image on the face of the camera. "No."

"Ah." Jasil fiddled with a stylus. "Very difficult to write a trust for a gen. If that's what you have in mind. And I would say, given his propensity for violence, probably better that he clearly remain property."

"What are you talking about?"

"You haven't seen the vids?"

"No." If the confrontation with the vidders hadn't been a triumph it had certainly gone well.

Jasil drew a circle with the stylus. It appeared floating over his left shoulder in the display. "Norrey's security chief got fired. I gather Beyba didn't waste time or money making it a sweet departure. And he sold the story of his trip from Holk Station to Interdex." Jasil erased part of the circle, shaded in the rest. "They synthesized a picture. It's been on the channels since last night."

"I would have though Rogany had more sense. He'll never get another job."

"I think Beyba told him that beforehand. Maybe he believed it. Anyway, he's done quite well for himself. Enough to get out-system and look around."

"What did he say?" It came out flat and tired.

Jasil looked uncomfortable. "You and Beyba stole this gen in the confusion on Holk, brutalized him while the pair of you were trapped in a shelter, then tried to get him medical treatment in advance of badly injured human beings—some of whom died. Then you set the creature on Rogany for sport and Beyba fired him for defending himself a little too well." Jasil moved a quarter of the circle, tried to redraw the missing three-quarters, gave up, and looked straight into Del's eyes. "What did happen?"

Del told him.

Jasil shifted a clutter of file-rods. "So there is actually reasonable doubt about his civil status. And—this is important, Del, people get foolish about their pets—"

Del opened his mouth to protest.

Jasil raised his hand to stop him. "I know, Del. I know you. But you may have to prove it to other people."

"Jasil, he can communicate. He just hasn't spoken."

"*Can* he speak?"

"He hasn't."

Jasil's fingertips sought one another. "Is it obvious to an observer that you're not just," his fingers flicked in the air, "making up something—" Jasil's eyes focused behind Del's back.

Del turned around, fast.

Teyr, who had been carefully impressed he must stay out of com range on the *Forrei*, stepped back, out of sight.

"That's a gen?" said Jasil.

"We're not sure."

"You see my problem," said Jasil. "And Rogany walking around with gouges on his ribs claiming his throat was nearly chewed out—" Jasil's eyes shifted to his left where the security monitor would be.

"Problem?" said Del.

"No." There was a hint of doubt. "But I think you better come in. You're a focus of attention, and it's worth some trouble to get a good story."

"Leaving now," said Del, and flipped off the com.

Jasil's image mouthed something polite as it shivered out of existence.

Emerging from Jasil's office half a shift later, Del felt back in control of things. Hanro's immediate problems had been solved, and if the judge presiding thought there was anything peculiar about Del's paying to stop a suit against himself she kept her thought to herself. *Probably thinks I pushed him into it*, thought Del. Jasil had a list of "suitable properties," and they had mapped out a campaign in the Rogany matter. A good day's work.

Amazing how quickly one's affairs went to ruin.

Del paused, insulated boots ankle deep in freezing slush, and looked across the plaza to the government offices. He looked at his escort: eight. He'd brought everyone easily available without weakening the estate's security, in case they should encounter the media. The government plaza was officially off-limits.

But so was Norrey Corporation property, and Beyba was a lot less friendly about encroachments than the easy-going government guards.

It might be a good idea to drop in on my office. Unannounced.

The eight guards shifted uncomfortably. Sitting outside Jasil's in damp boots was dull and miserable. They were ready to go home.

Del stated his decision and watched the covert looks of resignation. "I expect they've gotten pretty slack," he unfastened his coded keys, "in my absence. I'd like to find out exactly what's been going on. Horres, I want you to go in the back, with—three?—others."

The guards' expressions had changed. This was going to be more than a perfunctory walk-through.

"Asen," Seobel said, accepting the keys with satisfaction. "Two will be enough. Seal the back?"

"No, go right on in. Make sure no one gets a message onto the net. The rest of us will come in by the portico from the trade delegation building."

"No force," said his chief of security.

"Announce yourselves. Anyone disobeys, they are in violation of the applicable regulations, which allow reasonable restraints. Don't make an incident. But I want them frozen in place until I know what everyone in that office was doing when I walked in."

By now the guards were eager.

In a low, intense voice Seobal said, "You heard the Asen. We're to freeze them as they stand, impound business in progress. We're looking for evidence of improper activities: that covers everything from sleeping on the job to dealing trade secrets. Do it neat, tight, polite, don't let them get a complaint on you."

Deltander nodded.

There was a mutter of coordinating times and Del's little black-and-grey force split and took its two ways in the gusting sleet.

It was Seobal who actually stepped through the seldom-used side door first and announced, "This is a security inspection under the authority of Asen Deltander Entaneray Solt Permund. You will remain as you are. Any attempt to communicate with anyone inside or outside of this office will be interpreted as an admission of guilt and referenced to the commission on internal affairs—"

Since the last time most of these people had faced the commission was when they were approved for this job, the forlorn little group looked scared. Del did a head count. Even at that they were in better positions than the four, five, six—one woman scuttled through the door—five people who were not in the office. From their vague responses, which became more specific with a little prodding, it became apparent the missing people had not been in today, and in two cases, hadn't been in for the past four or five days. It was possible to work from home, as Del had from the *Forrei*, but none of these people were authorized to do so.

Seobal's group prowled through the room enjoying themselves.

There were the usual unauthorized games, and improperly secured consoles.

Del could hear shouting from his private office that promised something more interesting. The glances among the clerks suggested they had a good idea what.

Del left them to the none-too-tender mercies of Seobal.

Yber heaved back a security door and beckoned, silent.

Del had put quite a number of his own personal credits into making his office comfortable, impressive, and secure, and had been rather proud of its dark, severe elegance. An elegance that was considerably spoiled by the clutter of stale food and scattered file-rods.

He sniffed the air, heavy with rith. Government offices, sealed against the city police, made excellent places for drugging out when their own security was lax. And embarrassing stories when the news hit the media. But that was a minor inconvenience, no what Del was checking for.

Entequil, on his knees with Horres standing over him, had apparently been returning quite a number of rods to the main files. Without touching, Del read their tagging.

"We'll check to see who's been handling them, Asen."

Del nodded.

Everything on the pending negotiations of the disputes between Everei Corporation and the field authorities at Kican. At least some of the material on the pending negotiated settlement between Acaco and Welerin. Plus an interesting miscellany that suggested Entequil was running a business rather than yielding to one well-financed temptation. In any case a matter for the commission, not something Del could handle in-house.

"Call the guard," said Del. All the petty offenders in the outer office, innocent or guilty of complicity, would be swept up, too. Their hard luck, perhaps, but they had to have had some idea what was going on.

"Asen."

Entequil tried to stand and was forced back to his knees. "I can explain, Asen—" He saw Del's face and fell silent.

He was checking to be sure everything looked right when I made my usual surprise visit a few days from now, thought Del. He looked at the bowed neck, streaked with sweaty hair, and turned away to the window overlooking the governmental plaza. A smart man would have had everything in order before the *Forrei* grounded.

Entequil would be lucky to end as a data-entry specialist in a restricted off-world colony. And as for whatever would happen to his dependents—there were five or six. Del tasted bile. He couldn't do a thing for them without leaving himself open to accusation.

Del studied the dark, carved wood panels that had cost half a year of his governmental salary. It had been an error to hire Entequil, breaking the tradition of preferring only the children of the well to do. Del had thought Entequil smart enough to understand he would eventually be compensated as other aides were compensated, by discreet opportunities for investment, advice, and suggestions.

He glared at the hanging head. *Stupid. Why couldn't you be loyal and wait?* At least he'd been out of town when this happened. The onus would fall on Tarany, who was responsible for supervising them when Deltander was away.

And the story would drive Rogany's complaints off the channels. *Indeed*, mused Del, turning to watch a solitary figure leave dark footprints in the plaza's slush, *it will be plausible to imply that Rogany's statements were part of a set-up to discredit him. It might even be true. It would not be the first time*.

An honest magistrate is an inconvenience if you have enough money to buy the right decisions as a business expense. That Entequil would be destroyed to score a few points among the bigger players would not have been given a thought. Slum trash, good riddance.

The government guards arrived, noisy and officious, to take charge. Del sat, stone-faced, watching and waiting until his own security would be free to accompany him home.

The wind-whipped path down to his own house from the landing pad had become rough and treacherous with frozen slush. The furry, swelling buds of the tolnen were glazed with ice, metallic in the light from the door to the main reception chamber. Del's guards crowded in, stamping feet and shaking off sleet as they commented on the day. Half in, they stopped.

Someone had taken two of the spare floatation pads for the skimmers and inflated them in the inlaid floor. A scattering of nervous-looking servants was peering up into the gilded fretwork of the dome. Jyse came forward, looking very relieved that Del was home.

Jyse's cheekbones looked thin and fragile as eggshells under the line-webbed skin. *He's not going to space many more times*, thought Del. Spacing robbed the bones of strength, no matter how careful you were to exercise and stay in the artificial fields. In the harsh overhead light it was plain Jyse had only a few more good years.

"Teyr's—" Jyse stopped, eyes on Deltander's face, seeing the pity there.

Del would have given days of his own life for Jyse to fail to understand his expression.

Jyse was silent.

The guards and servants stared, uncomprehending.

Del took Jyse by the arm and went into the small, flower-filled room where guests prepared themselves before being received. He took the thin, cold hands. "Jyse?"

The fragrance of tolnen was overwhelming. The floor was littered with it. He could hear the twittering in the reception hall. *They think I'm disciplining him*, thought Del.

Jyse indicated the crushed flowers with a jerk of his chin. "Asen. He did this, and Fior hit him. Of course she says she didn't."

"Yes," said Del, releasing Jyse's hands, glad of the distraction of the present.

Fior had a constant problem with the younger staff and the few children that lived with their parents. The large garden and the greenhouses were wonderful places to play: strange and mysterious to city-bred children. No amount of rule making prevented them from getting into the plantings, and there was always damage visible to Fior's critical eye. That she often lost her temper and gave a few cuts with anything handy had turned harassing her into a rough sport for some of the older children.

And Teyr had run afoul of her.

"What has Andur done?"

"Asen, he went out before you."

Del cursed with a fluency considerably improved by confinement with Beyba. Of course he had. Andur had spent the last two ten-days with the same people, all of them male. He'd have been off into the city as soon as Seobal gave him leave.

"Asen?"

Del put a hand on Jyse's frail shoulder as he thought. With Andur out, only Jyse could communicate with Teyr, and Jyse's understanding was limited. Del could feel the old man quivering. His whole life had been spent serving the Permunds, and that Del have reason to be displeased with him was unusual and terrible.

"He's in the roof?" said Del.

"Asen, he's gotten up behind the carvings near the service access." Jyse twisted his hands together. "I was afraid to send someone up after him." He looked at the littered floor. "And I was afraid to crawl out there myself." It was a fifteen-foot drop to the stone floor and the gilded carving would offer no protection.

"I'm glad you didn't try. He's all right?"

Jyse nodded. "Itor says she wouldn't stop hitting him, and he wouldn't hit her."

"Ah," said Del. So Teyr'd staged a strategic retreat. He started pulling off his outer robe. Jyse reached to help.

"Asen, what are you going to do?"

"Tell him to come down," said Del, stripped to shirt and pants.

The access way was a generous fit even for his broad figure, but it was dusty enough to leave his arms streaked with grime. Del had an excellent idea what a fool he was going to look when he emerged.

The hatch popped open under his hand.

Behind the nearly three-dimensional carvings that decorated the entrance hall dome, a walkway for cleaning and machinery access had been built. It was onto this Del crawled and leaned back against the wall, beating dust out of his clothes, waiting for his eyes to adjust to the dim light. Fine grey grit lay smooth and undisturbed in both directions.

Teyr had gotten in by climbing up the outside.

Del stood, mouth half-open, listening.

Was that a cautious whisper of sound to his left?

"Teyr?" breathed Del.

He wanted the boy to stay still. If he hid in the maze of service tunnels it would be difficult, even dangerous, to have him followed. "Teyr?" Del looked to his left. He jumped and shivered as something touched his hair.

Del turned, slowly, and looked up.

Even in arm's reach, Teyr was nothing but a dark shadow on darkness. The top of Del's head must have passed no more than a finger-length beneath him. He'd blacked his face and hands with grime. The slim-bladed knife Andur had given him was naked in his hand.

Del felt his guts loosen. *Glad you waited.* Come down, said Del with his hands.

The blade was sheathed with a click and there was a slither of cloth. Teyr slid down and hugged him.

Del hugged back and nearly laughed with relief until he saw the dark mark under the grit. Fior had hit the boy down across the forehead and cheek, his eye protected only by its bony socket. Del tilted Teyr's head to the light. At least the eye wasn't damaged.

You must, thought Del, gently rubbing the mark with his sleeve, *have rolled in the tolnen*. There were red, purple, and yellow stains and splashes of golden pollen worked into the grey-and-black clothes. *Fior had no idea what she might have set off.*

Teyr endured Del's attention, stoic.

Del grabbed his shoulders. "You did the right thing," he said.

Teyr looked away. Del's words had no meaning to him.

"The right thing," said Del, pressing his face against the dusty hair. And, silently, *Tomorrow we're going to start to find out what you are. So Jasil can see you have protection, and my brother can't try any more bright, borrowed ideas.*

"Asen?" Jyse's worried voice rang around the dome. "Are you all right?"

"Coming," said Del.

Teyr's tongue tidily licked the corners of his mouth as he picked up another joint. Del poured a dollop of syrup into his kentor, sipped. He jumped slightly at the crack of a bone being twisted open.

Teyr looked up apologetically from trying to get the marrow from its cavity.

Del sipped again.

They were sitting in the little room where Del usually ate before going to work. The air was filled with the aroma of fruit, sauces and grilled meat. Just the smell was nourishing.

Gern proffered a dampened towel to Teyr, who carefully wiped his hands. The overservant then hinted an application to the face was in order. Teyr dabbed aimlessly.

"*Gern*," said Del.

Gern, who had scrubbed Del's face when he was a boy, produced a clean face in one smooth pass. Or two if you counted the teasing dab under the chin.

Teyr wandered around the room, then settled on the padded window still overlooking the dark, icy garden.

Del helped himself to another cake.

Tomorrow we diet.

Gern discreetly freshened the table. "Asen?"

"You can go."

When he was gone, Teyr gestured, hungry.

Del put his cup down and gave up brooding over the problem of Fior. He would have to have Hanro give her a job on the new estate.

Hungry? gestured Del.

Teyr's stomach bulged, even if his cheeks were hollow.

It was Andur who had discovered Teyr would respond to hand motions where verbal commands met with blank incomprehension. Andur had an abbreviated system of hand motions designed for the giving of silent commands. On the trip home Teyr had picked up enough to make a simple exchange of wants and needs possible.

None of them had made any progress in the Teyr's own quick and complicated system. Though his hands often flew to speak, they stopped. The swift series of gestures Teyr made now meant nothing to Del, who even had trouble sorting out individual signs in the smooth flow of motion.

Del sighed and put down his cup, about to start the slow process of defining the thing wanted by question and example, when it occurred to him that the kitchen, filled with everything available if not imaginable, was the place to settle the matter.

A high-pitched laugh cut off abruptly as the door slide shut behind them. Someone in the cold store had gotten word of Del's arrival a little too late.

Vicke, the cook, didn't bother to stop chopping. Del was a regular visitor. "Asen."

"This is Teyr."

Vicke nodded.

"He says," Del pulled over a backless stool to rest his legs, "he's hungry."

Vicke looked startled. Few people in his household complained of hunger after a meal.

"I think he means for something specific."

Vicke's expression relaxed. Requests were something more usual. His knife gathered the fluffy bits of green together and carried them to the bowl he was filling. "For what, Asen?"

"I don't know." Del gestured a few questions. Whatever it was, it was round. Sort of. That uncertain hand waggle covered a lot of territory.

Vicke was dubious. "An egg?"

The bowl of pink-dappled eggs was carefully scrutinized.

Vicke picked one up, cracked it, and flipped the raw contents into his mouth. Teyr followed his example, and Del hastily went to admire the pastry chef's efforts. There were limits to his cosmopolitanism. He watched sugar being stretched and pulled into ribbons and bows, while listening to the crack of shells behind him.

When it stopped, he turned round.

Teyr licked a dribble of yolk from his upper lip.

Del beckoned him, thanked Vicke, and started for the stairs, acutely aware that the butchering room, with its fascinating bits of this and that, was an area he would rather Teyr explored without him.

It was Andur, coming back late from the city, who brought the news about Rogany.

Dead.

I was not prepared for the shattered body in the holobloc. It might be impossible to determine the cause. It had required gene typing to determine the identity.

"Norrey's a rough player," said Andur, rotating the image.

I looked away and asked if he thought Beyba had him killed.

Andur shrugged. "Asen Norrey had a problem. His security solved it."

Just like cargo manifests that weren't being posted promptly enough: something to be straightened out without being ordered.

The com chirped and voiced a request I enter my reason for interest in this matter. I reached for the device, and was forestalled by Andur, who gave his name and said, "Personal acquaintance." He shut the image off. "Don't leave a fingerprint in the system, Asen. There'll be enough speculation without that."

Del ran a thumb down the stack of thick creamy paper. *Less. Definitely less than yesterday.*

There was no one in the household who was truly literate beside himself. Although reading facilitated Del's job—not all the old records were machine-comprehensible—it was primarily an odd hobby, the subject of jokes among his friends. Nonetheless, someone was taking paper from his desk. Not a lot, but steadily, and his stylus needed refilling again.

The door slid back and the only person, besides himself, who had free access to Del's desk backed through, arms heavy with rod-files in their cases. Andur followed, directing Teyr where to go, and pushing the portable reader. Coming to the thick rug, Andur grunted and lifted the thing bodily into place.

Del eyed the cumbersome machine without favor. He was working through his vacation because of the disruption of the investigation.

"Thank you," said Del, measuring the stack of paper again.

His tone caught Andur's ear. "Something wrong?"

Del glanced at Teyr, who was patiently sorting through the files: separating them into piles of like and like as any clerk would before reaching for a reader and voice-in-the-ear to find what they meant. "Is there some reason he'd be using my paper?"

"Not that I know of." Andur walked over and looked at the stack. "I can check his room."

Del refrained from looking at Teyr. He did not understand spoken language, but he was very quick to read gesture and facial expression. "Without his knowing."

"Keep him busy," said Andur.

Del watched Teyr's fingers shift the rods. He was as efficient as one of the clerks. Del had been thinking of trying to teach him to read. He was quick enough at remembering the coded symbols. There were so many things Del wanted to know—

Andur, out of sight in the room beyond, said, "I think you should look at this, Asen."

Teyr looked likely to be busy for a while yet.

The room was almost painfully bare, stripped after the last of Del's companions had been dismissed. Del reminded himself again that the place should be redone.

Andur pointed up to the grillwork running around the top of the wall: wood, old, and beautifully carved. Del had paid a substantial price for it to reduce the raw newness of the house, and reserved the best for use throughout his private suite. Del looked closer. Nearly matching the cream of the walls, the sheets, slipped behind the grill, were invisible in plain sight.

Andur left, presumably to check on Teyr.

Del carefully worked an end sheet out, acutely conscious that he wasn't comfortable sneaking a look, and that it might be worse to just ask—

The back of the sheet, facing out, was blank. But the front, against the wall, was covered, top to bottom, with minute, flowing symbols.

Del tilted the sheet to the light.

He couldn't recognize one, and yet he was sure they were symbols, not just attempts to scribble something like his own writing. Riana had done that when she was very young, and Del had half-hoped she might be interested in learning. It would have been fun to have someone share his avocation. Nothing had come of it.

No, this was writing. Smooth, uniformly formed, and repeated in groups. There was an occasional sputter from the stylus as if the tool was not adapted to produce what the writer had in mind, and had rebelled at the tight curves and shifts of direction.

Some of the problem, thought Del, carefully sliding the sheet back into place, *may be the scale*. On this sheet, at least, Teyr had used every inch of surface, as if trying to use as little paper as possible. *Why is he doing this?*

Del moved along the wall, searching. He wanted to find something earlier. He reached through, rolling another sheet to pull it out. *This one looks older*. The writing was bigger, and the characters irregular. Teyr had been struggling to control the stylus.

Here, tucked behind the others, there were drawings. One was of Andur, quite recognizable, with all the markings on his face diagramed separately in an abstract design. Del looked, thinking, *I never thought of it that way*. The pattern was, quite clearly, that of the jaws of some beast gripping Andur's head so that his scar-embellished face showed between its teeth.

Others were people Del did not know. He flipped through pages, half-listening for any sound from the next room. One man was drawn repeatedly, front and side, chin in hand and a half-smile on his lips.

There was a landscape, broken by a huge building, its scale indicated by the tiny human figures that climbed the steps before it. It looked too cyclopean to be real.

But Del was sure it was real: the details were too precise. One step was broken, and the right and left wings had different decorative patterns incised in the stone.

These are things he wants to remember.

Andur hadn't come back.

Which might mean he was having to keep Teyr busy.

Andur looked openly relieved when Del came in. Teyr glanced up from the sorted piles and stood, waiting." You can go, Andur." Del sat down in his chair. Teyr started to follow. You stay, Del added by hand.

Teyr remained, looking a little puzzled. He knew something was going on, but was not sure it involved him.

Del pulled a sheet of paper from his desk. Using this, question, signed Del.

Teyr was, Del saw, really tempted to say no. Which meant Del had chosen the wrong way to go about it.

Yes, reluctant.

Del's hands wanted to shape why. Instead he simply pulled a block of sheets off the stack, put the stylus on top, and handed it all to Teyr. He signed, You want more, ask me.

May I go? Awkwardly one-handed.

Yes.

Del stared at the closed door, frustrated. There was nothing he wanted more than to be able to read those pages.

Beyba picked a fruit at random and drove his belt knife into it in three precise cuts. The he spiked the wedge, pulled it free, and sampled it. "So he can write. You think." Beyba wiped his mouth. "Hate this stuff. You've checked the databank?"

Del nodded, attention on the swaying cargo pods in the high-speed line overhead. They had been repainted. Dents and scratches showed they had originally belonged to Venterox, which was currently forbidden to trade in Belsyrtis for various infractions dangerous to the port. Like shipping undeclared explosives. They might just be selling off local assets, but it could be worthwhile to check if that sloppy white logo slapped over Venterox's wasn't just a front.

"Well?" said Beyba, unlatching an end-flap and prodding the contents of another crate.

"Nothing. But," Del pulled his attention away from the pods, "he's writing in script. It's possible that what we've got's machine printing. It might look quite different. Ours does."

"Ptah!" Beyba spat out a chewed sample. "Have them code it. The groupings will look the same. Try this."

This was red and drippy and very good. Del leaned forward, trying to keep his robe clean. "I don't want to hire someone. Whatever they found would be on the vid channels a shift later."

Beyba nodded and cut another sample.

Del wiped his hands.

Beyba gave him an oblique look, then said to the interior of a crate. "I have someone. If you get a sample."

Del signaled for a servant to place a folding stool and sat down. Another pod of fruit was opened for Beyba's inspection, and the porters stepped back out of easy earshot again.

Beyba pulped a bit between his fingers, and sniffed.

"You're not going to be easy until you find out."

"Um," said Del.

Beyba wiped his hands and cut another wedge. "So the question isn't whether or not, but how and when." He scraped a rind with his knife and found the results unsatisfactory. "You could just ask him."

"No," said Del, looking over the vast expanse of the Norrey docking bay, loud with the clash and rattle of loaders and freight lines. "He hid it. If I hadn't been on vacation and using the paper more than usual I would never have noticed. I might do better to leave it alone."

Beyba snorted. "Del, you're going to sit and argue with yourself until you justify it. Why not skip the preliminaries?" He yelled for the porters to pull another pod. "You want a good reason? Suppose something happens you could have prevented if only you'd known," Beyba's long forefinger prodded the air, "this. Or that. You'd never forgive yourself." He grinned. "The question is, when and how, not whether."

"Leave me a few illusions about myself."

"Wastes time." Beyba punched the override key home and the porters cracked the pod. The sweet overripe smell made Beyba curse vigorously. "How many of these do we have?"

The question was semaphored across the floor.

The answer made Beyba wince. "Dump them. We'll pay," he said to the anxious floor manager holding the humming master list.

"Asen, I suggest we check a few more—"

Beyba turned slowly around and stared at the man, who swallowed, and said, "Yes, Asen."

Del watched Beyba's order reach the far wall where the piercing whine of the uncouplers began immediately.

"Why so many," asked Del.

"It's all full ripe or worse. By the time it's offloaded and rechilled it'll have spoiled." Beyba wiped his hands and beckoned another pod forward.

Del shifted on his seat.

Without turning around, Beyba said, "You can wait up in the office if you want. I'll be done in a bit." He rammed the key home. "This can't wait."

"I'm all right."

"Suit yourself." Beyba gave his attention to the contents of the pod.

Ordinarily Del would have enjoyed waiting. Beybaken Norrey in action was instructive: for all his wealth, he supervised his business closely. Watching him work gave Del an unaccustomed look into the practical realities of running a business. By the time most disputes got to Del, everything had been reduced to a tidy file of assertions and counter-assertions, evidence, and a summary of precedents. The gritty routine of unloading, appraisal, and price setting was a corrective. But today Del was restless. He wanted Beyba's advice and was having to stand second in line to a cargo of perishables.

He sat watching the systematic stripping of the pods—there was something awesome in such wholesale destruction. The crew moved from pod to pod, tagging them. The floor crew followed simply sucking the contents into the waste machines: fruit, crates, tags, and all. The pods jounced away to be cleaned and slotted into the loading line.

Some of the stuff was still good enough to be sold to other, lesser dealers to pick through. But that would undercut Beyba's prices for the higher quality, and Beyba had opted for simple destruction. Del wondered if he had precise figures to back his decision, or if he was playing by well-tuned ear. *Tongue, in this case*, thought Del, standing and stretching.

He moved along the gallery to the far end where he could see the multi-colored logos of the small freighters pulled into the older docking facilities. Del searched the designs for any he didn't know. So many, their relative poverty easy to guess by the complication of their emblems. It took credits to register and retain the bold, simple designs of the majors, and they defended their symbols savagely against even accidental confusion. Norrey might not be able to register every orange logo, but his men of business could make anyone using one painfully sorry.

Del stood musing on the inequities of a supposedly fair port system until Beyba put a hand on his shoulder. "I said: 'Hey.' Left you too long, didn't I."

Del had startled.

"You have that black, brooding look."

"I was wondering how they survive."

Beyba laughed a single hard syllable. "Some of them don't. Most of them scrape a living. I docked right over there the first time I brought a ship into Belsyrtis," Beyba's heavy robes swung as he lifted an arm, "and I thought I'd never be back if I could ever get them to let me leave."

"Ah?" said Del.

"Freighting wooldref."

Del started laughing.

"Yeah. No license. Well, nobody told me I needed one." Beyba shook his head. "By the time they'd fined me, had me pay disposal costs, and I'd paid the docking fees and the overtime for the unloaders I never got to use because I had to pay the port for the privilege of having their *bonded* team handle it—" Beyba keyed open a door and ushered Del through. "It would have been cheaper to sell the fucking ship. Except—"

"You would still have had to pay," finished Del.

"I've always thought port authorities had a lot of nerve calling independent traders pirates." He punched a code and a door opened in an apparently seamless wall. "In here."

The lights came on.

Beyba's private office was in stark contrast to his flamboyant robes. Del ran his usual appreciative eye over the smooth surfaces and muted colors. The only clutter was in the wall-high cabinets of objects that filled two sides of the room. Del drifted along the collection, admiring.

"This is new," said Beyba, opening a cabinet. "Came in yesterday." He handed Del the rosy, nacreous nodule.

"Henohir," said Del, rubbing his fingers on the smooth surface. "Very fine."

"But flawed," said Beyba. "Look here." He held the piece to the light.

There was a single dark fleck embedded in the heart of the stone.

Del took it back and looked for himself. "You'd hardly notice."

"No. And it's uncut." Beyba returned it to its cradle and closed the door on it. "But I'll sell it when I get the chance." He slipped off his heavy robe and motioned for Del to do the same.

In shirts and pants they sat down.

"Now," said Beyba, opening a box, "are you going to tell me why I'm in the shit? Or do I get to go on playing guessing games?"

"I wanted to get some advice," said Del.

Beyba measured the fine brown powder out with a spatula no longer than his little finger. "You've been extremely polite ever since we got back from Holk."

"I'm usually polite," said Del, dryly.

Beyba, fingers busy packing the tiny tube, frowned and said, "I know when I'm being chilled. I want to know why." He lit the tube and blew a cloud of smoke, offered it to Del.

Who accepted and inhaled. He felt drowsy with the drug in seconds. "I wanted your advice."

"Ahh," Beyba breathed out. "I can lend you someone who can run a code check, so you'll know if we have anything like a language and take a look in the general databanks." Beyba passed the fuming tube.

Del took a long last pull and killed the pipe.

Beyba began cleaning out the tube, knocking the ash into another box and twisting it closed. "Now you tell me what's wrong, Del."

Del looked at the bony face and couldn't meet Beyba's eyes.

The oath Beyba rapped out was startling in its violence. "I hated this place when I first came and it hasn't changed. I pick up a cup the wrong way and all the aristos titter and make sure I never get near the bidding. Bunch of shits." His voice went louder. "I'd like to know what I did, Del," the volume lessened. "In simple, crude language the ignorant might understand." Beyba dug his hands into the hair at the nape of his neck.

"Nothing," said Del.

"Fuck it," said Beyba, flat, tired. "Del?"

Rogany's death shouldn't have surprised me, thought Del. *I knew how he did business.* "Did you have Rogany killed?" The words popped out. Del looked up, appalled at himself.

Beyba took his hand from the back of his neck and laughed. "Is that what's bothering you. No." He leaned back and considered the arrangement, pipe and two boxes, in front of him. Then, more slowly. "No. Although I wouldn't be surprised to learn one of my employees did."

Del, trying to find something for his nervous hands to do, picked up the round box and unscrewed and rescrewed the top twice before he spilled the ash out, fiddling. He tried to push it into a tidy heap.

"Leave it alone." Beyba swept the rith-ash off the table with one impatient movement. "Rogany had too many credits and too little wits. He was a dead man when he walked out my gates."

"Why?" said Del.

"He was unemployable, so nobody was going to protect him, and he had a nice chunk of unassigned credits—"

"*Unassigned*," said Del.

"I said he was stupid. He flashed the chit all over the zone."

"Doesn't make sense."

"Yeah, it does, if you knew Rogany. He figured he'd gotten the best of the deal, and wanted to enjoy it."

"Why unassigned credits?"

Beyba shrugged. "That's what he asked for. I think he thought he'd change his name, work his way back up into someone's security. You can buy good false records on Gneiss. They have a set-up that makes it almost legal."

Del tried to dust off his hands.

"You'll have to wash it off," said Beyba. "What are you going to do about Teyr?"

Del stopped scrubbing his hands together and considered. "I thought I might teach him one of the scripts I know—"

Beyba reached for a flask and Del held out his hands. "That should put off the problem for a year or two." Beyba shook a few drops into Del's palm.

Del wiped his hands together and accepted the square of paper Beyba offered. The fragrance of tolnen almost overcame the odor of rith in the room. "It shouldn't take that long," said Del.

"Teach him two or three, then." Beyba sat up. "Look. You want to know, I'll help. You don't want to know, stop worrying it."

Del folded the paper with finicky care.

"What are you afraid of?"

"He had a rough time—"

"Oh, I didn't know, didn't know," wailed Beyba in falsetto.

"Don't!" Del, jarred through, wiped his over-scented hand across his mouth. "Don't."

"You've wanted to talk to him ever since you found him. Now that it looks like you can, you're dithering. Why?"

"What if he says, 'I want to go home'?"

"Ah," said Beyba, settling himself elaborately against the back of the seat. "Now we come to it. Say no."

Del gave him a distracted look as he rose and began pacing.

Beyba, watching, said, "Someone sent him on a trip that a grown man would think hard before taking. Wherever he was going, it wasn't home." Beyba stood up. "I don't want to shatter any romantic notions of yours, Del, but Teyr is sophisticated enough to conceal that he can read and write. And he knows you can. That's not a naive choice."

Del fingered the latch on a cabinet. "I trust him."

"But he's no innocent." Beyba came and stood behind him. Del could see his reflection in the glass. "What makes you think he wants to go?"

"I don't know."

"What?"

Del turned around, annoyed.

"You don't know why you think he wants to go? Or you don't know that he does?"

"He thinks about it, draws pictures."

"I think about the slums of Gneiss. Which doesn't mean I want to go back. I'll send Kartor around. Have Andur copy a sample for him."

"Thank you."

Beyba was pushing his arms up his sleeves. He straightened his robe's heavy yoke.

Del began pulling his own on, thinking.

Beyba, waiting by the door, reached to adjust Del's yoke. "Del. Don't waste—" He stopped and rephrased. "Don't wait for something to show you what to do. Make it happen."

Del shook his head, tired.

Beyba gave him a friendly thump on the shoulder. "Let's get going."

Del's office had a strange, barren feeling stripped of half its personnel. This time scandal had passed him by. Or, possibly Entequil had kept Del's name clear in the hope of some clemency. The testimony that nothing had happened until Asen Permund was aboard ship, out-bound from Syrtis, was so conveniently unambiguous.

Perhaps it was just that Entequil had to wait until there was time to safely sit and sort through the sheer volume of material. Nearly every important case for the past twenty ten-days was compromised.

Clearly everyone wants the best justice credits can get, thought Del with a sour smile for the old, old saw. The problem was there were so many credits involved. The amounts were staggering. Ten, fifteen times Del's own capital worth. A little loose change from some of these people would make a clerk rich beyond his wildest hopes, instantly. In some of these cases—Del shoved the file-rods together disgustedly—a person could afford to be permanently censured and still go home to his own district with honor, it being understood that you'd taken the blame for someone with a reputation to protect and credits to spend.

Del rose and paced, moving his body because his mind refused to come up with new solutions. If he didn't come up with something, he'd be caught. If not next time, then the time after, or the time after that. Honest magistrates have as many enemies as crooked. Maybe more. Del suspected some of Hanro's troubles were attempts to get at him.

He still needed to hire new staff.

Del began working his way through his options again.

He had tried hiring from the established pools: the eager young of well-off families with generations of people in government work. If they were never impeccably honest, they knew enough to be discreet and set their prices high.

And he had tried hiring from the clever members of the underclass, hoping that preference would make them loyal in self-interest. Anyone brought from outside was a risk. The ins and outs of Belsyrtis had to be lived to be appreciated.

Beyba had lived in the city, wealthy, clever, and a perpetual outsider for the past two ten-years. He still cautiously did most of his business off-world. Del's friendship was worth cold, hard credits to him.

When Del was enmeshed in his brother's bankruptcy, standing in the petitioners' room, waiting to be called to declare how much of their joint debts he could cover, he had been handed Beyba's note-of-hand with a limit so high it was meaningless. And Del had walked away, followed by no more than a fading cloud of rumors judged in time to be unfounded. Pity about his brother, the gossip ran, but he covered it—

Calling to assure Beyba he would repay every credit, no matter how long it took him, Beyba had flipped his guarantee into the disposer and said, "If you want. But it's a business expense. I can't operate in Belsyrtis without knowing one honest trade magistrate. I can't afford to buy every decision." Beyba had laughed at Del's expression, then gone sober. "But get Carnath going on Hanro. You may be fireproof, but he's," Beyba's long fingers fluttered up, "flammable."

Del studied the plaza beneath him, almost empty except for someone's clerk jogging his way from the courts building to trades, both arms straight down with heavy, presumably confidential, files. Otherwise they would have gone over the comnet. Del rested his palm against the glass and watched the clouds fly beneath his hand. The pale glow of a rising shuttle made the glass darken slightly in response to its invisible radiation.

Hiring anyone from off world was a risk.

Anyone from the lower world was a risk.

Those from the up world were locked in webs of business and family affiliation: debts owed, favors paid.

Exasperated, Del considered orphan members of the upper world— He was thirty seconds into the fantasy before he laughed and went back to his console to shut it down. Time to go home. Beyba's man should have made his report.

The drift of thread-flowers, yellow-green and fuzzy, over the path to his house said warm spring was finally here to stay. Del glanced at the delicate strands clinging like embroidery to his sleeves and refrained from brushing them away. By the steps up to the main house the plump sticky buds of hetips and orthys had cracked open, hinting at the white explosion of blossom in the next ten-days.

Andur, face smudged with pollen, paced beside him, humming a cheerful tune that had words better left unspoken in polite company. Andur was spending a lot of time off the estate, which meant he was on the outs with Seobal, which meant ructions and trouble. Seobal was fonder of her tall, blond second-in-command than he was of her.

Del remembered his grandfather's dicta: a master should know everything and notice nothing about his servants' private lives. He generally knew nothing and suspected much—

It was too nice a day to spoil.

Del sniffed the wind, and spared a glance, with the merest jab of guilt, for the empty main house. Hanro send daily bulletins on the trials of opening the newly purchased house at Daranfel, where he was apparently providing employment for entire clans of stoneworkers and gardeners.

It was still cheaper than keeping him in the great house.

Del was looking forward to the official severing of financial ties in two ten-days. Meanwhile Jasil was under orders to complain about everything and pay most of it—

Andur stopped humming. "What's going on?"

The front of Del's house swarmed with people. There was usually one source of that intense an excitement: Teyr.

Del and Andur both broke into a trot.

"Go!" said Del, and Andur passed him effortlessly. Del saw him reach the seething mob and question a servant, turn, and start back up the slope, but not before Del had picked Teyr's dark head out of the mass of people.

Del slowed down. Whatever was going on, Teyr was safe enough, already running up the hill after Andur. Andur looked over his shoulder and speeded up. Teyr was closing the distance when they both reached Del, who kept moving at a steadily slowing speed. Time to let his heart slow down.

Teyr's shoulder under his hand, Del settled to a dignified pace.

"Hanro's here," said Andur. "Trying to collect your property." He started to correct himself, then didn't bother when Del swept past him, saying, "Call Carnath."

"Asen," said Andur, long strides carrying him toward the main house, where he could use the comnet without interference.

Hanro had brought a crowd of his own retainers and they had pulled apart the decorations of the entrance hall. Half-filled packing pods sat everywhere. Del's household guard, faced with laying hands on his brother or watching Del robbed, had sealed off the house. Nothing was leaving, but the disruption and damage were enormous.

"Hanro?" said Asen Deltander Permund.

99

Hanro turned around, red-faced, sweating, and ineffectual. "Ah, Del." He gave a shifty glance at a dark-robed man standing to one side. "This is Derrak Hobst. He's here to supervise the division of the estate."

Del gave Hobst a though looking-over. He'd not seen him to know him, but he did know the kind of case his name appeared on. *Hanro would fish this one out of the trash.* "Call the city guard," said Del.

"Asen?" said Seobal.

"Call the city guard."

"Asen." Seobal did not look pleased: allowing the city guard in was usually an admission of failure on the part of private security.

Del wanted there to be no way Hobst could complain about the handling he received. Hanro was a fool to let this slippery character handle his affairs.

Del watched Hanro's guards' nervous hands as they continued packing, Hanro's own jerky pacing, and Hobst's greasy half-smile.

Until Jasil and the city guard arrived it was best to do nothing.

He gritted his teeth as one man pulled a carving from the wall in a shower of frescoed plaster. *I'll have every credit out of you, Hanro. I swear it. This is the last time.*

The arrival of Carnath and the city guard forced a trip to the courts when the purpose of Hanro's effort became clear. He was trying to claim a share of Teyr's worth by forcing Del to sell Teyr.

Hanro, you witless, greedy fool, I'll never forgive you. As they waited for the judge, Del clasped his hands to keep them from shaking with rage. He *must* appear calm—

Jasil was presenting their counter-case using nothing but experience and quick wits, when Del saw Hobst twitch to attention. The spectators' gallery had filled with grim men with belts and harnesses with the empty loops of the temporarily disarmed. Del had never been gladder to see Beyba's orange uniforms. He didn't recognize the dark, well-dressed woman who was with the Norrey guards.

But plainly Hobst did.

And Jasil saw that, too. "If I might take a moment to speak with my client?"

He came close to Del. "Who is that?"

"I don't know," said Del, as the two of them turned to stand side-by-side rather than face-to-face and surveyed the gallery.

"Is she with Norrey's people, or does it just look that way?"

She was standing more than an arm's length away from them, but even that degree of closeness was unusual. Almost any woman would keep a distance from Beyba's guards: they were not known for their courtesy to women.

"Beyba's in town?" said Jasil.

"No," said Del.

"No?"

"On his way to Agevenis for a ten-days."

"Ah. So what's going on—" Jasil put his fingertips together. "Would Norrey put a watch on you?"

Del shrugged. "Maybe. He thinks I'm a little too, cultured?"

"Not a fault of his, certainly," said Jasil, dryly. "Does he think he deserves a share of Teyr?"

"Andur said I should watch for that, but I don't think—"

"You didn't think Hanro would, either."

"Beyba wouldn't want the credits."

"But he might want Teyr."

Del remembered Beyba's excited face at the dinner on the *Forrei*. "No," said Del with finality. Beyba wasn't a man to let lust interfere with profit and he had a substantial investment in Del.

"Who's she, then?" said Jasil.

The woman came to the rail, and in the change of light, Del knew her. She'd helped carry him off Holk. "She was one of his guard."

"Beyba's?" Jasil's voice was threaded through with incredulity.

"Yes," said Del. He lifted one hand.

The woman nodded, and made her way along the gallery, down the stair and was stopped at the foot. But by then Jasil had crossed to speak for her. She came onto the floor. "Asen Permund." It was a pleasant voice, clear and light.

Del waited.

"I have some information about Asen," there was a nice degree of contempt on that honorific, "Hobst."

Jasil had prudently moved himself back out of earshot. He was required to report any information on illegal dealings to the court.

Del's position gave him discretion, and, consequently, bargaining power.

"What," said Del, without inflection.

The brief summary of Hobst's business dealings was precisely tailored to the occasion. Enough to convince Hobst to drop the matter, and yet suggest there were greater resources he would be wise to leave untouched.

"Did Asen Norrey send you?" asked Del. He was puzzled by the unexpected, unasked for, aid.

"No, Asen. I," if the pause was intended to be meaningful it wasn't, "look after some of his interests when he is away."

"Ah," said Del, noncommittally. He'd like to check that with Beyba. Meanwhile—

Jasil, seeing the conference ended, came forward.

"Ask for a postponement," said Del.

"We-have-new-information," said Jasil in a dull monotone, lifting an eyebrow.

"Something like that," said Del.

Jasil went to delay the battle.

At home in his suite, Del picked at the problem. Jasil had finished the day's work at court by saying, "Del, if you can get him civil status, you'd better."

Assuming he was a gen, and property, Teyr was valuable. But it was a value difficult to realize in the economy of Belsyrtis: he was simply too costly. And he couldn't be split and sold in smaller lots. Dividing him into shares for a syndicate was useless unless there was a market for some service he could perform for credits to be divided among the shareholders.

Del couldn't think of what that could be that would justify the expensive fees. Anything Teyr could do, or be forced to, could be had far more cheaply and with far less trouble.

He was sure he could feel the tug of foreign interests. The move didn't make sense by local standards, therefore there must be something else in play. Somebody else with an interest. Del wondered who that might be.

I may not have time to wait and find out.

The only fast way to Teyr's status was to get a special bill authorized. It would tip his hand, but he couldn't afford to be subtle.

If his suspicions had any basis, then whoever wanted the boy would also be maneuvering. Del's only advantage might be the favors he could call in immediately. Before credits could be marshaled against him.

I suppose that if I had thought it would be an easy job I would have tried a special bill to confirm Teyr's civil status as soon as I brought him to Belsyrtis. Hanro's being drawn into some maneuver was more of a surprise than it should have been. Teyr's worth guaranteed that something would be tried but I had no way of estimating his value.

I don't know what a local syndicate could have done with him: perhaps put him into an arena to fight. Betting and concessions might have brought the take to a sufficiently high level.

But the truth is, I could not think of him as a gen, and that crippled my judgment. Gene-analysis was ambiguous, and told me nothing I could not see for myself. He looked human. The matter might well come to nothing but definitions.

I never believed it was a local attempt to take control of Teyr. From the first I think G-R was trying to recover its dangerous bit of property. If Hobst had forced Teyr's sale I know they would have paid any price for him.

Having an independent, recognized court rule Teyr and his kind had civil status was the last thing G-R wanted. Better the Teyr be killed, and the rest of their investment preserved.

It has gone quiet outside: a bad sign. They are starting to think, looking for the flaws in our defense. If they find them, we will die. There is no hope of help from the city guards.

My hands are quite steady now.

Teyr and Andur have gone to sleep, leaving me alone to watch.

"Litjin Varriel." Deltander said it aloud, sounding the pronunciation code. He pressed his shaking hands against the console top and replayed the message.

He was summoned to the court of claims, "—with the disputed property, the gene-sculpture known as 'Teyr,' to satisfy the court that this gene-sculpture is not the one designed by Litjin Varriel and owned by Geffund-Raq Corporation designated—" There followed a long string of numbers and specifications that Deltander skipped over in a shrill chittering.

"This property was unlawfully removed from the possession of the agent of Geffund-Raq Corporation on Soltan V on or about—" Del went fast forward through the complicated universal reckoning. "—and fraudulently sold to—" Del skipped again. "—then transported to Holk Station, a biological facility located at—" The specification was overly exact, as if the man of business framing the document had never heard of the place and assumed no one else had either. "—where it became subject to a salvage claim correctly filed in the courts at Belsyrtis on Syrtis, star,"—string of numbers—"called 'Nevis.' No wrong-doing is alleged against the salvage claimant, Deltander Entaneray Solt Permund—"

Del punched the call and convey to Beyba, adding an urgent priority.

Beyba, when he appeared, was nude to at least the waist and wet. "This better be important, Del."

"Listen," said Del, his voice shaking.

Beyba bent forward, wiping water from his lower face with an equally wet hand. "Shit," he said, and accepted a towel from someone out of camera range. He rubbed the towel down his face and torso, eyes abstracted over the message. Finally he looked up and into the camera. "I don't suppose there's some good reason you can't present him this morning?"

"Is there any reason to delay?" said Del.

"There's nothing to gain by hurrying."

"I'm an official, subject to imprisonment, not fines, if I 'knowingly impede the swift execution of justice.'"

"Yeah, well, if they're smart they've set someone to watch you anyway," said Beyba. He accepted a cup, sipped, and spat back into it. "What is this?" Vague murmur out of pickup range. Beyba looked into the cup as if something were looking back and put it down. "Del, the best you can do is show up, on time, with Carnath. If we can get him on short notice. Have you called?"

"No," said Del.

Beyba fiddled with something on his console, glanced into the camera, and then down again. "We can try to buy him."

"I can hardly pay my brother's bills."

"I'll put up the price, if you take a consulting position with my company."

Norrey's tame magistrate. Del remembered Teyr, shivering, battered. *What sort of people had sent him across star system after star system, unguarded? But this said he had been stolen. Maybe Teyr would want to go.*

With an almost noiseless gasp, Del winced at the tearing pain in his chest. He forced himself upright. *All Teyr had to do was tell me, and he didn't. He doesn't. He can't*— "Whatever it takes, Beyba," said Asen Permund, voice made colorless by resignation.

"Del." Beyba ran both hands through his hair. "I don't mean—fuck it. Get Carnath. I'll do what I can about money. But if this is true, there's nothing to contest."

"I can't give him up," said Del.

"You may not have a choice." Beyba ground his palm over his chin. "I'll meet you there, don't go in before I come. Are you listening, Del?"

"Yes," said Del, controlling his face. The pain in his chest had twisted itself into a manageable knot.

Neat and trim in dark, formal clothes, Jasil Carnath met Deltander, Teyr, and Andur outside the court. Their two security escorts pooled together and began chatting as they set up the new defense. Jasil and Del's forces had been working together since the two men trained together. This morning there was a furrow between Jasil's brows and he seemed distracted.

"I'm sorry to interrupt your schedule," Del said mechanically. Teyr kept pulling out of his anxious grasp. Del wasn't sure what Andur had told him.

"Perfectly all right," said Jasil, equally mechanically, eyes searching the walk. He brightened. A small woman in the dark robes of an assistant was coming toward them so quickly that she was catching the attention of passersby. She came up and handed over a set of file-rods, breathing deeply. "Asens."

"Everything?" said Jasil.

"Yes. Even the speculative material from your private files."

"Good," said Jasil. "Thank you." He slipped the carrier under his arm. "Keep track of things at the office. If we're lucky I'll be very late."

She started off without another word.

Andur was checking the shadows in the entryway. In reaction, Jasil looked nervously behind himself. *They won't do anything like that,* Andur, thought Del.

Jasil tapped on the file-carrier. "We might as well go in."

Deltander thought of the open floor of the court where they would stand and wait, naked to the cameras of the vidders, the curious stares of the spectators, and the scrutiny of the people claiming Teyr. "Beyba said to wait for him here."

Jasil tapped softly at his carrier. "It'd help if I had some time to get their feel."

Without another word, Del started in, guiding hand on Teyr's upper arm. Teyr looked at him, offended by the constraint. Andur pressed forward behind them, stripping his weapons as he walked. The court forbade weapons on the floor or in the spectator's gallery.

There was no difficulty in picking out the party from Geffund-Raq. They had not bothered to buy or borrow the formal robes current on Belsyrtis, and their full trousers and skin-tight shirts looked subtly disrespectful despite their rich fabric.

Deltander picked out three of them from their security: two young, hard-faced executives, one male, one female, and an older man with his back to Del. When he sat down and rested his chin in his hand Del tensed with recognition. That was the profile in Teyr's drawing: arc of a nose over a bitter, fine-cut mouth, deep-set eyes.

Del hated the sight of him.

Andur, uncomfortable with a threatening situation where his skills were forbidden, eased his belt with its short-bladed gentleman's knife, supposedly useless as a weapon, so the utilitarian sheath, worn glossy with use, was convenient to his hand.

Teyr, who had been at Andur's right, retreated behind him so deftly that it was a moment before Del was sure he had deliberately hidden himself. He rubbed his chest. Del had hoped that if he had to yield Teyr, it would be to friends.

Andur glanced over his shoulder, then at Del, mouth sour.

Erta Buness, magistrate for the day, swept into her place in a flurry of official robes. Her staff was dropped into the socket in the floor, and the court was in session.

The woman executive stood forth to speak for Geffund-Raq.

Buness waved her back, and said, "Litjin Varriel."

Varriel rose, surveying the barbarians around him, and stepped into place.

Not much to look at, for all his poise, thought Del. Medium height and build. Brown hair gone grey in streaks and thinning at the temples. He hadn't bothered to have it corrected. By their expensive fabric, his offensive clothes were probably costly, but his nails were short, the hands those of a man who does more than manipulate his stylus and com. He looked like a small-time merchant, or an upper-middle class professional. Not someone to be reckoned with in Del's scale of things.

He could claim Teyr.

Attracted by Del's inspection, Varriel looked directly at him. Seen head on, his eyes had the flat, hard glare of a predator. Del swallowed, uncomfortable.

And jumped slightly as his own name was called. Without stepping forward, he designated Jasil Carnath to represent him. Buness did not look pleased. She obviously wanted the two best-informed principals to settle this simple matter between them, without legal artifice. She gestured Del into the brighter light at the foot of her chair, started to speak, and then stared at him. Del tried to keep his face impassive and knew he had failed. He could feel the corners of his mouth quiver.

Until that moment Buness must have had no idea that there was more at stake than a simple restoration of property. She nodded agreement, and Del withdrew, knowing he must be very pale, feeling sweat bead and run down his sides. He pressed the flat of his hand to his chest unobtrusively.

In the brighter light at the center of the court, Varriel appraised Carnath head to toe, then gave his complete attention to Buness.

Jasil handed his accreditation to a court aide and stood, relaxed and easy.

Del wished he believed Jasil was as confident as he looked. He'd stood like that too many times himself to put any faith in appearances.

Buness inquired if Carnath was contesting the matter. "If not," she said, "perhaps we can go directly to the matter of the Asen's expenses and finder's fee—"

And wrap this whole thing up before shift-break, added Del mentally.

Anticipating Carnath's agreement, Varriel stepped back, yielding place to one of the others to handle the technical points of an exchange.

Jasil spoke. "Asen Buness, we do not, at this time, wish to contest the facts as entered in the claim, but we do question the civil status of the boy, Teyr."

Buness' expression cracked open with surprise.

Varriel moved back into place with a small, tense, very pleased smile.

Del clamped a neutral expression on. *Jasil! Of course he has to make the claim now, or lose the chance. But we have nothing but rags of conjecture for a case.*

"Make your case," said Buness, easing herself back in her seat.

Jasil began to speak.

For the rest of his life Del would remember Jasil standing in the pit of the court making the case of his career entirely out of his head. It was like watching a man lift some improbable weight that would crush him if he relaxed an instant.

Varriel watched with complete concentration.

The rest of the court was so silent Del could hear the shifting of boot-soles on the gallery floor.

But it went on far too long.

Sometime later Del wondered if the entire brilliant performance had only one purpose: delay.

Later still, and Jasil had lost his audience, but not the thread of his discourse. The magistrate was fiddling with water, when Jasil abruptly ended his argument and asked Buness' permission to confer with a colleague. His colleague, Del saw, was Beyba, who practically lifted Jasil across the barrier and into conference.

Varriel gave his attention to a ray of sunlight creeping across the inlaid floor. Andur shifted his alert posture for the ten-thousandth tiny increment. Del tried to peer into the comparative darkness behind the railing.

There were two, no, three, other people with Jasil and Beyba, hooded, dark-clad figures that eluded careful examination. Del guessed they were professional informers from the port where knowing who had a cargo competitive with yours, who had lost a sale, who needed to make a sale, often made the difference between profit and loss.

Finally Jasil re-entered the pit, and thanked the magistrate for her indulgence.

"I'm glad you understand it is indulgence," said Buness, dryly.

There was a sanctimonious titter from the spectators, silenced with excessive zeal by the bored attendants.

Jasil requested permission to question Asen Varriel.

Buness inquired if Varriel was willing.

He made a gesture of agreement. "If I might remain seated?"

Jasil would be pleased to question the Asen in any posture he cared to assume.

Varriel draped himself over the back of his chair, a position that should have been insolent and actually suggested something habitual.

Jasil turned to look at Del, dark robes giving an emphatic swirl. He was, Del saw, really sure he was on to something. Del couldn't imagine what.

Teyr pulled his shoulder from Del's tense grip.

Carnath turned back to Varriel, paused a moment, then began. "It's my understanding that you have a mature specimen of this gene-sculpture with your party. Is this correct?"

Del jerked with surprise.

Varriel sat up. He said, "Yes," despite a flutter of protesting hands from the two executives.

Buness had seen that, too. "I remind all the parties to this case that the penalties for knowingly misrepresenting or concealing facts are severe."

Considering his next point, Jasil moved away, turned, came back. "It is impossible to question Teyr: he cannot speak. Even if he could, he is immature, traumatized. However, we might gain some insight into his civil status by questioning his mature clone-brother. You can communicate?"

"Yes." Varriel looked cheerful.

The two executives looked dismayed.

"Will you consent to be sworn as an officer of this court to facilitate questioning? You understand the penalties if you are at any time in the future found to have knowingly impeded justice—"

Buness interrupted to deliver the caution officially.

Varriel shrugged with disdain, and stood to make his formal affirmation. The two executives attempted to confer with Varriel and were waved back. Varriel was sworn and one of the Geffund-Raq security left the floor.

They all sat waiting.

Long enough to take the speed-strip down and back from the port hotel complex.

The mature gen gave Deltander the same exotic shock he had experienced when he first saw Teyr. There was the absolute, artificial contrast of white skin and black hair. The pale grey eyes. A fine-cut, dreamy face, although here the mouth had gone hard.

Andur was alert, appraising, heel of hand on the hilt of the tiny gentleman's purse-tool, its blade shorter than a little finger.

As the gen came to stand before Varriel with an elegant economy of motion, Del saw what had caught Andur's attention: the three metal balls swinging in their cord loops were a weapon, not the ornaments some court attendant had assumed them to be. Teyr started to go to him and was stopped by a gesture so fast Del wasn't sure he had seen it. Teyr stood, chin up, in front of Del and Andur, for all the world as if he were guarding them.

Maybe he is, thought Del.

Varriel looked amused, and said, "This is Bondre."

"He can communicate with the boy?" Jasil hadn't missed the exchange between the two.

The woman from G-R protested calling the gene-sculpture a boy.

Jasil did not directly contest the correction. "He can communicate with Teyr?"

"Yes." Varriel's hands moved, fast.

Bondre responded.

Jasil requested Bondre ask Teyr what happened to him.

It was a faster process than most translations Del had sat through. Either Teyr's narrative was very concise, or Bondre or Varriel was a capable editor on the wing. Del had the feeling that some things were being left out. There was no mention of why Teyr had been traveling in the first place, or whom, if anyone, he had been with—

The court was silent as Varriel's dry, expressionless voice spoke and paused and spoke and paused. But when Teyr began describing how he was attacked Bondre became more and more agitated. He finally stopped and conferred with an irritated Varriel.

Up to that point, Bondre had been so self-effacing that Del doubted anyone in the audience had wondered about him: their attention was focused on the story itself. Upset, Bondre invested his gestures with such passion that the urgency of his message did not need translation. Del could see the vidcams following his every move.

Under the onslaught, Varriel shifted in his seat with the first sign of awkwardness Deltander had seen in him. "Bondre would like a few moments to speak with Evtan."

"'Evtan,'" thought Del, wondering what, if anything, it meant.

"Granted," said Buness, without bothering to confer with Jasil.

Jasil motioned to Bondre, but he had already started for Teyr.

Jasil was carefully not looking smug. Buness' failure to query him was one possible point in a retrial request. *But that's not what he's pleased about*, Del thought with abrupt insight. When the questioning had started, Bondre was nothing but a biologically based machine, as good as invisible to the court. Now he was a vivid personality.

It was a tight little conference, odd because Bondre and Teyr stood close together, watching each other's hands rather than their faces. Bondre looked up, once, at Andur, who did something Del had never thought he would see: Andur deliberately displayed his open, empty hands and backed a half step.

Bondre was very angry.

And Bondre was as tall as Andur, and might, Del guessed, have years more of the training that enabled Teyr to give Andur a hard fight in a friendly match.

He glittered danger.

Del moistened his lips.

Teyr touched his arm and gestured.

Bondre's hard, bright gaze went back to their discussion.

Del saw Andur take a deep breath.

Jasil had certainly established Bondre was no machine.

But he had also established that Teyr—*Evtan*, corrected Del—was the one Varriel and company were seeking.

It might be an emotional victory, but it did not foreshadow a legal victory. Buness was not likely to be distracted. Del rubbed his chest. *Jasil is no fool, what does he think he is doing?*

Del's hand dropped to his side, dismayed. He knew.

It had been a sunny afternoon long ago, with Carnath, senior, safely tied up in court for the next shift and the ceaseless shuffle of office work in the competent hands of the clerks. He and Jasil had been reviewing the general code for their upcoming verbal examinations. Most of it they could recite from memory because they cited its provisions every day. Only one unused section required their attention, and Jasil had been fascinated with it.

The section dealing with alien contact.

It did nothing so crude as refer to aliens. Del projected himself backward in time, remembering the sharp slats of the folding seat against the backs of his knees, the smell of dust and ozone from the cranky reader, the drone of Jasil's voice mimicking the bored monotone of his father. "—sentient, moral beings of non-human origin."

Del skimmed the passage in his mind. He was sure it did not specify that the being need be a natural creation. *And that*, thought Del, mind finally leaping ahead, *is what Varriel wants. Proof he has created sentients.*

Between them, Carnath and Varriel were setting up the perfect legal case.

Bondre, upset, angry, armed, trusted, trying to intervene for Evtan, made a powerful statement.

That might be too sophisticated for this court.

Erta Buness had a habit of strict legal interpretation. She would have to be convinced that there was some reason for her to go beyond simply verifying Teyr was the stolen property that G-R's representatives claimed title to.

Bondre finished, put one hand on Teyr's shoulder for a moment, and went back.

The questioning resumed.

Del stood in a haze, concentrating on keeping his knees straight, his face impassive.

The lights under the edge of the dome had come on by the time the arguments petered down.

Buness inquired if they had completed their cases.

The two from G-R conferred with each other. They had.

"Asen Varriel?"

A gesture of agreement.

"I take it that means yes."

Varriel stood with stiff courtesy. "Yes, Magistrate."

"Asen Carnath?"

Jasil agreed.

"Asen Permund?"

Del's voice sounded hoarse and uncertain. "Yes." He touched Teyr's back, feeling the hard-muscled, live warmth.

Teyr looked him, puzzled.

Maybe, hoped Del, *he won't mind going back. I can stand it if he doesn't mind. I think I can stand—*

Buness shifted uncomfortably in her seat—it had been a long day without a break—consulted the timer on her note-file, then stood and ruled.

That the question of Teyr's civil status was no part of the matter brought before this court, and that Evtan, called Teyr, was clearly the property in question and so awarded to Geffund-Raq.

Geffund-Raq security personnel closed around Teyr, shouldering Deltander and Andur out of the way.

They planned this, thought Del, struggling to keep his footing.

Teyr looked around, wide-eyed and tried to pull free, then kicked the woman holding his right arm smartly on the knee, the man on the other side somewhat higher up, and bolted for the door.

Spectators hung over the gallery, cheering him on, offering hands up, advice, and assistance he would have been foolish to take even if he could have understood any of it.

The court guards blocked the entrance.

Teyr turned around, trying to reach Del and Andur, and was casually hit sideways by one of the Geffund-Raq guards.

On his feet, Litjin Varriel said something incomprehensible, angrily motioning Bondre into the fray.

Bondre held up his hands, heavy nails sharp as claws, and declined.

Mouth moving, inaudible in the noise, Varriel waded in, emerging in the center of a circle of panting guards with a still struggling Teyr by one arm.

Bondre kept trying to get Teyr to pay attention to him.

Teyr looked away, refusing to take heed. Shorter than the guards, Teyr vanished in the press of bodies.

Del rubbed the pain in his chest. *Stay calm, it'll only make it worse if he sees you distressed.* The pain was crushing. He might even have cried out. Certainly the next thing he knew was that he was staring up at the ornate filigree of the court dome, a total stranger releasing his wrist. "He's just fainted."

"Del?" Beyba's face was white.

Del struggled to sit up. "Sorry."

Andur put an arm across Del's back and got him to his feet.

Del staggered, bewildered.

"Get him home," said Beyba. "Let Carnath earn his fee for the rest."

"Teyr?"

"Gone," said Beyba. "I'll do what I can."

Del went to work the next day, and every day thereafter. He had no idea if he did any good: simply staying home in the empty house was too much to bear. He spent his evenings, lap full of papers he couldn't read, slowly turning page after page, trying to see some kindness in Varriel's often-sketched face.

Beyba's offer to negotiate a price was refused outright.

Del hoped they would at least let him bid a proper farewell, but his messages, too, went unanswered. Beyba's corps of informers reported that Teyr was kept in isolation in the G-R group's hotel suite, separate from Varriel and Bondre, while they waited for their ship to be prepared for the short haul to the jump point and the longer haul to Kumaman.

All Beyba's money and influence could do was to make it one of the longest refittings in the history of the port.

Which seemed like pointless wrath to Del, except he could not bear to tell Beyba to stop. Every day gained was another day he knew that Teyr was safe and well.

Bondre was a wary and somewhat dangerous observer of Beyba's information gathering. *It would*, Del thought, dropping the voice-in-the-ear with the day's report onto the table at his elbow, *be easier if we could make Bondre understand our interest.*

For Bondre got around quite handily with a hand-held device that spoke for him, buying small goods and arranging matters with the hotel personnel, who reported the group expected to take ship in five days, even if the refitting was not complete. Anything left undone would be completed in one of the out ports.

Alone in his office with his newest clerk, Del marked another file-rod for adjudication and stoically pushed the next into the reader. Maybe it was better if he didn't see Teyr. Maybe it would—

The file slipped from Del's fingers and shattered on the floor.

"Fuck it," said Del with such venom the Filip started.

"I'll get another copy." She hurried out of the room, anxious to get away. His mostly-new staff was trying hard to be sympathetic but Del's uncertain temper was difficult to bear.

Del bent over to pick up the pieces and cut his hand. He was sitting, watching the cut drip into the floor when Filip returned. She sat the new file down and called the floor cleaner.

"Asen," she said, "Teyr's missing and Geffund-Raq is asking that you meet them and discuss where he might be."

"Where do they want to meet?" If he held his hand in the air, the bleeding slowed.

"They're here, now." She knit her hands. "They've already got the port police searching the building in case he's hidden here."

"Who authorized that!" Del stood so fast his chair went over backward.

Filip cowered away from him. "I don't know."

"*You* didn't?"

"No, Asen." She licked nervous lips. "They're not inclined to listen to anything. Gerrien thinks they've been bribed."

Del watched the floor cleaner slurp up another drop of his blood. He stood, holding the hand in the air. "First," he said, hunting for something to wrap it in, "no one is ever to examine these offices without proper authority. You and I are liable to severe penalties. So call the city guard and protest until they send an army. Second," he was in the grip of a rage so pure it was almost ecstatic, "you and the rest of the staff are to guard our files. Third," he started for the door, "I'll talk to them."

Filip skittered out of the room.

The commanding officer of the port guard was accompanied by the man who had caught Teyr a blow. Del recited the city regulations and penalties with cold fury but no interest and the officer did not pretend to listen. The farce finished, Del asked to talk to his superiors.

"Unavailable," said the man.

A few minutes' work with the com established that they were, indeed, available, and angry. But not at the invasion of Del's offices. They were angry the officer had revealed Teyr was missing.

Del had no problem with that.

Teyr was like an unlimited credit chit. The best that G-R could hope for was that someone would hold him for ransom. The worst was that someone might try to realize his true value, then panic and kill him.

Varriel's cold, arrogant presence probably had a great deal to do with the effusive length of the G-R rep's apologies. He kept checking to see if Varriel, not Del, was satisfied. It was a relief to Del when the man got the sign to stop.

Del was puzzled by Varriel's evident authority.

G-R was listed as Teyr's owner.

Varriel as his creator.

But on some things Varriel could overrule the two reps, and plainly he had no respect for them. He sent them from the room before speaking further with Del. Show of power or pre-arranged attempt to win Del's confidence?

Bondre, standing to one side, seemed to keep asking something. Del wished they could converse directly, for, although Varriel's moving hands may have been translating what Del said, he made no effort to let Del know what Bondre commented.

"Where do you think he might have gone?" Varriel was blunt.

Del shook his head, and began explaining Teyr's utter inexperience in the city. He had never traveled anywhere without a guard, always in private transport.

As Varriel questioned Del, the G-R guards came and went, reporting on the progress of their search. They had established that Teyr had not left the port by any of the guarded entrances and exits. That, theoretically, guaranteed he was still in the port itself. In practice it meant the guards would now have the concentrate on the zone, and the illegal routes over the warehouses and through the surrounding slums: territory as shifting and trackless as any jungle, an area even Andur would need good reason to enter alone.

Del rubbed his painful chest.

He had thought nothing could be worse than seeing Teyr taken away. But knowing what might, no, Del said cruelly to himself, what probably would happen to him in Belsyrtis' slums or even in the port zone was worse.

The more Del explained, the angrier Varriel grew, and another time Del would have been fascinated by the play of power between the G-R executives and Varriel. But Teyr was lost.

And he had very little experience to fall back on. Everything had gone wrong on the boy's first trip away from Varriel's estate at Kumaman.

That much, at least, Del had learned from Varriel's comments and instructions to the G-R guard. If he had been able to understand Varriel's conversation with Bondre, Del was convinced he would have learned much more.

Drained of ideas and information Del went home and instructed his guards they to join in the search. Searching the slums would be left to last because it took well-armed guards and would alert the entire city something was up. The port guards and the people from G-R could search the vast complex of warehouses and loading areas very efficiently.

But, although it had been years since he had been to the port zone in anything other than his official capacity, Del did know it thoroughly. It was there he would concentrate his people's efforts.

Every major port had something like it. It was not lawless, although it fell under the jurisdiction of off-planet negotiators like Del rather than the local government. Within the port the laws of Belsyrtis did not apply, only the port's own regulations and the guidelines of interworld trade.

Local men and women often went masked in the zone, and the convention was that you did not recognize anyone you had not entered with. It was where Belsyrtis went to experience the pleasures and practice the depravities forbidden in the city proper.

A lot of what went on was foolish, nothing more than you might have found in the city itself, other than the transactions were often for credits, and the proceedings spiced with intrigue.

Some of it was disgusting but harmless, infantile play by adults.

And some of it was obscene, only technically legal even here. Del had dealt with a rush of cases in the last standard involving people mutilated in accordance with signed contracts seeking damages, claiming they were drugged or brainwashed into agreement. There had been that one legal, outright murder—

Deltander sniffed the air at the open gate, fragrant with heated fruit-flavored alcohol, and felt the ghost of old adventures stir. Inside, there was the feverish glitter and activity. It had all changed enormously and not changed at all. Del had spent a good deal of time and credits here as a young man, much to his father's distress. It had seemed much more benign and exotic then.

He knew too much about it now.

Andur motioned his little troop tight around Del, and surveyed the street. This area was far too cheap to credibly interest Del in his own persona, but shielded by the mask, he hoped to be, not more convincing—everything from his hands to his way of walking would proclaim his social status—but less conspicuous. A gentleman satisfying a vulgar whim.

An ordinary figure here.

Del surveyed the scene from behind the mask that made his face one smooth reflective curve. The fashions had metamorphosed so many times they seemed to cycle back to their beginnings. Right now the girls were modestly clad—some even veiled—except for the cutouts that let them do business. Their licenses, dated for the night, were locked on their wrists.

A small boy, no, a dwarf—no child could have a face so preternaturally wise—chanted his way down the arcaded street with a curiously plaintive air. He was advertising the more costly establishments along Paval Park, the garden strip that had originally been intended to soften the harsh industrialism of the warehouses and loading areas at the rim of the port and now provided a pleasant green setting for the zone's exclusive brothels, the ones you had to reveal your identity and give a credit rating to enter.

The dwarf was stopped by a masked, redheaded boy in the blue glow of light from the arcade. Despite his gilded makeup Del could see the harsh light pick out the slick scars where his arms had been surgically shortened. Del could see the golden, wizened face reflected in the boy's mask as the two talked. There were fashions in oddities that came and went, but there were always a few dwarfs, grotesque as imagination and surgical skill could make them.

The well-dressed boy made some urgent plea, credit rod in hand. The dwarf scratched his rump while listening, then laughed and readjusted his flaring collar. He said, "Maybe later, sweetheart," and walked away, raising his voice again, listing prices and pleasures.

Jingle-jangle boys, good for a few moments or an evening, passed by, laughing and joking, not yet settled to the night's work. The smell of rift and burning talik buds began to fill the street. By dawn's ruddy light the clouds of smoke would cast drifting shadows on the pavement.

Del felt numbed by the onslaught of sound and smell. His appetites had become far more sophisticated, if unsubdued. Perhaps you had to be young to find sheer blatant variety appealing.

"Let's get started," he said.

Andur began working his way along the line of faces, freshly made-up if not fresh, offering cash for information about a dark-haired youth. The girls giggled, accepted credits, and made suggestions.

They would, Del hoped, think he was looking for some runaway contract-breaker. He tried to carry himself like a man out to satisfy offended pride, or coax a half-willing partner back. Showing emotion might make it more difficult to find Teyr: certainly it would make it worthwhile for someone to hold him and bargain.

Del didn't think Teyr could cope with being sold.

Or raped.

Most other things here, yes. He was quick and strong. He could disarm any five or six of these trumpery bullyboys without breaking his stride.

Del was startled at the violence of his thoughts.

He could see the ripple of gossip spread up the street. Some people changed direction. The cheaper vendors, disturbed, drifting off to the less visible stands, the clusters of painted faces, veiled with translucent drapery, quietly changed from female to male as girls moved on and boys moved in. A tall woman, half-naked in articulated metal, passed with a cortege of boys, rouged at nipples, groin, and all four cheeks, their unchanged voices singing their prices.

There were a lot of metamorphs among the restless throng.

They were forbidden the city proper, but Yens Enfahss, marshal of the district, tolerated them, supposedly as part of the port's free-trade position.

A woman, arms sinuous, boneless, legs lengthened, silted by, dark-rimmed eyes picking through the crowd. She wouldn't be too expensive, those were cheap, common modifications. The boyish androgyne with female organs would be slightly more. The man with feathers and useless wings would be very costly and fussy about his customers: broken feathers would be painful to replace.

Del watched from behind his mask and let Andur deal with the offers of dark-haired boys. He was tired of looking into so many eyes, pleading, bold, frightened, black, brown, blue, none of them the grey ones he was looking for.

But they didn't really expect Teyr to be out on the street.

Andur's face was tired when he came back.

"If he's here, Asen, he's hidden or in hiding. We can try cruising the streets closer to the free district, but we'll need more guards and I think I should do it alone. We'll take you home and start first thing next shift."

"No," said Del. "I'll go home if you want—" he would be a burden in any rough stuff "—but you start now." If Teyr saw them, he might come to them, but they had to make themselves seen. The odds were, if he was here, Teyr wouldn't be moving.

Andur rubbed his eyes with thumb and forefinger. "Asen, we—" He looked at Del and shut up.

The guards were tired, but they didn't have any time left.

Del went home, the shifts passed, and they went from looking for hiding places to sweeping the port perimeter with sniffers to merely attempting to get news, and at the last semi-legally sieving hundreds of accounts to locate any rumor of the boy.

There was nothing.

The morning of the fifth day came. The G-R reps informed Varriel that was their decision that their ship would leave that evening.

Judging from his flushed face, Varriel had argued hard, but he was resigned to leaving by the time he called Del to inform him that, title to Teyr having been returned to him, he could make any necessary arrangements if anything was found—Del assumed he meant a body—and he was giving title to Del.

By now, for all their care, the predators of the port knew there was prey and a reward. Nothing having turned up, it was a fair assumption that Teyr was no longer alive, his captors panicked by the publicity surrounding a case where the prestige of the port and city guards was publicly at stake.

Del saw no one for two days.

On Belsyrtis we assumed that political forces toward the cluster's heart were as isolated from us as we were from them. In fact, the comparatively shorter distances led to a strong interest in developing information and travel-related technology. It was only a matter of time until they turned their attention to the rich, placid backwater of Belsyrtis and its allies. Geffund-Raq's appearance was the storm-froth blown before a wind of change.

None of which mattered to me when they claimed Teyr.

I was not prepared for my reaction: I had known all of my friends and most of my acquaintances since we were children. The occasional companions I took into my home came and went without impinging on this stable core.

Beyba was the only exception until Teyr.

I went through a ten-days in which I did nothing I remember. I got up, went to work, came home, and lay down to stare at the ceiling, but the comments I recorded, the decisions I made, are as new to my eyes as any stranger's. If the decisions were uninspired they were also unexceptional.

But it took all of Beyba's persuasive powers to get me to accept his dinner invitation, and if I had not felt I would have damaged our friendship by refusing I would have stayed home.

Del rubbed the edge of the table, rough with carving. Curious how his fingertips could not discern the pattern so clear to his eyes.

Beyba signaled the servant to refill Del's glass. Del placed his hand in the way. "I have to work tomorrow."

Beyba dismissed the servant with an impatient jerk. "You haven't taken a day off," he paused, and went on in a different tone, "in a while."

Since Teyr went, thought Del. "No," he said, rubbing his chest absently: it didn't quite hurt. Yet another series of tests had shown nothing wrong with him but nerves.

Behind the screen there was the thrum of stringed instrument accidently bumped, and the soft, hissing reproaches of the master musician.

Del prepared to look like he was paying attention.

He and Beyba had dined alone in a stately splendor that was a relief because it required a formal style of conversation long since become mechanical to Del, who had kept up his end with polite determination. He had managed to behave with seeming normality, but the entertainment could scarcely have counted a success by any ordinary standard.

Someone behind the stage screen played a run up and down, stopped and plucked a note, retuned.

Del could hear the slither and rustle of fabric, then silence.

Ready.

Beyba took a deep breath. "I was going to make this a big surprise, but I'm not so sure it's a good idea—"

Del reached for the decanter and poured himself a substantial drink: there was relief in the thought of being too miserable to face his barren office in the morning. "Go on—" Del took a big swallow.

Beyba made three indecisive movements, took a gulp from his own drink, then signaled the stage.

Beyba's troop of dancers, all boys, had achieved a fame of its own. He was lavish in paying to find the best, and the production costs were enormous. There was no tinsel or trumpery backdrops. Beyba paid for real jewelry and fine paintings, details that showed plainly in the intimate settings where they performed. Poor Prit had never mastered disciplined subordination to the whole, and had never qualified as one of the troop.

People who would never have spoken to Beybaken Norrey in the ordinary way of social dealings maneuvered to get invitations to their semi-public performances, came, marveled, and continued to despise Norrey as an uncultured nouveau-riche fortunately exploited by clever artists.

But while everything else Beyba owned might be at the service of his commercial interests and, by extension, his social ambitions, the intimate performances were exempt. If you were invited to see the dancers in Beyba's private theater, then Beyba accounted you a real friend.

Del, who had only to express idle curiosity to get an invitation, was aware he undervalued the privilege. But his interest in watching young bodies leap and turn and pose was limited. And in the best classical mode, the stylized make-up and heavy wigs stripped the face and head of any individuality.

Everything had to be said with the body.

There was a soft shudder of a drumbeat. Del shifted his shoulders against his chair back, knotty with carving, and prepared for a long evening.

The four boys, faces white and lips reddened, came onto the stage in pairs, danced, quarreled and re-paired, ending intertwined in a nosegay of faces. The stage went dark.

Del poured himself another drink in the dimness. From the smell he judged he'd missed the cup with some of it. He could see Beyba's shadowy shape jerk nervously. "Sorry," said Del, starting to mop with his sleeve and thinking the better of it.

There was the high, sweet chime of the zantros. Del braced himself against the chair back: he was pretty drunk. He sipped, then determinedly took a larger swallow. He could not allow himself the luxury of getting sloppy in front of his own servants, but Beyba wouldn't care.

The zantros had begun a steady figure that repeated and repeated. Del recognized the opening of the affilade, the one dance he always enjoyed seeing. Given sufficient incentive, Andur would perform it, or rather the opening section. It was always a relief and a disappointment when Andur reached the point where the mysteries began and simply stopped and walked away—

The masked dancer who took the stage was electrifying, with all of Andur's fire, head whipping back and forth as he hunted an unseen prey. Del felt his drink spilling over his fingers and blindly shoved the cup onto the table.

The music chimed up to its climax.

The zantros pealed, once, twice.

The dancer froze.

Deltander sat back in his seat at the expected end.

There was a low note that vibrated along the marrow of his bones and the music continued. The masked head, turned, searched, looking, hunting.

Del shivered, unable to look away.

The hidden eyes fixed on Del, the dancer pulled the mask up and off and leaped, knife in one hand, mask in the other, from the stage.

At Del.

Who stood up, hearing at some vast distance the crash of decanter and cup on the floor, and reached for the face, pale without powder, even after exertion.

Teyr.

Face buried in the hard braids wound tight to the head for the mask, Del said, "Where?"

Beyba signaled the lights to quarter power, shoved the table aside. "My office at the port."

Del, wiping sweat with his sleeve—Teyr endured but did not welcome the attention—said, "What?"

"He came to my office." Beyba leaned back and stretched out his long legs. "As well as we can figure out, G-R security got bored and went up to play the lickaton holos. They gave him a fistful of credits to amuse himself around the gaming room. When the set got going he wandered off, bought himself some makeup and a disposable work suit from a vending machine, changed and took the speed strip to my offices where they let him in—"

Knowing your interest in personable boys, thought Del.

Beyba had promptly impounded all of his staff Teyr might have passed, sent them to duties off-planet, and smuggled Teyr to his own home. Where Teyr had stayed while G-R personnel, the city and the port guard, and Del's own security had combed Belsyrtis.

"Andur got on to me fast," said Beyba. "And he's a tough man to bribe."

Andur, who had slipped in to stand against the wall at the back, gave Beybaken a cold look. "Asen."

Beyba laughed at Andur's anger. "I had to get Jasil Carnath to do some fancy talking—he's an expensive boy when he consents to deal with a mere parvenu—that if he," Beyba pointed at Teyr, "had civil status then informing you," Beyba's long forefinger pointed at Del, "where he was would force you, as an official, to inform on him and would endanger the pursuit of his legal interests." Beyba sat up. "Or something like that. It worked and it should have: it cost me enough."

"He didn't want to go," said Andur.

Which probably summarizes Andur's thinking completely, thought Del. Whatever Jasil said wouldn't have mattered except to tell Andur there was some legal folderol to drape the naked truth in. He held on to Teyr's hard, solid weight, smelling musk and sweat.

"We couldn't tell you. Carnath was absolute. You'd have had to inform G-R, and we weren't about to waste Teyr's good work." Beyba drew a face in the spilled liquor, smiling to himself.

Del held on tight. "I still have to tell them."

Beyba stood up so fast he had to grab the edge of the table for balance. "Are you crazy?" Beyba's eyes shot to Andur.

Andur came off the wall to say, "He doesn't want to go, Asen."

Beyba said, "Del, if he's property, you have title. If he isn't—"

"Then he isn't of age, and Varriel is probably his legal guardian, although that might be—"

"No," said Beyba. "Carnath said something else."

"Carnath's not a specialist in trade law: I am. When I want to juggle words I can do it for myself."

"Well, fuck it, Del what do you want?" Beyba's hand hit the fragile tabletop so hard it cracked. "You've been walking around here like a dead man!"

Teyr pulled away and looked at Del.

"I don't know," said Del, rubbing his chest.

Beyba sat down and slid his legs to their full extension. "You can take this," his hand cut the air with disdain, "'follow the rules' too far. You guys sit here in Belsyrtis and most of you are on the take and the rest are so busy worrying about not being on the take that you never have any time to think."

Beyba pulled his legs in and leaned forward. "And I'm sick of it. He stays here until you work it out with that twitchy conscience of yours."

Del looked at Andur who folded his arms and leaned back against the wall.

"I could sue," said Del.

Beyba kissed his middle finger.

Del looked away, and wiped his mouth with the flat of his hand: his lips felt numb.

"Talk it over with Carnath, Del. Just because it hurts doesn't mean it's right." Beyba stood. "Meanwhile you go home to that empty house."

Stunned—he had never imagined being dismissed by Beybaken Norrey—Del looked at Andur, who was briskly gesturing away at Teyr, hands moving faster than Del could follow.

Teyr looked at Del, who winced, unable to meet his eyes.

Beyba said, "Well?"

Del looked at him.

"What are you afraid of, Del? That they're all going to laugh and say they finally know Permund's price?"

Del rubbed his mouth. He knew what they were going to say. He'd found a valuable piece of property and concealed it when the rightful owner attempted to claim it. Then gotten the rights to it by a ruse. "I have to notify them he's alive," said Del.

"And if they take that as 'Ha, ha, fooled you,' and come back in force? You're not rich enough to take on G-R. Even if you have a perfect case, they'll just grind you into bankruptcy."

Del shook his head, "I have to respect the law."

Beyba thumped both fists on the cracked table. "I don't. Justice, maybe. Where's the justice in sending him back? Varriel gave him up to secure a business loan."

"What?"

"Oh, yeah. He needed money for his research, so he transferred his rights in Evtan to G-R. For two trialliads worth of credit." Beyba pulled a chair around and sat down. "To give him his due, I think he intended to get him back as fast as he could scrape the credits together." Beyba's hands gripped the chair arms. "When he knew he couldn't get him back, he sat there and did his damndest to give the case to Jasil."

"I," Del stopped.

"He was dumb enough to listen to what they were saying instead of what he was thumb printing."

Del swayed—he'd had a lot to drink—and Andur pushed a chair behind him.

"They did a lot of loud fighting about it," said Beyba, "and the hotel staff heard most of it."

Del gripped the chair arms to steady the rocking walls.

"You're too drunk to think, Del. Let Andur get you to bed. We'll argue in the morning."

When he woke Del lay still trying to sort out what had happened the night before. He'd gotten very drunk—his pounding head assured him of that—and made a fool of himself over one of Beyba's dancer's who looked like—

Teyr.

He whipped the covers back and looked around the strange room. The first set of double doors led to the personal. The second was a vast, mostly empty, wardrobe. The third—

The doors thudded open, and Teyr, startled awake, snarled, saw who it was, and subsided into his nest of bedding.

Del took one deep calming breath.

And yelled at the top of his lungs, "ANDUR!"

Andur came through the door like as man expecting an army on the other side. He looked around the room, and began rehanging his weapons methodically. "Asen," he said, between pants.

"Tell me what happened last night."

Andur's eyes hunted over the floor.

"Besides my making a fool of myself." Del sat down, cautiously. It was the sharp, piercing pain behind the right eye that hurt most.

Andur put one finger under a strap and eased his heavy harness. "I think maybe Asen Norrey could give a better—"

"Andur."

Andur turned to Teyr with a quick series of gestures and Teyr climbed out of bed and went into the personal. Del, trying to massage his temples while holding his head very still, accepted the cup of water Teyr offered, broke three of the ampoules he'd brought into it, and downed the bitter mixture in one forced series of swallows.

As he handed the cup back he noticed the haze of dark fuzz on Teyr's upper lip. That was new. Del measured the shoulders against the hips as Teyr walked away. Bondre had broad shoulders and lean, hollow hips, too.

"The office," said Del.

"I had Jyse call you in sick."

Del ran his tongue around the inside of his mouth. From the taste, something had died there several days ago. "Beyba?"

"Asen Norrey left for his office at the port half a shift ago."

"What time is it?"

Andur told him.

"Huh," said Del, in astonishment.

Andur's stolid expression was flawed by traces of amusement.

The outrageous pain in Del's head was easing enough that Asen Permund was able to form a criminal intent for the first time in his life. "Andur," said Del. "How many people know about Teyr?"

"You, me, Asen Norrey. The household staff: there are only four at the moment. Some of Norrey's office personnel saw him, but Norrey doesn't think they would recognize him, and in any case he's sent them all to off-planet duty."

"Call my office and say—"

"Asen, the com doesn't work."

"What?"

"Asen Norrey disabled it before he left."

That sounded like Beyba. "Well, fix it."

"He disabled it by throwing a chair into it."

That would do it. Del considered Andur.

Andur looked coolly back.

"And just what else did Asen Norrey have to say?"

Andur licked his lips, once, and thought how to phrase it. Then he settled on an unadorned quote. "That I better keep you out of trouble when you woke up. And Teyr better be here when he got back."

"And what did he mean by that?"

"Asen, I don't know if you remember last night. You had a lot to drink. But you were saying you had to notify G-R that Teyr is alive—"

Del, watching Teyr, who was watching him, said, "I spent a ten-days trying to convince myself that what I had to do was what I wanted to do. It takes a few minutes to—" *junk the principles of a lifetime*— "—adjust," finished Del. "What did you tell Teyr?"

"Nothing," said Andur. "We had to carry you to bed."

Teyr was prowling the suite, opening doors and cabinets, sniffing at the disused air in the wardrobe. He found the sound system and Del covered his ears. "Off," he said, tersely.

Andur's hands moved and the sound died.

"So I'm under house arrest?"

"Asen—" Andur hitched his weapons harness. "Asen Norrey went to explore some possible courses of action and wanted you to wait for his input before you began considering appropriate ways of dealing with the situation."

"You've been spending too much time with diplomats."

Andur made an embarrassed sound.

"I suppose Beyba has no objection to our feeding and amusing ourselves?"

"No, Asen," said Andur. "He gave the staff orders—" Andur stopped.

Del laughed. And regretted it. "Let's look around."

The exercise room looked shiny and unused, and as far as Del was concerned, it could stay that way. But it was as good a spot as any to pass the time until Beyba decided to get home. There was a large comfortable chair.

"Uh," grunted Andur, teeth bared. He began pushing back slowly. Teyr braced his whole weight against him. Andur rocked, and flipped. Teyr placed the tip of the practice knife under Andur's chin with loving care. Andur, panting, released his grip and turned his head to side. Teyr stood up.

"Shit," said Beyba. "He beat you."

Andur, moping sweat from his glossy body, nodded. He rubbed the towel over his head.

"What are you going to when he gets heavier?"

"Make sure we're on the same side," said Andur. "I can only win half the time now and I know what to expect. He'd win the first time by surprise with a new opponent."

"And in a real fight?" Beyba helped himself to the juice Del was drinking.

"I hope I never find out." Andur pulled on a shirt.

Beyba pursed his lips. "The claws."

"The teeth," said Andur. "You rip somebody's throat open it doesn't matter what he weighs. He's a dead man."

Teyr smiled.

Beyba appraised the white, sharp dentition. "I see."

"What did you find out?" said Andur.

Del gave him a look.

Beyba accepted the familiarity. "A lot of things. But first we have to convince Del, here, he wants to forget his grief with a long vacation off-planet."

"I do?" said Del.

"You'd better," said Beyba.

Andur nodded agreement. "Your brother, for one, Asen, usually needs credits."

Del put down his cup with a click. Hanro. A kaleidoscope of possibilities spun in his mind, none of them good. "Yes. Where?"

"I thought you might combine business with pleasure, get a little practical experience, accompany me on a prospecting trip. In fact," Beyba offered Andur juice, "I told the servants last night."

"Uh," said Del.

"You've been distressed, Asen, I'm sure your office would find the explanation creditable." Andur accepted the cup.

I may have liked you better strong and silent, Andur, thought Del. *But you're right*. "You're both ahead of me. Well?"

Beyba looked to Andur, who nodded. "I've called the *Andeno* to the High Syrtis Two. We can go up next shift—send Andur and Teyr with the luggage."

"Teyr in the luggage?" said Del.

"Yeah," said Beyba. "Andur's been training him."

"Um," said Del.

"And after that, we can improvise as necessary."

Del looked at Andur.

"We've worked it out," said Andur. "I'll stay right with him."

"He's not going to like being in a box."

"He's not going to like being back in G-R's hands, either," said Andur.

"They had plans for him," said Beyba, "and whatever they were, Varriel was furious."

"I'm not sure about the box," said Del. "It's a long trip. And even with Andur providing backup, there's no real failsafe."

"Asen," said Andur. "What do you suggest?"

"Can you take him with you, Beyba? As a companion?"

Beyba looked thoughtful. "He'd have to be made-up—and he's extremely muscular—" he frowned. "I think," Beyba propped long fingers together, I think we could bring him as a dancer." He moved his hands apart.

Teyr, sensing decision, looked at the three of them, one by one.

He made a striking blond, thought Del, and the spray-on bronzer looked convincingly appropriate as the make-up it was. The tacked-on braid kept ticking him in the back, however, and he moved around restlessly until Andur wound it into a warrior's knot at the nape of his neck. Then Teyr started hunching his shoulders, annoyed at the off-balance tug. At which point Andur gave a swift series of gestures that produced complete stillness.

"What did you say," said Del.

"Nothing," said Andur.

Del opened his mouth.

"Not now," said Beyba. "We're on, and I hope the vidders don't catch sight of us."

"No problem," said Andur.

The blond Etalazian dancer scratched his jaw, defiantly.

Andur glared.

Tongue-tip between teeth, Beyba touched up the coating. The skimmer hit with a thump. "Shit," said Beyba, who'd bitten himself.

Del started rubbing his chest.

Andur reached and flipped down Teyr's veil of beads.

The door opened and they were in public view.

Del would have been happier if Beyba hadn't looked so contented with his arm across Teyr's shoulders. That Teyr was smiling tight-lipped was only a reflection of Andur's instructions—keep your mouth closed—and didn't console Del in the least. But they were on their way down the station reception lounge before the resident vidders, probably alerted from the ground, got into action in an explosion of lights and sound.

Del was gladder than usual for Andur's solid muscle at his back as they pushed the lights into his face and mercilessly shouted questions, most of which could be ignored in the din. Del beamed like a death's-head, face innocent of make-up. From the way they were moving the lights around they were competing to see who could get the most ghastly shot.

Del hadn't viewed his appearance in court, and had no intention of doing so, ever. His departure from Syrtis Two was another event that might be in the history records, but was going to be unviewed as far as Del was concerned.

When the doors to the restricted boarding area closed, Del rubbed his hand over his mouth and said, "Where's Beyba?"

Beyba had been altogether too happy to play the besotted patron.

"They've boarded," said Andur, moving briskly.

But on the *Andeno* Beyba was busy giving orders to the crew and Teyr was nowhere in sight. "About time," said Beyba. "What took so long?"

"They left no question unasked," said Del. "Where's—"

"Show the Asen to his quarters, Effed."

"Asen."

The quarters were in stark contrast to any ship Del had ever been on: big, and elaborately lighted, with a ventilation system that rippled the wall hangings. Andur began checking the luggage methodically as Effed inquired if the Asen would require any personal servants.

Del thought of Jyse, left home without a word, and shook his head. "No."

"Asen." Effed was out the door and away.

Teyr, face pink with scrubbing, appeared from the personal.

The walls rang with decoupling.

"Better lie down," said Andur, tumbling a near-empty borrowed case into a luggage store. "Asen Norrey likes smart departures."

Del felt the angle of the floor shift, and hastily reached the bed. The *Andeno* was underway. Teyr rose slowly off the floor in the fading gravity and floated, the pale blond of his bleached hair drifting around his head. He looked supremely happy clinging with one foot to the wall. As Andur reached to get Teyr to strap down, Del closed his eyes and tried not to think about his stomach.

Beyba traced a complicated pattern into the holo. "Something like that," he said, with satisfaction.

Del looked it over. While he had been grinding mindlessly back and forth to the office, Beyba and Andur had been very busy indeed. It was unsettling to see how well they worked together. It had never occurred to Del that Andur was capable of directing an enterprise with such unobtrusive skill. Beyba was quite comfortable following Andur. Del wasn't, and knew why. He felt stupid.

If he had thought about it, he would have known that Andur, a capable leader, would be able to put his thoughts both precisely and persuasively. What Del wasn't happy about was the fact that he felt as if Andur had pulled off a years' long practical joke on him.

His strong, silent, retro-savage was a formidable, sophisticated agent in his own right. His eyes had a quiet amusement at Del's discomfort. Del was left wondering what went on behind Teyr's perpetual silence.

Del had spent his life considering the martially trained as tools of the intellectual. A few shifts of the new Andur and Del was wondering who manipulated whom. And why. And how the Kel picked those they allowed to employ them.

Feeling a little paranoid, aren't we, thought Del, and gave his attention to the chart.

Beyba began explaining the rational behind the route. "Andur thinks," he said, shading a sector, "that G-R is pressing out in this direction because they foresee certain events in the cluster core."

"What?" said Del.

"I think Teyr has something to do with it."

"Teyr?"

Andur looked at his hands on the console, then up at Del. "We think there may be a lot of others like him. He's got a language, Asen. It just isn't verbal, and I'm not very good at learning it."

"What," asked Del.

"His gestures."

"That's too simple to qualify as a language. Go there. Come here."

Andur shook his head. "He can say a lot more than that. We can't understand him."

"It's true," said Beyba. "I was watching him talk to Andur. He keeps trying to teach Andur to speak." Beyba grinned. "He must consider us idiots."

Andur made a motion of agreement.

Del wrestled with his expectations. "But why?"

Andur sat forward, warming to his explanation. "I think there's a natural bias toward silence, heavily reinforced by training. Once he was past the receptive age he wouldn't break the barrier. Might not be able to make the sounds."

"Even if there were nothing wrong physically."

"Or mentally," said Andur. "You don't see him in action often, Asen. He's very capable."

"I didn't think he wasn't," said Del.

Andur didn't answer.

"I didn't," said Del, irritated.

"You think of him as younger than he is," said Andur.

Del was silent. *I think of him as innocent, Andur.*

Teyr looked from face to face, locked behind a wall of silence.

Beyba said, "Let me explain what I had in mind—"

Del gave him his fullest attention. The other would keep. These were decisions that would change his life forever.

If we had been provincial up to now, the greater world of the core suns and their convoluted politics began to intrude all too insistently on our microcosm.

I had always been aware that there were larger interests, but they made little difference in the short term to us on Belsyrtis, and their long-term effects were like the changes of the seasons: invisible from day to day.

Entirely apart from the matter of Teyr, Beyba could scarcely have picked a better time to move away from the core: there was something going on, that caused a general expansion hard to ignore once you were away from placid Belsyrtis.

The first thing I had noticed was that a large number of the wealthy were traveling, taking vacations further away then usual, moving to build new bases unobtrusively. Nothing seemed to be happening in the news, and yet the climate had changed. People were on the move. We could only watch, wonder, and wait. Unless, like Beyba, one was prepared to act on instinct alone.

I cast my lot with Beyba.

Neither Beyba nor I thought it a good sign that so few of the wealthy came to Belsyrtis. "It's true," said Beyba, "the profits are better further out: but these are entire families. You'd think they'd want a little civilization."

And the general flow of trade had begun to change. Not every ship came back, some moved to new routes farther out, shuttling between ports that had been no more than emergency landing fields scraped down to bedrock with AI beacons a standard before.

Andur says I should sleep now, if I can, and he will watch.

It is so quiet that I hoped night had come and dispersed the mob. But my chrono says it is the middle of the second shift: broad daylight. If we go to the first story, we could use the security system to survey the plaza.

I will leave that decision to Andur, who stands at the foot of the stairs, listening.

Del surveyed the rough slabs leading down to the still-bare earth of the garden, wistfully remembering the manicured grounds of his estate on Belsyrtis. *Maybe Hanro will enough decency not to occupy my house.*

He walked down the steps, grit squeaking underfoot, and looked up at the synthetic sky of the dome, hearing the low humming that meant a fierce wind was stressing the thin material. Lybayos' atmosphere was not poisonous, but wind-blown sand scoured everything.

He caught himself testing his balance: the lighter gravity was pleasant, it even tempted one to foolishness. Del seated himself on a dust-covered bench, and laughed quietly to himself.

Or at himself.

I spent my whole life wanting this and not knowing it. It is such a pleasure to get up and wonder what different is going to happen. To worry, not about which sum of credits went where, but about how a life-support system should be backed up and how big the reserves should be.

Under Beyba's cautious direction these were not urgent, but always necessary, questions. Del had spent years wondering how some of the—well, think of Inte—how some of Holk's problems had been allowed to occur. Now he knew. But he also knew that his intuition that he could do this was right.

"You look happy," said Beyba, ostentatiously dusting a patch and sitting down on the bench.

"I am," said Del.

"Good," said Beyba, "enjoy it another moment. I've got the cargo reports."

"What's missing?" said Del, reaching for the file rods. It was one thing to order something, and another to actually claim it at the port. There were always agents bidding for newly arrived goods and if you weren't there to claim your own it was apt to turn up missing, sold to the highest bidder.

Del stood, and Beyba brushed vigorously at the seat of his robe. "Skip the small stuff. Make sure we get our l-s backup. You know who to sweeten."

Del flipped open his belt pouch and thumbed through the stiff universal credit chits.

Beyba watched him count, then reached for his own. "Here. Take these. Get it even if you overpay."

Del nodded, counting and recounting. The dirt-filled wind destroyed equipment at a fantastic rate: three or even four backups were not extravagant. "I'll get it," he said.

Beyba grinned.

Del gave him a reproving look.

Beyba tried to stop and ending laughing. "Grandfather must have been a real pirate."

Del tucked the credits away. "He was a good businessman."

"That's what I said."

They went up the steps to the house.

"I need to know what else is in," Beyba keyed the door, "so if you get a chance, walk around a bit. Better, take Teyr. He and Andur can get all over the place."

Del frowned.

"It's safe enough," said Beyba.

Del shrugged. The port was tough by local standards, but that wasn't what worried him. It was just that, defined as property, Teyr represented a lot of credits, an enormous temptation.

But he was unsalable here. Lybayos was tolerant of pretty sharp practice, but her population walked safe streets: justice was summary. Your pocket might be picked, but the cargo handler sleeping off rift had no doubt he'd wake up.

Teyr and Andur roamed the streets at will, and Del had, finally, put Andur on his honor, strapped a communicator to the pair, and settled for being able to locate them most of the time.

Having never been out of calling range of his security in his life, Del found Andur's casual assumption anything that bothered him would be sorry—or dead—made him nervous. A nervousness Del was gradually becoming more comfortable with as he realized there were rules to the game, here as on Belsyrtis.

In fact, thought Del, coming through the double, dust-proofed entrance to the port concourse in a haze of powdered dirt, *living here is like being a player in a giant, unending gambling game*. People came and went, the stakes went up and down, but the game was on, night and day, without pause.

Del could see two, three, four figures crane to see who he was then run off in different directions: alerting their bosses Permund was here. Del noted their number, speed and direction with a practiced eye. Nothing unusual. He turned toward the inflated building that was temporary headquarters for Norreyco. If the hardening foam ever arrived, it would become the permanent headquarters.

Meanwhile the hiss and sigh as he passed through the door-lock reminded Del that every cycle sent wearing dirt into the machinery.

"Asen." Flamburt Delorn rose behind his desk—two cargo pods fused together and littered with com equipment.

"Delorn," acknowledged Del.

"What's the program?" Delorn shoved a crude chair forward and sat down again without further courtesy.

"The backup l-s is in. I'm here to see we get it."

"Anarey has already approached Hent."

Del punched a file rod into a reader and tilted his head to the high-pitched whisper. "How do you know?"

"Hent asked me if I'd like to make a counter-offer."

Del laughed. "What did you say?"

"'Sure.'"

Del looked up from the flickering figures, inquiring.

"I offered that if he fulfilled his contract we'd manage not to drop his water precips when we got around to delivering them." Delorn leaned back, robe collapsing into his concave belly. "And I sent Jass over to stand around and watch."

Del nodded, and punched the summary for the file. "Can we deliver today?"

"Slow things down a bit."

"I want that l-s in our hands, nobody else's."

Delorn nodded.

Del pulled the rod out, entered another. "Anything here I really need to know before I go over?"

"Hent's shipment hasn't come in."

Del looked up with interest. "Why?"

"That's the interesting part. It was sent. The ship hasn't reported."

Del stopped the file. "The ship hasn't reported?"

"Third in a ten-days."

"I'll get this settled. When Norrey comes in, tell him we need to talk."

"Asen." Delorn rose, leaning forward on the desk, and watched him out.

Del strode down the concourse, alert to the traffic around him as he never had been when cocooned by security. The loaders at the next two companies down were dusty: unused. A bad sign. And the normally bustling freight lines for Anarey's Novacorp were running at about half speed, and underutilized at that.

Del walked faster. They might need everything on that freighter if trade was going to be disrupted.

He turned in under the garish logo.

Three idle clerks leaped to their feet, and one said, "Asen Permund. What a pleasure! I'll just tell the Asen you're here—"

"I'll announce myself."

Del pushed open the door to the inner office. Anarey didn't even jump when Del came through the door.

"I want my shipment delivered this shift, Hent."

Zandro Hent took his feet off the desk and stood up. "Ah. That might be problem, Del. There seems to have been a shortage—"

"I'm sure you'll discover it's a clerk's error." Del refused the folding chair proffered by a sweating aide. Anarey was foolish to waste cargo space on such frippery now. "This shift."

Hent's glance flickered to Elinda Anarey, who smoothed her robes and smiled coldly. "I'll pay twenty-five percent over cost now and cover your port charges for the next unit. Will you sell?"

It was a good offer, and a little pressure would make it better. Del shook his head. "I'm sorry, Elinda, we've already got a whine in our main unit." It was a fluent lie. "We may be down to the backup by this evening." Or at least in three ten-days before the next unit might arrive if it was ordered immediately. If freight was still arriving then.

Elinda smoothed the fabric across her knees. "We have a unit on order, Del. I'll sell it to you below cost if I can take delivery now."

Del saw Hent blink with surprise. "I am sorry, Elinda. We need it now."

Del turned to Hent. "You'll be wanting delivery of those water precips. If you send your own labor teams, we can both have our equipment by the end of the next shift."

Hent had caught the implications in Anarey's offer. He leaned to the com unit. "Lett? Start loading the l-s for Norrey. We're to collect our precips at the same time, take a small hauler and a team." He flipped the com off with a solid thunk.

Elinda Anarey rose and shook her robes into place. "There's a meeting at Quarrail's tonight. Small traders pooling what we know. Maybe you big guys would like to send someone."

"When?" said Del.

"End of the next shift."

"Someone will be there," said Del. This was apt to be Beyba's kind of affair. Del was too stiff to win confidences in that freewheeling crowd.

The low-ceilinged room was hot, and smelled of crowded, rather drunk, humanity. Drunk because alcohol could be manufactured anywhere there was food. Drugs were imported and expensive on Lybayos.

Del trailed in Beyba's brisk wake until they found a place against a wall near an exit. Beyba craned his neck and looked around. Del was too short to see more than nearby backs.

"Big crowd," said Beyba.

Del put his shoulders against the wall, resigned to listening. "Too many."

Beyba looked down. "Bad sign," he agreed shortly. "What's the news," he asked a broad back.

Genthar Deven looked around. "Beyba. I don't know. I'm here because I've been getting rumors all day. This is in short supply. And that hasn't been delivered." He maneuvered his heavy body to face them. "Del. Didn't see you."

Del made a resigned, wordless acknowledgement.

"I'm not sure anyone has any word. It's just," he sniffed loudly, "a cold smell on the wind. Same sort of thing that sent us out here."

Beyba looked at Del and back at Genthar. "Some sharp noses here."

"Yeah." Genthar looked around, eyes pausing at three or four people. He looked back at Beyba. "You and me not the least."

Del made himself unobtrusive, and wasn't entirely pleased when Beyba took him by the upper arm and moved both of them close to Deven. Deven's breath reeked of rift. "Thar," Beyba's voice was pitched so low Del had trouble hearing it. "Are you getting anything from further in?"

Genthar looked evasive. "All the usual stuff. Automatic traffic, ships in, ships out, situation reports."

Beyba leaned closer and Del admired his strong stomach. "But the open traffic? Ship to ship? Coded commercial?"

Thar rocked back on his heels. "You noticed? Thin."

He and Beyba stood almost nose-to-nose.

Genthar made the opening move. "What do you think?"

Beyba shrugged. "It's interesting."

"Interesting."

"Suggestive."

"Yeah." Genthar took Beyba's shoulders and pulled him so close their mouths were finger's breadth from each other's ears.

Del couldn't hear the discussion that followed.

Finally Beyba stepped back. "All right," he said, agreeing to something.

Thar nodded and moved away through the crowd.

"We're leaving," said Beyba.

Del bit back, "Why?" and followed.

Beyba's fierce face went in and out of light and darkness as they passed the float-lights along the main street.

"Don't we need to know what they're going to say?" asked Del.

"No." Beyba's long stride made Del scurry at his side. "There's some sort of trouble further in."

"I guessed that," said Del dryly.

"It involves G-R and something called the Varr."

"What?" Del stopped in the street, feeling the warm, gritty air brush his face.

"Keep moving," said Beyba. "We want to get home."

Del started rubbing the old, familiar pain at his sternum that he'd almost forgotten. He lengthened his stride. The Varr. Litjin Varriel. Too similar to be accidental.

Beyba caught him by the elbow. "Look calm, Del. Some one might be watching."

Andur was startled when they keyed their way in. "I thought you'd be gone longer."

"We found out what we needed to know."

Andur, catching Beyba's tone, got to his feet and started checking his weapons.

"Where's Teyr?" said Del.

"At Renchard's," said Andur, sliding a charge in and out.

"Outside our security," said Beyba. "Get him."

Andur's instant of hesitation was long for him; short for almost anybody else. He didn't bother with a filter mask, but jogged out the door without question.

"Sit down," said Beyba. "He'll be all right. It'll take them a while to think of it—" His anxious pacing to look through the dust-clouded glass at the empty street, its darkness broken by feeble pools of light, gave the lie to his words.

Del coughed to relieve the pressure behind his sternum.

Beyba looked back from his vantage point. "Relax," he snapped. "It's going to be fine."

Del nodded, chest too tight to speak.

Beyba left the room, dust swirling on the floor in his wake. "Anss? Anss!"

Del's vision blurred, and all his attention was concentrated on the hard knot of pain.

The sharp-nailed hands gripping his shoulders were familiar.

Teyr.

Del moaned and leaned into the hard, muscular body that smelled of dust, sweat, and musk. He could hear Andur's voice, sharp with anger, questioning Beyba.

Beyba, ignoring Andur, ordered house security brought to full strength.

All Del had attention for was the solid reality of Teyr.

The pain slowly eased.

He could feel sand and grit on Teyr's bare back. He moved his palm, puzzled, and pulled back to look Teyr over.

Teyr was wearing nothing but his trousers, and they were unfastened at the ankles and secured crooked at the waist.

Renchard's daughter is pretty, recalled Del, *and willing, or so they say*. Her father had the loudest and most vulgar mouth Del had ever heard. He sighed and released his hold; gestured, get dressed.

Teyr padded off, bare feet leaving dusty footprints on the polished floor, the autoclean following his trail, humming.

Del stood and caught his balance, hearing Beyba in the first stages of losing his temper, and Andur thumping at the recalcitrant security machinery. He poured himself some water, thinking.

Teyr was going to be a problem.

His own father had been strict: paying attentions to any of the staff was forbidden, the daughters of his father's friends off-limits, and the entertainment district proscribed.

His father had simply purchased a contract for a healthy, willing girl of suitable age—somewhat older than Del—and told Del that was it.

It wasn't.

It had been a considerable relief to his father to find his second son was more docile about such matters. Hanro was contract-bonded to Riana's mother before he was out of his mid-twenties.

Del lifted a loop-necked flask straight off one of Beyba's ships and added enough jart to color his water deep amber. Anss, who was taking a remarkably long time, would not approve—

Beyba, looking hot and angry, didn't approve either. "Bad idea, Del. Did Anss ask leave to go out?"

The household staff was required to ask, mostly to keep track of where to find them in case of need. As household doctor, Anss was more likely than most to get an emergency call.

"No," said Del.

"She's not here. Went out right after we did."

Del put his drink down. It was not going to help his suddenly dry mouth. Anss knew a great deal about Teyr, Del, Beyba, and their security. And she was a new hire. Del's doctor had preferred to stay on Belsyrtis; Beyba's had moved up to supervising conditions on the new additions to the Norreyco fleet.

Beyba picked up Del's drink and tossed it back.

Del poured himself a cup of water.

"Andur!" yelled Beyba.

Del could hear Andur coming. The clink and jingle of his unsecured weapons preceded him. He was fastening the loops and straps as he entered. "Asen Norrey," he said, looking at Del.

A reminder who employed him.

Beyba turned to Del, his mouth gone thin.

"Whatever, Beyba," said Del. Then, to Andur, "Where's Teyr?"

"Coming."

Teyr came silently through the door, a dark-haired version of Andur, down to the array of weapons clipped to his belt.

He looked frighteningly capable.

"All right." Beyba was unable to stand still. "I spoke to Thar Deven. He's gotten word there's trouble further in. G-R appears to be fighting a private war using something the messages call Varr."

Andur's eyes switched to Teyr.

"No," said Beyba. "These are furry, retractable claws, maybe semi-intelligent. Maybe not. Some of the Jertanth hard-liners are condemning them for producing semi-humans—"

The Jertanth had a fair-sized military force to argue for their religious convictions.

Del felt fear trickle down his spine.

Wars based on economics, on territory, even on offended pride, were negotiable. But religious wars were devastating because none of the ordinary restraints applied. What restrains a fanatic who believes he's going to his own personal paradise if he dies firm in his convictions while fighting for the cause?

The inevitable differences of humans across the long distances in space and time had been the focus of wars so destructive that humanity had survived only because it was so widely scattered.

But that scattering had produced a range of human-derived stocks, and only one universal law that human genes were not to be used in gene-sculptures. Teyr offended the standards in intention if not in fact being artificially created and close to the human norm.

Del believed Varriel had accomplished what he claimed. But a less-educated, less-well-informed person would be hard-pressed to make the distinction. And not likely to bother.

Del didn't know what G-R had unleashed. Or why. But it was a threat to Teyr. To Bondre and Teyr's kind. It raised passions better left unaroused.

Del sipped his water, listening to Beyba's summary and preparation with half an ear, trained by years of skimming file-rods. *Varriel is the key. If he needs credits for his projects, what would stop him from producing a gene-sculptured sub-race of soldiers? Possibly he created them to protect his other projects?*

Del took another sip of gritty water.

But Varriel had no stake in stirring things up. Carnath had the impression Varriel hoped to force recognition of Teyr's civil status in the court at Belsyrtis. That argued he considered his creations to have standing, even if G-R didn't. *Therefore, what? Varriel is in trouble?*

Beyba's voice stopped and Del looked up. Then he heard it: the formless sound of a large crowd. The door annunciator chimed. The servant who answered it was trembling. The four people who entered were all familiar, if not precisely friends. The fierce competition among the members of the tiny colony precluded easy friendships.

Bredi Obt stepped forward as spokesperson, grey-streaked hair powdered with dust, robe streaked from a day's hard labor. The Obts were not leisured. She took a wide-based stance and pointed with her chin. "We want to know what that is."

Beyba started to speak, then yielded to Del.

"You know Teyr," said Del neutrally. Force your opponent to make his own arguments.

"You left the meeting, you know what we're talking about." She glanced behind her for support. "Anyone can see he's not your child. What is he?"

Del studied the faces in front of him for an instant. They were, he saw with relief, genuinely asking. The standard year of seeing Teyr every day, following Andur, or Beyba, or Del, quiet, intent, made it harder for them to make the leap of equating him with the obscenities blurrily sketched in the reports from further in, particularly when there was no immediate threat.

Whatever I do, Del thought, *I must give them as little as possible.* There was no way to predict what facts might be turned against Teyr in the future, especially if their anger and fear grew. "We're not sure," said Del.

"What does that mean?" snapped Renchard, a man who thought he wanted clear answers, but might, if he was aware of his daughter's activities, prefer some suitable lies.

Del said smoothly, "Why don't you all sit down? Beyba?"

Beyba, taking his cue, moved toward the liquor.

Del toyed with his cup, afraid to get a refill and make it obvious he would be drinking only water. "I'll tell you what we know." Del made a point of being truthful, if spare. And if he mentioned Teyr met the norms and didn't mention the implications of the tattoo under the upper lip, he still couldn't easily be charged with lying or deliberate distortion.

I have my own ideas about where Anss might have gone and who she has talked to. It is, thought Del, *just possible she has never folded back Teyr's upper lip to see the mark. And there has been no reason for any of us to mention it—*

They had decided, back on Belsyrtis, not to do anything immediately about the tattoo. Erasure was painful, and Del had a half-formed notion that if Teyr met his own kind it would be better if his status was unambiguous to them.

Del talked on, soothing, apparently taking them into his confidence. Finding Teyr. His fears and worries about the boy. Simple, human things. Beyba, standing behind the seated group refilled his glass and gave Del a silent toast.

The group gradually relaxed, hearing things they wanted to hear, things that confirmed what they had believed. Renchard's face had lost its hard, fixed expression. They had another round of imported liquor and were almost cordial when Del showed them to the door.

Del came back and accepted a drink.

"Masterful," said Beyba.

"They could turn the other way just as fast," said Del.

"So? What do we do?"

"Wait. And hope we get some solid information fast."

Beyba shook his head. "And if it's true?"

"I'd bet it's true," said Del.

"Why?"

"There's a limited market for—" Del waved a hand, searching for a proper term.

"Exotic personal servants," supplied Beyba.

"But soldiers—"

"Are in short supply and high demand," finished Beyba. "And he's what, the model for the commanding officer?"

"I hadn't thought that far," said Del.

"But it fits," said Beyba.

Andur silently agree.

"Yes," said Del.

Teyr looked from face to face to face.

Andur's hands began moving.

It was nearly a ten-days later when Renchard asked to talk to Asen Permund.

Del hoped he didn't know what the visit was about. He offered a seat, liquor, and neutral small talk. He had seen to it Teyr was kept home, or in company, and he had hoped Renchard would be willing to let the matter pass officially unnoticed.

But Renchard did not have the angry glow of an outraged father. He was, in fact, extremely nervous.

Del was completely unprepared for what he had to say.

Renchard gripped his hands together and forced the words out. "My Irdese's pregnant by your Teyr."

Del felt his jaw drop, then closed his mouth hastily. "I'll pay support. If it tests out," he added with a dash of caution.

"I don't want your credits." Renchard was red-faced. "I want to know what it's going to do to her."

"What?" said Del.

Renchard lowered his head, stared at floor, and stubbornly kept talking. "She has nightmares it'll claw its way out of her, eat her alive from the inside—"

"If she feels that way—" *about Teyr*, finished Del silently, *what was she doing with him. I want Renchard on record to prevent a rape charge*. Del flicked on his personal recorder. It wouldn't take more than an sixth of a shift's testimony, but that should be enough to ensure that Renchard's initial approach hadn't been based on an accusation of force.

Renchard hadn't even noticed Del's aborted interruption and action. "—all in her head. They've tested. He's a healthy boy. Meets the norms." He took his drink in a series of forced swallows. "She's too scared. Teyr's not of age. We need your consent to end the pregnancy—"

No, thought Del. *We can't afford that. It'll be no secret and the rumors*— "No," said Del, quietly.

Renchard shook his head. "Asen, I know—"

What, thought Del.

"He would be my first grandchild. And a boy. But she hates it—"

Del went for the weak spot. "Renchard, she's young and in no state to make a decision. Those of us, older, with more experience, should take care for her—"

His principle advantage, thought Del, as the soothing words flowed from him, was that Renchard wanted to believe him. The Renchards were clannish, isolated from their own larger family, and the birth of any child, let alone a male, would signal success in continuing their line. Since they were strictly monogamous, Del was not sure why they prized males so highly, but it was better not to explore that now.

Del's own interests in the matter were not so easily publicly avowed. Teyr's fathering a child was the ultimate answer to whether he was human. Not only could Del not afford to see the opportunity thrown away, destroying the child would start rumors about what sort of monster it had been.

Renchard was assuring Del the tests were completely in order, Teyr was the father, the child was healthy—

Del listened with the polite skepticism of a wealthy man accustomed to resisting raids on his purse.

"You'll acknowledge him," pressed Renchard. It occurred to Del that at some time Renchard had probably been more than willing that his daughter force an informal alliance with the Permunds, and was, now, blaming himself.

"Yes," said Del, envying his father his secure grip on such problems.

Teyr accepted the news without interest.

Andur was flabbergasted.

"You knew this was going on," said Del. "Why didn't you tell me?"

"I didn't expect that—he's supposed to be a gen."

"Scratch that theory," said Beyba.

Andur licked his lips. "Asen, there may be more than one."

Beyba grinned into his drink.

"Just how many is more than one?" said Del.

When Andur started on the forefinger of his second hand, Beyba began to laugh. "Del, you're going to have to sell some of them to support the rest—" He sobered suddenly at Del's expression. "You're right, that isn't funny."

"Andur, I thought—"

Beyba sipped a little liquor. "Relax, Del. The rest of them probably were safed. Renchard's got religious quirks." Beyba swirled the liquid in his cup. "One's enough for your purposes, anyway."

Del sat back. "It settles a lot of questions."

"Raises a lot of others. Varriel lied. Why?"

"I don't think he lied," said Del.

"Why not? If I had to bet, I'd bet he did a little illegal fiddling and lied about it."

Del frowned. "You get a feel for these things. Varriel wanted to disclose every fact he could. The G-R people didn't. But Varriel was ready to take on the court."

"Then how do you explain—?" Beyba's hand described an ample curve in front of his own flat belly.

148

"You could build human gene sequences from raw material: cells do. But gene-sculptures are usually coded with non-functional sequences, difficult to remove and retain type and viability, to identify the copyright holder. If we knew Varriel's code, I think we'd find they're on Teyr's gene chart."

"Gene-tampering is illegal."

"That's the point, Beyba, and why I'm sure that Varriel can prove Teyr's a gen. If he's a gen, it's not illegal."

"I wouldn't advertise that analysis," said Beyba.

"No," said Del.

I should, Del supposed, *have more sympathy for the girl*. She was a forlorn, pretty figure, but too obviously the pawn in a maneuver of her father's. Teyr remained uninterested, which bothered Del more than it pleased him.

Irdese cried a lot, that was part of the problem. A bolder girl might have carried off her state with élan. But Irdese's dripping misery was hard to bear. Del ruthlessly saw that she was attended by the colony's most competent, very indiscreet doctor.

The child, when it was born, was a healthy, noisy cub, with the tips of two sharp teeth in its upper gum and sharp little nails that needed cutting. It promptly bit its nursing mother, who refused to have anything more to do with it.

Teyr, presented with it, sniffed it critically, and showed no further interest: it lacked scent glands. He was filling out himself, the dark shading on his upper lip emphasizing the sensual mouth. Irdese was not the only girl receptive to his attentions, and Andur had his hands full maintaining Del's restrictions.

Lybayos was still too small for anonymous eroticism. Who met whom and why was one of the main themes of conversation. Directly following the topic of the skirmishes near the core and the rumors of oncoming beast-men.

Del listened with sharp attention, combed the com messages for information. Nothing seemed to attach itself to Teyr, and yet Del remained worried.

Veness was as noisy as his father was silent, dark brown eyes following everything, light brown curls bobbing up everywhere at an unlikely speed. If his mother thought she hated him, plainly his grandmother and grandfather doted on the boy.

It was three standard years since they left Belsyrtis.

My grandfather would have unreservedly condemned our life-style on Lybayos as raw and graceless. But we were safer than those who stayed behind on Belsyrtis.

And there was Teyr. We might hope to influence public opinion in so small a place. Teyr was a person here, and a representative of a menace on Belsyrtis.

I was relieved when Renchard took his family and moved farther out. The girl was ready enough to give Veness up—children normally staying with the same-sex parent—but her father overruled her, and Renchard took his grandson with him.

A pretty child, active, lively, not obviously different. I thought he was likely to prove a sterile hybrid, but it would be years before that would be put to the test, and Renchard was fond of him. I had no fears for him. No special fears.

The situation grew slowly tenser and more difficult ten-days by ten-days. This unavailable. That ship missing. Beyba and I conferred over whether we should, as the phrase went, "look over our prospects," uneasily aware the hard-won comforts of our new home biased our judgment.

We were loading the ship when matters were taken out of our hands.

Even at the relatively small distances between stars in the cluster it was possible to see trouble coming for a long time. The com center on Arstep had been tracking three unidentified ships for three ten-days and speculation had run wild as to what they might be. Ordinary traffic identified itself constantly through automatic mechanisms, for the safety of the ship if for no other reason. Silence was a deliberate action.

Del and Beyba, who had picked through the stories from further in, spared no effort to strip the house and load the one ship they had in port. They watched their less completely prepared neighbors struggle to assemble necessities.

A few chose speed over caution and thundered into the sky with near-empty ships. Empty except for those goods they hoped would provide them with a credit base anywhere. Rare metals, machine modules, even jewelry and, in one case, pirated information. There was going to be a lot of trouble if the Delrans ever caught up with Lenert Dolle.

"When are we leaving, Beyba?" Del was restless. Sitting on the ground in tiny, ill-furnished port was not to his taste. He was neither comfortable nor improving his safety.

"I want to see what happens," said Beyba.

"You mean stay here?" Del looked around at the stripped-down clutter.

"No," grunted Beyba, heaving a pod into place. "There's an old saying. 'The first ships to leave a port are the richest.' If they're interested in picking ships off, I don't want to attract attention. We leave with the rest of the crowd."

Andur nodded.

Del activated his portable com and occupied himself.

From the very first, he had hoped to teach Teyr to read. Del found he was not apt at gestural language. Andur, who was, was not interested in the things Del wanted to know. It was difficult to convey abstract ideas.

Del knew Teyr's home was big, white, and cold. That ruled out the building he had seen in Teyr's drawings. He paused to wonder where those drawings were. Still behind the woodwork in Teyr's room on Belsyrtis, probably.

It was so painfully slow gathering information that Del had abandoned the effort on Belsyrtis in favor of making sure Teyr knew what he needed to get along. And since then there never seemed to be time. Andur was well in place as the one in charge of Teyr, and Del never seriously tried to interfere with the routine.

Although, thought Del, calling another entry with his stylus, *what Teyr and Andur seem to do, mostly, is work on different ways of killing things. Or avoid being killed. I hope these pods are actually where the lists say they are—*

There was beauty of a kind in the smooth motions of looping a garrote or throwing a knife that Del had come, reluctantly, to appreciate. And the strength and skill necessary to scale an apparently

smooth wall won his admiration. But the implications about the world
they were living in were not pleasant.

At least on this trip Del meant to make a good start on Teyr's
learning something else. *The problem is going to be*, thought Del,
watching Beyba horse a container away from the wall and inspect a
damaged securing clip, *that Teyr, not understanding spoken speech,
cannot not start with the realization that writing is a symbolic
transcription of sound. He will have to memorize the words as
individual symbols.*

Del was trying to produce a compact set of words that would have
the greatest use. *Motions. Colors. Objects? Most of those can be
simply pointed out—*

Beyba dropped something and cursed, without much force.

Teyr had already learned the common codes understood by the
illiterate general population: off, on, enter, exit, warning. And he
could follow the universal pictographs of the spaceports. *What else
does he need immediately?*

Del looked up as the lurch and whir of a passing loader vibrated
through the ship. The *Tonucan* was a far cry from the *Andeno*. A
hastily converted freighter where they would sleep strapped to the
walls, and undergo both extra-g and free-fall. He felt the tube of pills
through the thin material of his belt pouch. *I'm was going to need all
of these and more.*

He forced his mind and his fingers back to his work.

The inner hatch door slid back, admitting a cold, dusty gust from
the field. Del sniffed the sharp odors of solvents and dripping fuel.
The place smelled like it'd go up in a blaze of glory at any spark.
Rushed workers did sloppy work.

Del didn't lift his eyes as Andur and Teyr's black-clad legs went
by. Whatever they were doing, he would have to get Andur's attention
to get the answer to a simple question, then Andur would have to
explain it to Teyr. It was too much effort for plain curiosity. Too
much time wasted.

Del jumped at the heavy thump beside him.

They were finishing placing the living modules, tipping the man-
sized canisters into place and fastening them down with bolts. The
stench of quick adhesive was horrible: that explained the open door.
The smell from the port, even the dust that would have to be cleared

by the filter system, were less annoying than living with the adhesive's reek for the entire trip.

Del gathered his things together and moved to the other wall. Feeling grit underfoot, he, resigned, slipped his com into its case. Better to waste time here than be without the thing on the trip. They were carrying very few backups.

Besides, it was his job to clean up after the others.

He was the weakest of the four, the oldest, and the least skilled in terms of running a ship. It was frustrating to watch Teyr, who couldn't read most of symbols, confidently set and re-set the equipment while if he, who could, touched anything, Beyba and Andur would immediately check it.

But he could run the cleaning machines, and every bit of grit he picked up now was one less potential problem when they were in space. Dutifully, Del began running the used filters through the cleaner.

Andur went by, rolling a canister along its edge as Teyr pushed to change its orientation. Satisfied, they tripped it into place and began spraying glue. Del sneezed, and both of them looked at him.

Two lean, hard, predatory faces, smudged with dirt.

"You could glue," said Andur. "The sooner we're done, the sooner the smell's out. Beyba doesn't plan to wait."

Del switched off the cleaner and reached for the glue.

Andur made a brief series of gestures and Teyr began showing Del how to use the tool.

Teyr had, Del noticed, made a difference in the way they all worked: they tended to copy his rapid, efficient pantomimes.

One: check this.

Two: light on?

If so, then three.

If not, then—Teyr flipped the tool over—check this—

Finally he handed the tool to Del.

One, began Del—

Half a shift later, Del wiped his nose, and felt the tired muscles in his arm wince. Andur threw his weight on the canister, tried to rock it. It held. Del signed, add another coat?

Andur shook his head, no.

They looked at one another and laughed.

"Let's get the filters going," said Andur. "We better get cleaned up while the outside water lines are connected."

Teyr rolled a hand over, palm up, in query, and Andur's hands began moving in answer.

Eyes on the hose timer, Del began stripping.

On cleanup, Deltander was stowing everything into the lockers that covered the walls and what was, at the moment, the ceiling. Those in the floor had been filled first, their handles snapped down flush. It was an old rule of spacecraft design: you never built anything that was just a wall. Any loose object is a potential missile, and any missing object is useless.

Del circled, snapping down, activating the door-posted accounting vocs so the main control could add them to the endless list of what they had and where it was. He rubbed sore knuckles, and looked at his hands, then rubbed again: calluses. Jyse would have had a fit. Del missed the old man.

"Are you done down there?" yelled Beyba. "Help me with this."

"On my way!"

They were topping off their reserves for what seemed the hundredth time when Beyba looked at the incoming messages on the com. His hands flew down the accentuators for the automatic sequencers so quickly that Del dropped into the nearest seat, threw the restraint system, and reached for the com to warn Andur and Teyr.

"Not yet," said Beyba. "But we've got traffic, close in, where there wasn't anything a while ago."

Andur, alerted by the change in he ship's sounds, stuck his head in. "Trouble?"

"Maybe." Beyba pointed.

Andur looked and began punching in a simulation.

Teyr arrived, fitted one last object into a locker, and stood beside Andur, watching the three-d Andur was building with the new data. He tapped Andur's wrist for attention.

Andur waved him off.

Teyr gripped Andur and pulled him around by main force.

Andur, totally nonplused, watched Teyr's urgent signing, and began relaying. "He says, he knows those ships. We must leave, now, without waiting. They have," Andur shook his head, "something on board. They're," Andur broke off. "I can't get everything he's saying, but he's emphatic. We want to get out of here."

"Del?" said Beyba.

"I'd go along."

"Yeah. Andur?"

"No question."

Beyba's eyebrows rose and fell. "Power up." He flipped off the squawking voice from port control. "Going to be a rough rise. Secure yourselves."

At first the sound was so distant that Del thought another ship was taking its chances on getting away. But the monstrous thunder came walking down the field toward them. Del looked at Beyba, whose hands were jabbing at the controls, then at Andur. Andur's expression was odd and Del followed his gaze to Teyr.

Teyr was methodically bringing up the charge on each of his weapons. He kicked open a floor-locker and pulled up spare powerpaks.

Andur closed his mouth and accepted a handful, passed a weapon to Del, who turned it around, uncertain just how you'd use it safely on a ship.

Then Teyr gripped Del by the shoulders and pulled him from his seat. He signed urgently to Andur.

"He says we must leave the ship."

"Like shit," said Beyba, continuing to power up. "I'm not running around a spaceport in the middle of a bombardment. Get him strapped down."

Teyr slapped the emergency abort.

Beyba rose out of his seat so fast his robes flattened against his body. His right fist flashed out. Teyr dodged out of reach, hands talking frantically, and Beyba missed. "You little shit. You just ruined our best chance."

The main board took precious time to reset itself.

Del said, "Andur?"

"I can't follow it all."

Teyr pulled at Del, pleading.

Del pulled away and Teyr lunged at him. He stepped back to think about what was going on, and Teyr, meaning business, went for him. Del had the distinct impression Teyr was going to knock him out.

Del held his hands up in surrender and peeled out of his restraints.

"Asen," said Andur, "you can't go out there."

Del grabbed a flapping handful of weapons belt. If he couldn't use it, he could carry spares for Teyr.

Beyba, hands and eyes busy, said, "Del, he's panicking. I'll have us out of here—"

"He's right, Asen." Andur was releasing his seat restraints. "I can hold him. You get strapped in."

"You can stay if you want, Andur," said Del. He turned to Teyr, gesturing, lead.

"Del, he's just frightened—" Then, "Fuck it. Del!" Beyba was torn between the numbers racing up the screen and stopping Del. "Andur, get off your ass!"

Andur looked from Beyba to Del, mind turning over disobeying a direct order, when Del charged after Teyr, who was heading for the emergency exit.

The door on the compartment clanged shut on their two tightly packed bodies, cutting off Beyba's stream of imprecations.

The outer hatch opened on the intense heat venting from the priming engines. It made Teyr's expedite of simply grabbing the sides of the escape ladder and sliding look good to Del, too. On the ground, he was afraid to breathe for the scant instants it took them to sprint out of the ship's shadow.

Teyr took one quick look around, pointed toward a weather tower at the far end of the field and ran. Away from the town.

He wasn't panicking. His speed was nicely adjusted to the best Del could do steadily. He waved the older man on, out into the gritty red waste, as they passed the emergency bunker in the base of the weather tower. Del could hear the shelter's alarms go as he ran on, concentrating on making distance. *They're supplies there. That's what he's after.*

Later, Teyr—arms, laden, back humped with two packs—passed him again. Del concentrated on the tricky footing. They topped the crusted edge of one of the larger craters, and Teyr stopped, making sure of his bearings.

Del looked back at the field in time to see a ship attempt to take off without freeing its auxiliary lines. Tethered, it slewed off-course, igniting something—a fuel tank, another ship, Del couldn't see—that erupted in a black and gold fireball. Del could feel the flesh on his face sag at the sound. Teyr tugged his sleeve.

Deaf, half-blind, Del followed.

They circled left, below the crater's inner edge with the crust had cracked into a tumble of slabs and boulders. Coming on a hollow among the rocks, Teyr looked it, playing his beamer around, then signed Del in. He shoved his load after, and signaled, stay here. Del, ears ringing with the thunder of destruction from the field, agreed with his hands. Gesturing seemed the normal way to talk.

He lay very still, careful to keep every part of him under the overhanging stone. A stationary hot spot so close to the port could only be a man: all the wildlife would have fled long ago. Teyr, crawling and weaving across the dusty landscape, might be in less danger. Del shivered, cold in the sweltering heat. He thought very hard, *I'm a boulder, I'm a rock, I can lie here forever without moving*—

He jumped at Teyr's hand on his ankle.

Teyr crouched into the tiny space, and sorted through the water containers, binding them into to loads. Del reached for the heavier and was restrained.

He understood why when they started out again. Teyr was setting a stiff pace: jogging for a short distance, slowing to a swift walk, and then jogging again. Del, struggling to keep up, kept losing his footing in the loose splintered stone until he began following immediately behind Teyr, placing his feet as Teyr did.

A mindlessly long time later, Teyr stopped and put a hand on Del's shoulder. Del sank into a grateful crouch, thigh muscles twitching. Teyr, stomach to the sand, eeled his way over an outcrop and was out of sight. Del rubbed his legs and waited.

There was a crunch of hardened mud collapsing and Teyr slid over the bank, limp form hanging down his back. Del made himself rise, but Teyr waved him down and drew the long, slim blade from his belt.

Del looked away as the viscera slipped into the dirt.

When he looked back, the saty was an anonymous roast packaged in its own hide, bound with stretched gut. Teyr lifted two or three flat rocks over the snarl of innards and the accusatory stare of the head, and scrubbed his hands with sand. He stood, dusting off his fingers, and stared back in the direction of the port.

Del smelled the stiff breeze. There was a big fire back there. Standing, he could see the rising smoke: black, grey, and a sickly dun. A tap on his arm, and they started off again, weaving through the cover of the larger stones. They went a long way, mostly downhill in rough country, Del a mindless automaton at Teyr's heels. The feeble sun was well down the sky before Teyr slowed and began investigating the hollows and holes in the rocks around them.

Sitting in a beamer-scorched niche, Del could watch most of the process. Apparently Teyr wanted something large enough to take them both, with a small—defensible—entrance, but no passages leading further back.

Del wondered that Teyr didn't want a second way out. But he might consider Del no good at defending it, and Del had no idea what might be living in the deeper dens of the rocks.

Although, Del licked his lips and wished he could crack open one of the heavy water containers, *Teyr probably knows. He and Andur explored a lot of the area near the port.*

Teyr beckoned Del over.

It's going to be a tight fit, thought Del. But that might be an advantage in the cold night. And it did have a possible escape route— a short, rough tunnel relatively easy for an active youth, but a tight squeeze for Del. Teyr came in after Del, rubbing his hands through his hair and then on the wall. The sweet musk overlay the dry, rusty smell of the powdered soil.

Teyr went back out.

Del could hear the grate of stone on stone: then silence. "Teyr?" whispered Del. Nothing, of course. The escape tunnel had a queer closed feel. Del crouched, peering into it. "Teyr?"

There was a slow deliberate slide of something heavy on the gritty floor behind him. Del spun around. Tery was tugging a heavy slab half-over the opening.

What did you do?

Del followed the darting hands. Covered the far end of the escape tunnel so, things, living things, couldn't claw in. Del could have skipped the graphic rendition of claw.

Teyr sat in the entrance, unwrapped the bundled carcass, and began carving it into thin strips. Del looked at his near-transparent piece of raw meat, a luminous rose in the rapidly fading light, and bit. It was edible. Bland, tough, stringy, but edible.

He followed Teyr's example and ate all he could. It wouldn't keep and there would be nothing else but a few squares of concentrated rations until Teyr killed again.

Teyr sniffed the leftovers critically and gathered them into the hide. He was off and out into the fading light before Del could frame a question.

It was grey twilight before Teyr returned, dragging another large, flat slab. Del helped him maneuver it over half the entrance, and settled down with him against the back wall of their den.

Del pulled his chrono from his waist pouch. *A full shift and more until daylight.* Teyr took the instrument from him and turned it off. The darkness seemed absolute once that feeble glow was gone.

He awoke to the gurgle of water and put his hand out blindly for the flask. The moisture in the meat had helped his dry mouth, but done nothing about the water lost during his long, hot run.

Teyr flipped on the chrono and began to gesture. He was going to sleep now. Del was not to drink any more until he had finished his watch. Teyr pointed out the time.

Del moistened cracked lips and entered a plea for enough to moisten his mouth.

Flask to lips, he filled his mouth with the lukewarm water and held it there a long moment. He swallowed and gave it back, understanding the reasoning that let Teyr slowly drink his fill and left him dry-mouthed with thirst. It would keep him awake, counting the instants until he could awaken Teyr and get another sip.

Sometime later, staring at the lighter patch of darkness that was the entrance, Del ran a sticky tongue over gummy teeth for the millionth time and stopped. There was something moving out there.

Del put out a hand and touched Teyr's leg. He heard the pause in the sleeper's steady breathing, then Teyr sat up smoothly and silently.

As he eased his way through the gap, Del caught the faint gleam of light along a long blade.

Use a laser, thought Del, fiercely; then, *No*. A laser-flash would be visible a long way. And they were limited in how many times they could shoot. Del listened, mouth open. Nothing. There was thump, and a gurgling wheeze.

Teyr stooped and dragged something heavy through the low entrance.

Del recoiled at the strong, feral scent.

Teyr settled the body in the opening and rejoined Del.

That ought to scare off anything with a sense of smell, thought Del. He edged over to the current of air from the escape tunnel.

It was very cold towards dawn, and they sat huddled together, too chilled to sleep. It was a relief when the first pale hint of light appeared and Teyr shouldered his share of the water.

Glad to get moving, Del did the same.

The stinking body bounced down the slope when Teyr shoved it out of the way. Del caught a flash of long, efficient-looking teeth in the tumble of coarse, dark fur. Teyr picked it up by the hind legs on his way past.

Del sighed.

A long, hot day with that.

They stumbled down a dry watercourse, dried mud collapsing underfoot. Even Teyr caught his balance once, twice, and a third time. But the rapidly growing light made it possible to pick one's way more quickly and the still-cold air made fast walking a necessity.

Once his stiff muscles warmed up, Del found it numbly pleasant to keep up a good, brisk pace. Every step now was one he didn't have to make in the blistering heat of midday.

His body anesthetized if not comfortable, Del found his mind beginning to work again and a mass of questions began fermenting. Teyr's dusty back was uncommunicative. Del turned to formulating his questions as simply as possible.

First, did Teyr see anything when he went back for the second load of water? Second—maybe this should be first, thought Del, dodging a spiny plant—*where are we going?* Teyr's quick glances at the fading stars and his occasional climbs onto a higher boulder suggested he had a specific destination in mind.

Third—

Teyr had stopped and crouched. Del followed suit. There was a distant drone. Del heard a shrill, far-off whistle and the flat whack of a small explosion. Teyr pressed himself into the sand. So did Del.

There was another whack. A third, fourth, and, at an interval a fifth, possibly a sixth. Growing softer, moving away from them. Teyr cautiously gathered himself together and rose. Del got slowly to his knees, and watched as Teyr, stooped forward climb the nearest rise and settled on his belly.

He spent a long time there.

When he came back he changed the direction of their course completely. By the time the sun was forty degrees above the horizon, he had them both under the cover of an overhang chewing on the sharp, musky meat of last night's carcass.

Del gagged down his share, saving his water to take the taste from his mouth.

Where are we going? he signed to Teyr.

Del admired the elegant economy of motion with which Teyr suggested water, growing things, something dropped from the sky—

The terriformers.

The solar-powered housings, dropped into place all over the planet, had little impact on the climate as yet. But near them were small oasis formed by the drip of condensed water and gene-tailored bacteria. There were hundreds on this high landmass alone, thousands down in the rift where climatic change could take hold most rapidly.

And after that, signed Del.

Teyr counted off days.

Two ten-days. Plus five.

In twenty-five days they might start back. Del swilled the water around his mouth and swallowed. He felt the smooth curve of fat on his belly. *Your dieting problem is solved*, he thought.

Teyr was cutting away at the battered-looking carcass, stripping out what must be the scent glands in the crotch, peeling off the thick hide with its dense fur.

Seen in full light, the reddish-brown fur with its long, white-tipped guard hairs was beautiful.

It still stank.

And the meat had its own peculiar reek.

They stayed under the overhang through the hottest part of the day. Long enough for some of the tiny things of the desert to find the discarded carcass. They twisted and flowed up out of the sand, reducing the beast to a blind, staring skull on a framework of ribs and vertebra.

He was staring with weary fascination at the remains, wondering what he would look like, when Teyr tapped him on the shoulder and they started out again.

It was hot.

The steady breeze dried sweat instantly. Powdered rock flowed along the ground after they had passed. Del followed doggedly, counting one hundred steps over and over. *One more. You can do one more.*

He was trying to catch up to Teyr to sign for a rest when they topped a low rise and the terriformer was in sight.

Shattered.

Del felt his heart sink.

But Teyr was smiling, pleased.

The housing had broken on impact, spilling its contents haphazardly. On its side in a rocky hollow, half in shadow even this close to midday. Del looked at the blue-white sky.

This one might well be unmapped, written off as lost.

It was almost cool in the shade of the rock and Del could hear the slow dripping of a precip somewhere in the low jungle of plants that struggled with one another for survival.

Teyr uncapped a flask and drank, one long continuous series of swallows. Del did the same, sighed, and blinked. The savage thirst would take a while to abate. He opened a second flask and sipped slowly, afraid to take more.

Sorting through the leaves, Teyr reached and pulled, then again. He waded off through the rustling green. When he came back he had a fistful of wet, green leaves and two white, slightly sandy, tubers.

The leaves were vaguely soapy.

The tubers were crisp and tasteless.

Del ate it all. *No worse than the average diplomatic reception*, he thought wryly. *In fact*, he concluded, remembering the wriggling grubs that were one delegation's triumphantly offered delicacy, *better than some.*

It was comfortable, just sitting in the shade with all the water you could drink, and dinner was incautious enough to stop by the waterhole. Two, plump, scaly things that looked rather delicious once they were gutted and skinned. Del wistfully asked if they could cook them.

Teyr looked surprised.

But he nodded and went off into the dry, dusty waste. When he returned with his double handful of fuel, he built a stone-lined hollow. The stalks that fed the fire were so dry the tiny, smokeless flame was near invisible. Wrapped in leaves, the white-meated carcasses went directly on the coals and hot stones in a hiss of steam, then were covered with another rock.

Del's mouth flooded with water.

As he painstakingly peeled tubers, Teyr, streaked red-brown with sun-protective mud, dozed. Del rubbed the faint stinging on his own dark cheeks and watched a straddling, chitin-covered whatever drag away the peels one by one. The twisting trail in the sand was slowly erased by the breeze as Del crunched leaves, the grainy stuff oozing water at the pressure of his teeth.

The sun was low and the hollow completely in shadow when Teyr uncovered the meat. Del ripped the steaming flesh from the delicate bones, scraped the hot pulp from the shroud of cooked leaves with his teeth, and discarded the leathery, ash-coated skins.

Looking up at the lavender sky, Del wondered how they would spend the night. The dry waste came alive in darkness and surely the water would draw animals to drink, graze, and hunt.

Del asked.

Follow me, signed Teyr.

The damaged housing had an upper chamber that must, once, have contained its starter supply of water, long since run away into the soil, along with its scattered seeds in their timed-release packets. The metal was still sound, although wind-pitted and cracked on one side. The large opening could be closed by a plate from the crushed base.

Wrapped in dry leaves and surrounded by a pungent smell of unwashed man and youth, the former magistrate slept like a stone, and woke in the chill, clear desert dawn to sleep again.

As the days went by Del discovered it was possible to be fairly comfortable. His principle craving was to sit in a bath, rather than patiently wipe every inch of his skin with a damp, fraying rag. Otherwise, things were good.

There was nothing to do at night but sleep and watch the stars.

In the day they could, with suitable precautions, roam the dry washes and gullies, arguing silently and amiably over what to kill for dinner. They ate one hot meal a day, and its cold remains the following morning.

All of which left plenty of time for Del to sit, slowly drawing letters in the sand.

It went slowly.

Del gave Teyr points for patience, knowing he was not a good teacher. It was hard for him to see the obstacles, anticipate what would confuse Teyr. He missed the resources of his study. There were so many things it would have been easy to image in the holobloc. Here he was restricted to what he could draw and find.

Teyr could dutifully write up and down, right and left, plant—that took some work, he wanted it to be a specific name, rock—likewise, for him flat rocks were not rounded rocks and neither was the same as the rough-surfaced stones that the daily cycle of heat and cold cracked from the underlying bedrock.

It was seven or eight days before it occurred to Del that Teyr was a more skillful teacher than he was. Del was becoming quite good at improvising with his hands.

Teyr was amused when Del pointed this out.

His hands flowed through the equivocal motion that Del took to be the equivalent of a verbal speaker's uh or ah, then those-who-are-like-me can, Teyr's fingers opened and closed before his mouth.

"Talk," said Del, and got, as usual, no response.

Teyr looked away, ending the conversation.

Why not you, thought Del, pulling fibers from the yellow fruit that was everywhere today and would be shriveled and rotting by tomorrow. Frowning, Del licked his fingers, thinking.

He had a lot of questions.

They had time.

The skin Del pressed his cheek against was smooth and he inhaled its scent with every quickening breath. He gathered the warm body tightly to himself as his loins spasmed with pleasure.

His beloved jerked violently from his grasp.

Del awoke, genitals shriveling in the cold, confused.

He and Teyr had been asleep, tucked together for warmth, Teyr's back and hips cradled by Del's belly and thighs, Del's threadbare robe spread over both of them. The rocks piled at their feet had lost their heat; the metal floor sent a chill through the layer of dried plants that was their mattress.

I was asleep, thought Del, defensively, rising on one elbow. *Dreaming. But so were you.*

Now Teyr was somewhere across the hollow metal drum, unreachable by reason until the dawn light made talking possible. Breathing slowing, Del was afraid to touch. It would be too easy to be misunderstood.

Del pulled his robe over his shoulders and rolled on his side to stare at the blank darkness where the first thread of light would appear around their improvised hatch. He lay in cold misery.

He knew he must have slept when sometime later the growing warmth at his back told him he was not alone. He lifted the robe and shook it back over Teyr. A hard-muscled arm pulled him closer. Del sighed, clasped both hands around the cold, sharp-nailed fingers, and settled himself. Just as well. He hadn't been able to think of a way to explain.

Del crouched, intent on the gully below, as the saty walked almost beneath him. He dropped the heavy stone, and saw the animal stagger and fall. *Stunned*, thought Del, sliding down the steep side in a cloud of dust. The black eyes stared at him, unblinking, as Del drew his finger-length blade and considered where to strike, as he tried not to wish he had missed his aim.

There was a slither higher up the gully wall. Del looked up at Teyr, asking, what now?

Teyr briskly drew a finger across his throat.

Del squatted and sawed.

There was a great deal of blood and the hind legs ran an instant before the bowels and bladder released. Del backed away. *We need the hide. We need the meat.*

Tery descended the slope, trying not to raise dust. He dipped a finger in the blood and tapped Del between the eyebrows before Deltander could draw away. Then he drew his own blade and spilled the membrane-encased guts, peeled back the spotted skin, and took the choice meat, leaving a naked red ruin on the blood-soaked sand.

Back at their camp, he stretched the hide on an open square of four sticks and squatted, scraping flesh and fat, before doing something that involved urine and ashes. Del watched the fine, well-shaped hands, nails rimmed with dark blood, and remembered the easy days aboard ship.

Teyr's intent face looked as if it had been carved from some fine-grained local rock. Del scratched own chin and considered Teyr's. *He's never going to have a heavy beard.*

Teyr looked up quizzically, dark grey eyes looking translucent in the strong sunshine.

Del made himself smile.

Teyr gave a puzzled shrug and continued working.

Del remembered seeing the pupil contract in answer to his hand light's question.

He thought about the forlorn huddle of bone and viscera left behind in the gully, rose and walked away, not wanting Teyr to see his expression. There had been so many fixed, dead stares before Teyr. He turned around, almost into Teyr. Then held on, not even sure what he was crying for.

Not the saty, certainly.

You're taller than I am, thought Del, face against faded grey cloth so sun-baked and sweat-soaked it had a smell like the sea—

"Del?" said a deep, soft voice in Teyr's chest.

Del looked up, incredulous.

"I'm" said Teyr carefully, "sorry." Hesitant, shy, but a man's deep voice.

Del couldn't say anything at all.

"We're," pause, "slow—to—talk? I'm—not—"

Hugging his knees while Teyr methodically smothered every trace of their fire at sunset, Del said, "It'd go faster if you talked more."

Teyr poured another handful of sand onto the flat stone that closed their fire pit and preserved the coals for morning. "No," he said.

Del pressed his hands on the heated sand. Sometimes breakfast spent the night on this warm spot. "Why not?" Del stood reluctantly and felt the breeze whip warmth from his belly and thighs.

Teyr's hand swept the circle of the horizon, "Silence." He bent to his work again.

Puzzled but not worried, Del wrapped his arms around himself. It was going to be good to get into their shelter, reeking with half-cured furs, and out of the rising night-wind.

He woke with something scratching at their improvised hatch. Del could hear the metal cover shift. Teyr rolled away. Del heard the snick of a blade clearing its sheath. There was a horrific shriek and a feral howl. It was heartbeats before Del sorted out the sound of something wounded and Teyr's threat.

Then their shelter shook and boomed at the impact of a heavy, angry body. Teyr howled again, sound echoing off the metal walls. Del could feel an icy draft from the widening gap. He drew himself together, out of the way against the back wall, hand around the leather-wrapped hilt of his scrap metal knife.

The powder of stars in the visible patch of sky was eclipsed by something panted hoarsely. The hatch shrilled under fangs or claws. Whatever it was, it was bigger than anything Del had seen here before.

Del heard Teyr's intake of breath as he struck with all his strength.

There was a shriek and the shelter jerked and shuddered. Teyr, ululating loudly, pulled the hatch out of the way and went in pursuit. Del's grasping hands grabbed scored metal instants too late to hinder.

He could hear Teyr howl defiance.

Then the shelter shook as Teyr slid back in and repositioned the hatch.

It was about a quarter-shift to dawn, and Teyr, in the flickering, failing light of Del's chrono was obviously unharmed. He delicately touched his tongue to his gory blade, eyes narrowed, tasting the blood, then wiped it clean with a leaf before resheathing it.

Del let the light go out.

When the dun-colored, dusty domes of the town showed over the horizon, Del was surprised. He had thought of their hiding place as being at a great distance. *In fact*, he thought, crouching in the shelter of a boulder, *it is only a good day's run for a reasonably conditioned man with plenty of water.*

Which explained why Teyr had been so ready to head out into the desert. He must have found their hiding place long ago when Andur had given up supervising Teyr as closely as Del would have liked. Veness was part of that. By Andur's standards, Teyr was more of an adult than Del was. He could take care of himself in unknown conditions; he had fathered a child. It was against Andur's principles to bother ringing Teyr with precautions he was more than capable of eluding. Simpler to make him responsible for himself.

I can hardly complain.

There was a soft crunch of stone on stone as some weathered fragment failed under pressure. Del slid his knife from its improvised sheath, braced one knee against the rock and advanced the other to give himself a broader base. Something gave a single click. Del relaxed slightly.

Teyr slid into the shadow of the stone like one of the crook-legged desert beasts.

Del sheathed his knife. Well, asked one hand.

Teyr rinsed his mouth with water, and recapped the flask. His hands flowed through the air. Andur's there.

Del hadn't known how much he minded losing Andur until he could hope to see him again. Did you talk, he signed.

He didn't see me.

Why?

Teyr eased himself into the cooler strip next to the rock. I don't know that he was alone.

"Beyba?" said Del, loud in the quiet, and had to re-sign his question.

No.

Del had more questions, but Teyr had already closed his eyes. Del unsheathed his knife, glanced at his battered chrono, and settled himself to sharpen the blade while he took the first watch. *Next time, I'm getting a time piece I can charge manually.*

The house, when they entered it, smelled unused. Del sniffed and wondered if Teyr's guess that Beyba wasn't there was based on the staleness of his perfume in the downstairs rooms.

There were footprints in the dust of the uppermost hall. Big feet, long strides. Motionless, Teyr looked from door to door, listening. Del listened, too. There was nothing but the sigh and whisper of the air system.

Teyr's hands said, call Andur.

"Andur?" said Del, not loud.

Again, motioned Teyr.

"Andur?"

"Asen," said the voice behind him.

Del wasn't conscious of turning around. Andur looked dirty and grim, three stripes of reddish brown down one cheek. He looked from Del, to Teyr, and back again, a lock of his unbound and cut hair sliding on his shoulder, then he wet a finger and scrubbed one, two of the stripes from his cheek. The smudgy third remained.

"Beyba?" said Del.

Andur shook his head. "The whole field went up."

Del began rubbing his chest. Annoyed, he dropped his hand. He was tired of doing that.

Andur shrugged and began to question Teyr.

The face that stared out of the videoplane in the personal was darker, but his hair was so sun-bleached it looked luminous. Del automatically fingered his waist for the roll of fat. His fingers scraped his skin.

He turned, naked, examining himself.

He hadn't looked like that even when he was young.

If it weren't for the deep lines in the face—

He lifted his chin a bit, looked right side, left.

And laughed at the vain old man.

He had to wrap the sash from one of his robes around his pants to keep them up. He missed Jyse for the ten-millionth time. Although, judging by Andur, maybe clean, correct attire would have been conspicuous here, now.

There was a rhythmic thud, thud, thud from the hall.

Del sighed, his pleasure spoiled.

Those two were throwing knives.

Del sat down, and began, with old precision, to review what he knew. Andur had run down the exit way after Del and Teyr and not seen them. So he assumed Teyr had the immediate problem under control, and ran to escape the backwash from the ship's exhaust. Beyba had gotten the ship off the ground, Andur was sure of that, but the entire field had erupted in one huge fireball that climbed thousands of feet vertically, and spared Andur only because he had reached an emergency shelter instants before the blast.

When he had come out, Andur decided that Teyr and Del would have headed back to the house if they survived and had gone there as rapidly as possible.

Only their three servants and Anss had been there. Baffled, Andur had turned to setting the house in order: water stored, food gathered, half of that concealed, everybody moved into the upper story, so the lower floor appeared deserted.

Which hadn't done much good when the troops searched house to house. Andur, assuming his presence was provocative, had hidden himself in the grillwork above the reception hall.

Which gave him an excellent view of what happened.

"It never occurred to me that they were looking specially for him." Andur's chin jerked at Teyr.

"There were five of the furry guys—"

"Fesyls," said Teyr.

"—big as I am, fur, claws, teeth, tempers," said Andur.

"Human?" said Del.

Andur shrugged. "Is he?"

Del spilled air from his hands. I don't know.

Andur gathered the gesture to himself. Me either.

"The leader looked like Bondre. Or Teyr, now."

Del shivered.

"Sharp, efficient. He had those guys moving every instant, and not a motion wasted. They got rough with Embay, and found I was in the house, so I peeled out, up and over the roof, down the back and off. They gave me a pretty good run, before they decided to quit."

Andur slide his knife out a finger's-breadth and back with a click. "They would have gotten me if they wanted to. I think they quit when they were sure I wasn't going anyplace specific." Andur's eyes probed some inner horizon. He looked at Del, "Asen, don't tell me where you went."

Del rubbed his goose-fleshed arms.

"They could have had me talking, so fast—"

"Andur." Del stopped. *There's nothing to say.*

Andur shook his head.

"It's not your fault," said Del. Embay's body was buried in the garden. The rest had fled.

"He told us. If I'd spoken up, Beyba would have listened."

"To Beyba, he was just a boy."

Andur laughed, harsh, humorless. "No. They may not have taught him table manners, but they did teach him how to hunt and how to kill. He's never been a boy, Asen, he," Andur gripped the air, "he killed two men on the *Aeguit*. I've never been able to sort out why."

"Defending himself," said Del.

"No," said Andur, glancing at Teyr's impassive face, "he uses a different," Andur's fingers rippled, "for that. They were prey. Something hunted down. I think they put him on that ship to hunt, like a husti down a hole."

"Why?" said Del.

"That's what he was made for."

"No," said Del. He looked at the pattern of his interlocked hands. He shook his head quickly from side to side, denying. "No. He's— intelligent."

Andur's lips drew back without mirth. "The best predators are clever. And some of them learn to mimic their prey."

Teyr said nothing.

"Asen, we tell a story about a man who wanted the perfect servant and conjured a demon."

Del picked at the web of worn threads at his cuff. "What happened?" he asked the frayed cloth.

"It served out the bargain." Andur looked off into unseeable distances. "Then it ate him." Andur got slowly to his feet. "We should get out of here. I need time to talk to Teyr. It's better if we stay together."

Del followed silently.

I had not been frightened in the desert. I had not even noticed that I wasn't. But when we returned to the dusty town to find a subdued Andur hiding in our stripped and battered house, I was scared.

We gathered together what we could: food and clothes, mostly. We had abandoned the clutter of our lives on our move.

Then Andur conferred with Teyr.

I had become more fluent in the gestural language in my days alone with Teyr, and I could follow a substantial portion of the discussion.

Teyr thought we should turn ourselves in. Andur was reluctant to reject this outright only because events had proven Teyr right before.

We turned the idea over and over. The argument was finally resolved when I told Andur I would go with Teyr, and he must make his own decision.

At that, Andur gathered his things together, slung them from one shoulder and said, "Let's go."

The streets were empty, the heavy protective shutters lowered on the house and shop fronts. As they neared the port, Del sniffed the air. It was almost a relief to see the cause: a row of heads mounted on poles. Not all of them were human, some grinned with fangs.

Del thought, *so they do, perhaps, maintain some sort of rough justice.*

Teyr stopped and studied the display thoroughly.

Andur kept trying to question him, but Teyr ignored his moving hands, and gestured, this way.

They followed.

The guards at the port offices had shaggy faces and hands. The rest was covered by a slick-surfaced uniform. They were bored and willing to amuse themselves with the trio so ill advised as to put themselves in their way, until they got a good look at Teyr.

Then they pulled back, wary, and sent one of their number running into the building. The man who came reminded Del of Varriel's Bondre, but plainly was not: he had old scars no one had bothered to have repaired.

He asked Teyr something in a harsh, sibilant language, and was surprised to get a gestured response. His hand motions were slow and unpracticed.

Del could follow his questioning.

The first thing he asked was not, who are you? But, where were you?

Teyr's response was a single sign that Del didn't know. He looked at Andur.

That sign met with an equally succinct response. Come.

The corridors of the former port building were shabby and uncared for, sure evidence that the invaders, whatever they called themselves, were only in temporary residence.

Del wondered if it would have been foolish of them to simply collect Andur and return to their retreat in the desert until the occupying force left. *But he asked*, where were you. *They knew, they expected, Teyr would be all right.*

The man leading them opened a door and sounded a call, waved them through, and left, indifferent to the weapons on Teyr and Andur's harness, let alone Del's improvised knife.

The men who looked up from a glowing display were identical to the first, with Teyr's black hair, pale skin, and thin, haughty nose. One smiled and came forward eagerly, hands questioning so quickly Del guessed that he was not completing anything.

That one touched cheeks formally with Teyr, and led them all into a room beyond. He indicated seats and sat down himself. Their quick interchange of gestures left Del behind. He looked away to find Andur examining the walls and floor as if they were part of a trap.

"You are?" asked a heavily accented voice.

Del jumped and looked into the grey-eyed face. An eyebrow lifted.

"Deltander Permund. This is Andur, my bodyguard."

Del studied the face. The man bore the inspection with composure. The face was worn—fine lines at the corner of the eyes, deeper ones from nose to mouth corner; worry had made a hack-mark between the brows.

"I am Ibeigne," he said. "I command here." He turned to Teyr, then back to Del. "He tells me you have taken some care for him. You may leave with us. If you wish."

"And Teyr?" said Del, one hand rising to his chest.

"*Evtan* goes with us."

Del turned to Andur, who gestured. "Both of us."

Teyr questioned Ibeigne with a hand. And smiled.

"Good," said Ibeigne. The hack-mark deepened. "Since he is recovered, we will be sterilizing the area."

"Sterilizing," said Andur, flatly.

Del must have made a protesting noise.

"It is not my decision to make, " said Ibeigne, "and I do not approve. But it will be done." His hands talked with Teyr, quickly, briefly. Then Ibeigne shook his head and spoke to Del. "Are there any others?"

"There may be one," said Del. Beyba? he asked Teyr.

Without following the specifics, the very pace and style of the motioned exchange told Del there was little chance Beyba had survived, although Teyr merely signed, he is not here.

Ibeigne reached for something in the tangle of equipment at his elbow. "Be still," he said.

It made a cold, painful sting above Del's right eye. Del saw Andur look and flinch, then hold his own head still for the same. It left a miniature black and white design and a drop or two of blood.

Ibeigne switched the thing off with a flick. "Do what Evtan says." He replaced the tool in the tangle. "Try and learn our language. Very few of us understand yours and the," his hands moved, "will be difficult in its more complex forms." He paused. "I wish you well, but not everybody here will. Be very cautious." Ibeigne stood, a decisive dismissal.

Cautious, leaving the presence, Del backed the first few steps to the door, then passed by Teyr, turned to follow.

To Del's surprise they left the building, crossed the landing field. On the way they were passed by a group of rather hostile furry guards before entering a craft of a type Del had never seen before. It looked frail and elegant, with aerodynamic lines, but the swell of shielding aft said it was space-capable.

The passenger compartment was empty except for a nondescript man with a trembling mouth, who took one look at Teyr and retreated as far as possible from them. He remained immobile throughout the trip.

No sooner were they settled then Del was pressed into his seat momentarily by acceleration, then jerked forward by its sudden loss. The viewport had darkened abruptly. Some sort of protective reaction, thought Del. But Teyr released his restraints and stood up. Del started to follow—there were stars out the viewport—and was told to wait with an emphatic gesture.

The door closed behind Teyr with a solid thud.

"We're slaves," said Andur.

"We don't know that," said Del.

"Don't be diplomatic," said Andur.

"I think," said Del slowly, "it is more a matter of protective custody." He touched the painful swelling above his eye. "Like a clan-mark." He didn't add that his only reason to think so was that Teyr hadn't made any demure.

Andur gave Del a look of such disbelief that Del fell silent. In the quiet they could hear the thin-faced man's ragged breathing. Behind the screen of his fingers he was crying. Andur frowned and began stroking the whet down his smallest knife.

Del laced his fingers to prop on a paunch he no longer had, then rose and began pacing, toward the star-spangled darkness of the viewport, then back to the padded wall. Toward, away. Andur's sharpening made a tiny musical accompaniment.

Slaves. I don't know, Andur, he thought. *I suppose it says something that we still have a short, simple word for it, not something like those-who-are-property. Of course*, he turned and looked at the wall again, *'gen' is a short, simple word.*

The coupling with the mother ship was awesome. Del had never been in a ship where it was possible to look out as the two craft drifted closer and closer and then mated. Normally a ship's radiation shielding prevented any direct view.

The soft, springy impact was instantly followed by the faint popping of the ears that showed their ship had opened to the larger. Teyr still hadn't returned. Del sat still. Andur, starting to rise, reseated himself. "No initiative?"

Del shook his head, "We're supposed to be here."

Teyr opened the door behind them, signed, come.

They both rose and followed him away from the stifled sobbing.

It was a long walk, leaving Del plenty of time to speculate whether Teyr had been on this ship before. He moved unhesitatingly, and knew the equipment—no fumbling to call the transporter, no pauses to check the script stenciled on the walls.

It was hot, and the air had a sharp chemical smell that was explained when they passed one open door. There was tier upon tier of racked globes, spilling over with blue-green foliage. Some sort of recycling? Food supply? Both?

The room whose door opened to Teyr's palm was large enough for three, and adequately provided with facilities, but by no standard luxurious except in its spaciousness. Its very bareness argued that the ship's inhabitants spent their time elsewhere than in their quarters. Del looked at Andur, who settled on one open bunk as if he wouldn't move again.

Teyr appraised him.

Del gestured, *I want a shower. Anyone in front of me?*

Teyr shook his head.

"Andur?" said Del.

"Leave me alone."

Del did.

They settled in, although Andur remained apathetic. Del tried suggesting they ask questions, explore, but after that initial impulse in the lander's lounge, nothing moved Andur. He cared for himself mechanically and spent the rest of the time staring at the walls.

Teyr was gone a great deal of the time and not communicative about where he had been when he was around.

Frustrated, Del asked for passive access to the ship's com system and began picking his way through the messages logged. Most of the internal stuff was no more than gibberish to him. But there was plenty of external traffic in Beyal, and Del was puzzled by what it suggested.

There was a lot of traffic on its way out from the cluster core. Even more, proportionately, up from Belsyrtis. And there were second-hand reports of single ships found stripped and drifting. Not since the earliest days of commercial travel had so many ships sought the protection of convoys. Apparently there was safety in numbers, at least for a time.

Del wondered if the ship he was on—he still didn't know its name after six days on board—was the cause of the attacks, the attacker, or if it, too, was only fleeing ahead of whatever menace was making its way along the most travelled space lanes.

There was a soft tone, signaling the door was opening, Teyr and came in, looking preoccupied. He gave Andur a dismissive glance and motioned for Del to follow him.

They went through a section of the ship Del had not seen before, older, patched and repaired with care, but with the subtle signs of well-worn age, a glossiness to the places often touched, a darkening where feet had ground dirt into the colored foam on walls that were sometimes floors.

When the door with its twining tendrils and half-hidden faces opened inward Del found he was not at all surprised to face Litjin Varriel, sitting in a pool of light in a shadow-filled room. What did surprise him was how noticeably Varriel had aged. There was a faint quiver to the hands, and a scrawny, plucked look to the neck.

But the eyes were as commanding as ever, and the amused quirk of the mouth was almost contempt.

"Not surprised, Permund?"

Del shook his head.

"No," said Varriel. He made no move to offer Del a seat. "Evtan tells me you specialize in negotiations."

Del waited.

"We could use a good negotiator. There have been several regrettable incidents. Our intentions seem to be misunderstood."

Del stayed silent.

"You needn't be so cautious: Ibeigne gave you to Evtan. That keeps you safe enough, for the time being. But I, we," Varriel glanced at the three silent men behind him, "could use your skills. It would be to your advantage, and Teyr's, if we were more—secure in our holdings."

"I don't know anything about the situation," said Del.

Varriel placed the tips of his fingers together, which warmed Del with familiarity until he placed the gesture as Jasil's. "Come, Asen, that's not quite true. You've been examining what we have. You should be a little more forthcoming."

Del looked to Teyr, who stood to one side, face impassive.

"I'll add a little incentive," said Varriel. "You are too old to be fluent in the," the hands moved. "I could have the rest of his block against verbal speech removed."

Del knew his face gave him away. Permund's price. "I have to know what I'm agreeing to do."

There was an irritable stirring among the three men.

Varriel didn't look back, but held up a hand. "Don't be over-hasty. I'd mistrust a man who didn't raise a few points."

There was the slightest possible stress on "few." Varriel was warning him. More, Varriel was acting as spokesperson, not the man in charge. Del looked at Teyr, who moved, uncharacteristically, uneasily, shifting from one foot to another. His hands moved a fraction, then were still.

Teyr wanted, very much, to cue Deltander.

Del didn't dare to study him too closely. "How," he said carefully, "do you think I can help?"

Varriel's forced impassivity didn't cover his relief. "We have been searching," he said, with the fluency of a man launching a rehearsed presentation, "for a place sufficiently isolated that I and my creations can live quietly, yet not so distant that we cannot have the benefits of trade in goods and information. We are about two hundred, well-armed, and might be a valuable addition to a colony able to accept the unusual appearance that accompanies their peculiar talent."

The three men moved into the light.

Del winced.

Where Teyr looked merely exotic, these were different. Their jaws protruded and the back of the cranium bulged so that, unlike the upright egg-shape of a human being, the long axis appeared to be more horizontal.

But it was the fine, dark eyes under the melancholy brows that bothered Del the most: they were so obviously sapient.

There was nothing apologetic or awkward in their stance.

"I see," said Del. "What of the others?"

"Which?" said Varriel.

"The guards, with fur—"

"The fesyl are useful, but not essential. Providing a sufficiently good bargain could be struck."

Del looked down, thinking. "Nonessential. What does that mean?"

178

"Their existence is negotiable. They, we, understand they might form a considerable obstacle. Intuition has been confirmed by experience in that respect." Varriel looked over his shoulder. "On the other hand, with the right direction, they are a formidable asset."

Del wondered if the fesyl were really so indifferent to their own existence. He doubted it. *Varriel has at least one blind spot.*

The three behind had moved out of the light and made no motion.

"What we propose to do," said Varriel, "is give you complete access to what information we have, and ask your appraisal of the situation. We hope you will see several possibilities which we can then discuss."

Del nodded. "And Teyr?"

"That would be a reward, not an inducement."

Del swallowed. "It would be useful to have someone who was familiar with both cultures—" *Don't take him away from me.*

Varriel, his back to his three creations, almost smiled. "I will confer on that point." He looked back again, then said briskly, "You are dismissed."

Del bowed as low as he ever had to any delegation head.

Varriel signaled Teyr to take charge with a hand sweep.

Andur was just as they had left him.

Del took one look at his glassy stare and shivered. Andur had fled someplace far within. Teyr gently shook him by the shoulder.

"Wha?"

Teyr waited, patient.

Andur's hands fumbled through something.

Teyr's flowed through a long explanation.

Andur sighed, but his eyes focused on them. "You're going to work for them, Asen?"

"I don't know that I have much choice, realistically. It would be to both side's advantage, and we are, as Varriel didn't quite point out, in this too, now."

Andur considered the pattern on the floor. "There's not much I can do."

Del forced a laugh. "Only everything you usually do." Then, more meaningfully, "Especially security."

Andur looked puzzled, then swept his eyes around the room.

Andur, thought Del, *I think the reason Teyr's not telling us much is he knows we're being listened to and thinks we're safer naive and innocent.* He stared at Andur, willing the thoughts into his mind. *Think, Andur, think.*

Andur stood and stretched, ostentatiously. "This is a very old ship, Asen. They've put visual equipment in and not bothered to remove the old audio equipment." He looked around.

Which might be useful to us, thought Del, following his thought, but shaking his head in warning. He said, "I think they fled in a hurry, and this was the best they could do—" *Don't say too much, Andur.* "Varriel says they can remove the block to his talking," he said, diverting the conversation.

"Make sure he doesn't mean they'll inhibit the," his hands moved. "He needs that, and so do we." Andur ran his fingers through the loose hair at the sides of his face, forcing it back into the still braided hair. Del could see the clipped lock—Andur had burned a bit, Kel ritual for a departed friend. "What's been happening, Asen?"

"I don't know," said Del. "But they're going to have to tell me. If I don't bargain 'full knowledge and in good faith,' anything I work out can be reneged on."

Andur started to speak, then closed his mouth firmly. He began moving around, hands automatically checking his weapons.

Del looked at Teyr, who smiled, upper lip held down over his teeth, then grinned, lip lifting away.

Del grinned back.

It was good to see Andur come back to life: the Kel had so little experience in being helpless.

Del worked steadily, without fuss. Varriel sent for him every day. The possibility of standing before those three pitiless pairs of eyes without progress to report made Del nervous.

Why should they pity?

My kind had no pity for theirs.

The stories Del was pulling out of the com's accumulated data showed an instinctive embellishment of the unknown with the horrifying.

Del remembered Irdese's fear her baby would claw its way out of her. He had taken that for the nightmares of an inexperienced girl in a difficult situation. Now he knew she might have picked the ideas up from the port gossip.

If I had heard any of this, thought Del, *I would have had us out of Lybayos as fast as possible.* It was strong stuff, calculated to feed mob passions. Some of it was true. He did not speculate what came first. The atrocious mutilations of Varriel's creations. Or the ripped-out throats and the bodies with significant pieces missing.

Andur spent his time prowling the ship, apparently undisturbed by the necessity of appearing subservient when he had a purpose to sustain him. He intended to map the entire ship.

Teyr spent a great deal of time away, and came back groggy and out-of-sorts. There were tight lines of strain between his eyebrows, as if his head hurt him.

Varriel had warned that Teyr "—may never be very fluent. Some areas of the brain may be permanently dedicated to perceiving motion rather than sound. His voice may be odd."

Del bit back the news that had already heard Teyr's voice. "Odd?" he asked.

Varriel shrugged dismissively. "Harsh. Flat. If I could use more drastic measures we might get better results. But, if we want his long-term cooperation we must respect his objections."

Having failed to ask before, Del was afraid to question the procedures now. Yet he dreamed of subtle agonies and longed for things to be over. Del more than toyed with the idea of asking Varriel to stop the day Teyr and Andur ended up in an all-out fight.

The sodden thud of fist on flesh frightened Del into attempting to separate them. When they both repelled him, Del staggered back, shocked at the pain. *How did they stand it*, thought Del, mopping blood from his nose with his sleeve.

"Uun," said Andur, as Teyr got a solid blow to the mid-section in.

"Ice," snarled Teyr.

Andur broke and backed off, breathing heavily. "What?"

"He needs ice." Teyr had one arm down guarding his belly and the other ready to strike.

Andur lowered his hands. "Asen?"

"Mpft," said Del, tasting iron and salt. "I'm dizzy—" With any luck he could get them fussing over him instead of battering one another. He sat down hard and watched blood drip onto the floor.

"Lean your head back," said Andur. "Teyr—"

But Teyr had already gone for the ice.

"Asen, I— Is it worth all this just so he can speak?"

Del licked blood from the corner of his mouth.

Andur sat back on his heels. "I mean, he does perfectly well without—"

Del wiped at his face and started the bleeding again. He swallowed. "Andur, he can't spend his life as a professional assassin. He's got to communicate with people."

Andur said, "I didn't think you'd figured that out."

Del leaned forward again. He was going to start retching if he tasted much more of it. "It was set-up, wasn't it? And they didn't expect him to survive." Del pressed his fingers to the bridge of his nose. "Did he make the kill?"

Andur grinned. "Three grown men."

"Oh." Del licked his lips.

"Poor little boy," said Andur. "He bit one's throat out."

Del retched. *How the hell did he stand the taste?*

Teyr, clattering cup of ice in hand, swung the door to behind him.

Del leaned back as Teyr pressed the cold container against his forehead. *I don't have to ask how you got close enough to do that, do I*, thought Del, looking up at the foreshortened face.

"I'll wrap some of that in a cloth," said Andur.

Del felt the sharp tips of the Teyr's nails against his face: not painful, but there. "Teyr?" he said.

The dark eyebrows lifted and looked down.

Del could hear Andur rummaging in the personal. Everything they had was threadbare with use.

"What was his name?"

Teyr started to ask, and then didn't pretend. "Mikarl Avenein," he said, slowly. "He owned a lot of G-R."

Del wiped another smear of blood across his face.

"Avenein was planning to stop production."

Andur positioned the improvised ice bag.

Del wondered if Avenein had been fond of Teyr. *Had he any idea what happened to him? Or did he die, unknowing, in a blaze of sleep-bewildered pain?*

"He said," Teyr's diction was precise, "it was unethical to create us."

Del shifted the cold chill over his eyes, and felt the cold water run down his temples. *Unethical to create you.* He could feel for Mikarl Avenein.

But he couldn't have destroyed Varriel's creations.

They were far too wonderful.

"He was a fool," said Del.

Teyr's hands tightened slightly

The prick of the nails on Del's face approached pain. "He was—"

Del put a hand to the cold fingers holding the ice in place. *I'm sorry, Teyr. It helps to be older when you have to make that kind of choice. But not much.*

"Want a pain-killer?" said Andur. "I think we have something."

"No," said Del. He felt like hurting.

It was a hard trip.

Not that we were deprived of anything. Varriel's provisioning had been thorough. But Andur and I were plunged into a strange society.

A non-human society.

No matter that I had wanted to see Teyr as human, or that he could mimic human behavior closely enough to keep me and Andur comfortable, there were fundamental differences.

Varriel had created Teyr and his kind, not in imitation of human beings, but because in some deep, inner part of himself these were what he admired: strong, hot-tempered, and intelligent.

And Varriel expected them to clash with humans.

He intended they should win.

I was to help.

Teyr came in smelling of sex as he had for the past ten-days, curled up on the lounge and went to sleep. Del glanced at Andur, who had half-roused then resettled himself in his corner.

The two of them had discussed whether Teyr had a mate, or whether there were simply accessible females somewhere on the ship. They had become very cautious about asking questions: so often the answers left them bewildered.

Del gave half his attention back to the list of arguments he was checking. When the time came to negotiate he wanted more at hand than his own fuddled wits.

Andur's last solo expedition had ended in a disastrous fight with a fesyl. Varriel had ruled Andur could only move about with an escort. The only escort he could communicate with was Teyr and Teyr had other interests. Confinement was hard on Andur. He lived for the chance to train with the young Varr, or even just for the chance to follow him out and around the ship.

Not, thought Del, calling yesterday's work to meld it with today's, *that Teyr neglects us*.

It was that Andur was out of resources and the fight with the fesyl had stripped him of confidence. Face torn open, blood dripping from his chin, Andur had said, "He was playing with me," before submitting to Del's painful attempts at medication. Teyr, coming in moments later, and probably not by chance, was much more effective.

But not, Del reflected, *very sympathetic*. It was possible that it was Teyr who had suggested to Varriel that Andur be confined. *If so*, thought Del, starting a new cross-reference, *it is best Andur not know*.

Andur already found it hard to accept orders from Varriel. Orders from the man he had trained as a boy would strain his thin-stretched pride. It was not a situation one of Andur's people would ever expect to face. You died or were retired, but your juniors did not pass you in rank.

Del made a note of two good ideas, and set a reminder for next shift's work. "Andur?"

The blond head came up from the crossed arms.

"Do you want to play kenvise?"

Andur reached for the board.

They must have played hundreds of games by now; each knew the other's tactics so thoroughly that there was seldom a surprise. But there was not much else to do, and once in a while one of them came up with a new twist that inspired a run of ten or fifteen games that were genuinely exciting.

The board hummed and clicked as Andur set it up.

Del juggled the modules and then held out his two closed hands.

Andur took the left and plugged it in.

They coaxed the ancient, balky randomizer into giving them dispositions. This time they got reasonably equal resources. Sometimes the randomizer failed halfway through its calculations and one or the other got little or nothing. At first, they had painstaking set the game up again and again until it seemed fair. Now they played with whatever the machine gave them, jockeying discolored icons across wavering power fields.

They were well into it when Teyr woke from his nap.

He yawned and stretched and came to watch Andur, who drafted him to help manipulate the board.

Del, outmatched, held his peace. Teyr used bizarre strategies that often worked—if for no other reason than they induced complete confusion in Del.

Del cautiously offered a piece and saw it snapped up. *So we are taking pieces today. Why?* Yesterday nothing would tempt Teyr until he cleaned the board in one fast sweep—tap, tap, tappity tap.

Del carefully maneuvered for position as Andur gave Teyr suggestions in a hoarse, perfectly audible whisper. Teyr amiably entered them all, considered them gravely, and made two alterations.

Andur hissed with feigned disgust.

Del flexed his hand.

They played with a timer. The faster you got a move onto the board, the more time you had later in the game when strategies shaped up. Of course, errors in the beginning could destroy you later, but speed added a certain dash to the competition.

They punched the randomizer.

First move to Del.

He advanced his line.

Teyr shifted his sideways.

Del frowned. That was new.

Teyr stared back, not quite impassive.

Working on something, aren't you, thought Del. He shrugged and entered his next move.

Second round.

The warning siren wailed up and down the scale.

Andur was on his feet, plucking emergency gear from its locker, tossing it to them. Del struggled to fasten the unfamiliar latches. Teyr, gear in place, pushed Del's fumbling hands aside and mounted the helmet. *One day*, thought Del, smelling his own fear in the close space, *there won't be anyone to help me. I've got to get faster at this*.

The escape pod felt crowded and noisy. The four other occupants had already cracked their helmets and settled to a dicing game on the grimy floor.

Teyr, Andur and Del, fully suited, backed against the wall and fastened the safety harness.

Time passed slowly.

Del could feel the sweat dripping down his back. He caught a restless motion from Andur. *This is taking too long*. Varriel was a stickler for frequent safety drills—the patched and worn condition of the ship explained his obsession—but he had never kept them waiting.

There was a growing rumble and Del was slammed against his harness. They were launched. Three dies flew down the length of the pod and shattered on the rear bulkhead, followed by the four who had been dicing. They hit and sagged like soft clay in their suits. Del felt his stomach give a sick heave.

None of the four moved again.

Then they went from heavy to weightless in an instant. Some time later, Del sucked the helmet teat, bitter with anti-nausea drugs. It was going to be a long trip, but they were secure in place. That was all they could do.

When he awoke from drug-induced sleep, Del was hanging in the harness, sagging sideways. A pleasant surprise: gravity. There was a distant whisper from outside the hull. They were in atmosphere and on their way down. Following some beacon, if they were lucky.

The landing was soft enough that Del was certain some port monitoring system had snagged them. All to the good. Wherever they were, there would be air, water, and food.

The indicators flickered green: breathable atmosphere. They peeled out of their suits and drank the sticky-sweet emergency concentrate, then sat, waiting for its energy burst to hit. A tremor went through the hull, then there was the high-pitched whine of a cutter. Andur, crouched against the wall, reached for Teyr, and struck him, hard, across the side of the head.

All Del could think for a moment was that Andur was taking revenge on Teyr for his misery on Varriel's ship. "Andur! He—"

Andur dragged the dazed Varr out flat, and said to him, "Lie still, " and then, to Del, "Cut his nails. Quick." He opened a machine port, ran his hands into its filth, and smeared Teyr's pale complexion. Then he hit him again, over the eye, where both Del and Andur carried the black and white brand.

"Uh," said Teyr, but he didn't move.

Del pulled his tiny knife from his belt pouch and went to work in fumbling haste.

"Make a good job of it," said Andur. He tilted Teyr's head, considered the rapidly swelling eye. It distorted Teyr's face considerably. He decided not to go for a third blow, but wiped off some of the grime.

Del caught the flash of grey eyes: Teyr was getting angry. He gripped the hand he had been working on as Andur used his whole weight to hold Teyr down. Teyr bared his teeth. Del shoved his arm in the way. "Andur, this was not the best way to do this."

"You want to sit around and debate," said Andur, knife in hand, clipping the long, stiff hairs above Teyr's ears, "pick another time." He dug another gobbet of filth from the machinery. "Darken his hands." Andur was methodically putting the long hairs into his belt pouch, checking the floor for nail fragments.

Teyr, still groggy, made it to a sitting position as Del worked on his hands. He made a puzzled noise.

"Clean your hands," said Andur to Del, giving the example. He refitted the hatch to the machinery.

There was a scraping that vibrated the hull. Someone was working their way in and they didn't know how to open the hatch system.

Del looked at Andur.

"I don't know where we are," said Andur, "but I'd bet they," his chin designated Teyr, "aren't welcome."

There was a dull clank, and the percussive rattle of a drag chain being threaded into place.

"Primitive," said Andur. He pulled a leather strand from his belt pouch and began braiding Teyr's hair. Done, he whipped it around with the leather and tied it. Then he worked his hands back and forth over Teyr's head, undoing half his work.

Thud. Boom. Silence.

There was a chill inrush of air.

"Anyone there?" said a woman's voice.

They weren't looked over too carefully in the rush to locate survivors. Which was just as well, for Teyr's make-shift disguise wouldn't stand up to inspection by someone knowledgeable.

They were fortunate, Del found. The majority of the refugees from the damaged ship had been picked up by a patrol that knew how to separate Varrs from humans and had old scores to settle.

The pictures on the jerky, blurred newsvid in the med section showed the battered faces of Varriel's creations. It was a horrible relief to Del to see they had not captured any of Teyr's type. Dead or alive they represented the greatest threat to Teyr. Del looked into the doctor's guileless eyes and hoped she did not learn what to look for.

He counted heads on the screen. Whatever had happened, less than a tenth of the Varr had been captured. And the ship had not been secured, although it seemed to have broken into several parts.

If, thought Del, *you wanted a space structure with maximum survivability, the first thing you did was insure that there were several independent sections. And if*, he continued, *you needed a very large structure that could be assembled in space, then one fast way to get it would be to fasten together several ships. That would explain the Bast's lumpy, patched appearance.*

An attack would explain the sudden systems failure that sent the three of them to the escape pod. Who and why were not yet clear to him. Del watched the animated recreation of the failure of the *Bast*, listened to the triumphant commentary as the ship broke apart and drifted.

Andur hunched together, grim.

Teyr dozed.

They roused themselves when the head of the medic section—which must be all of five people—introduced herself as Castolan and reached to examine Teyr's face.

Del thought his heart would stop.

Andur unfolded himself and reached for the foamer she was holding. "He's not to be touched by," Andur's tone implied polite censorship, but probably reflected a fast search for an excuse, "strangers."

Castolan looked puzzled, but yielded the tool.

Del sighed with relief, and inadvertently drew her attention. "Andur's a Kel," he offered.

"What does that mean?"

Really in the out worlds here.

"They're security personnel, bodyguards. Andur was working for me when we were captured. He's training Teyr." *Not one lie*, thought Del. Now, if she drew a false conclusion, then he was in a position of deniability. Although since no one would be recording the conversation that might not be much help. It would be her word against his. It was essential to develop her good will.

She was young to be in charge of a department.

Del made a venture. "Does your family live here?"

"My mother's station head." She said it with the resignation of somebody already used to the assumption that she attained her post through pull rather than competence. She didn't mention her father and Del decided that might be best left alone. "Ah," he said, noncommittally.

Andur was having a hard time applying foam over oil.

Castolan was watching, prepared to intervene.

Del grunted and got to his feet, intending to stroll toward the window to redirect her attention. The ploy was far more effective than he intended: he caught his breath at the sudden pain in his chest.

Castolan turned around and said, "Are you having trouble breathing, Seret?"

Presently, stripped to a paper kilt, streaked with sensor paste, and hung with leads, Del was undergoing a complete examination.

"Chest pain? What kind of chest pain?" She was hot on the trail. "Were you taking medication? Using a support system?"

"No, I," Del gave an account of his faint at Teyr's court hearing without mentioning the cause of his distress.

As Castolan turned to hunt for another tool, Del looked at Andur, expecting a glance of complicity, but Andur gave him a serious, considering stare, glad to have Del thoroughly examined.

Castolan punched more information into her diagnostic and got another series of tests to run.

Del sat and rubbed a stiff shoulder—he must have hit the pod wall harder than he'd noticed. At least she was diverted from Teyr for the moment. Surely Andur could think of some way to further disguise him. First, they needed something to change the skin color—

Andur stretched, and got an appreciative look.

Del managed not to smile. Andur was a good-looking man, despite the scarred face.

Teyr was nicely impassive.

The blips and lines on the monitor danced as Andur charmed away. Castolan measured probed, and fussed. Del sat and watched his bare feet grow pale with cold. Finally, he yawned hugely, and apologized. He was exhausted.

Castolan took the hint and began wrapping up Del's exam. "The station head will want to interview you."

Del hoped his expression didn't reveal how unwelcome the prospect was. "Perhaps we could go to your guest quarters and get cleaned up first?"

"There will be a vid team, too," added Castolan.

Del looked down at himself, ruefully. "It might be better if I looked less like," his hand flicked back and forth, "a refugee."

"I think," said Castolan with a crisp hardness that startled Del, "that's exactly how mother will want you to look." She clipped a tool home in its case with a sharp shove. "She wants to be sure everyone stays alert."

"A little hard on my dignity," said Del.

Castolan didn't bother to look up.

"I see," said Del, tired. "You two," he spoke briskly, hoping Castolan didn't have the nerve to challenge him, "go to our quarters."

Del wanted to keep Teyr's face off the vid at almost any price. If Castolan didn't see what Teyr was, there were plenty who would. Maybe even some of their own former shipmates who would not be slow to identify what kind of company the former Beyal councilor had been keeping.

It would be the performance of a lifetime.

It would have to be.

A quarter shift later, Del sat down heavily in the guest quarters, and ran his hand down his face.

Ser Shona Prissew had an agenda.

190

Everyone else in the crowded room had been frightened and avid with an unhealthy curiosity about what living at close quarters with the Varr was like.

Hard pressed, Del had unconsciously begun to rub his sternum and won a reprieve. Shona Castolan might be the station head's daughter but she had a professional reputation to maintain.

Del listened to the sounds from the personal. Andur had the water on, full force. From his behavior, Andur suspected that the place was live for sound and sight. He had insisted on moving what scant furniture there was around into odd, inconvenient positions. Then he took Teyr into the personal, where they were apparently having a fight—not much surveillance equipment was designed to withstand having a heavy man fall against it repeatedly. And the sounds in any listening system would be painful.

There was a signal at the door. "Enter," said Del. The guard who entered inquired if there was a problem. "No," said Del in counterpoint to Andur's muffled, unintelligible fury.

The woman looked in the direction of the noise. "What's that?"

Del glanced negligently at the closed door. "I don't interfere in Kel discipline."

There was the sound of something shattering. The guard did a jittery two-step, toward, away.

"Was there something else?"

The woman looked at him, then decided to beat a retreat for further instructions. "No. Seret."

Del waved a hand in release.

The door hummed shut.

Del stood and redraped his robes, then moved unhurriedly to the personal.

The claustrophobically small space had confined two strong, frustrated men for longer than was good for it. What had been a vidplane that produced an unflattering infinity of views of whoever was inside was now a set of blank walls decorated with pressure-induced starbursts.

What? asked Andur's hands.

Questions, answered Del's.

Andur grinned.

Teyr was already stripping down, scrubbing oil off his skin. Andur kneaded and twisted at the heavy-duty medfoam pack: the stuff would make any skin tone look strange.

Andur was generous with the goo, leaving uncovered only the choicer bruises on the face and arms, lying by implication.

Teyr looked like he'd had a severe beating.

Andur looked at his handiwork with satisfaction as Teyr limped into their disordered room.

Del said dryly, for the microphones, "Use quieter methods: we're attracting attention."

Andur grunted savagely, and began prowling.

The vision sensors were probably in the wainscoting where the floor-edge nightlight would illuminate most of the room. Teyr shifted about, avoiding Andur's angry progress. Del sat down on an out-of-position chair, and lifted a supercilious eyebrow.

The door signal went.

Andur stepped into the personal.

"Enter," said Del.

The man who came in was, by his clothes, an upper servant. By his expression he was not happy. In fact, he was terrified. "Seret, is everything in order?"

An interesting way to put it, thought Del, *since everything most definitely is not in order.* "We could use something to eat," he said.

The man closed his mouth, which had sprung open like a jarred cabinet. "Seret." He looked at Teyr.

In the personal, Andur let out a shout Del recognized as a preliminary to a practice bout.

The man retreated to the door in what looked like one convulsive leap.

Teyr limped painfully to answer.

Andur gave tongue again and hit, Del thought, the padded surround of the bath. Whatever it was made a meaty smack.

"I'll see you're sent something." The man was halfway through the door before he added, "Seret."

Del could hear a mumble of voices before the door closed fully.

He was not surprised that the servant who delivered the food was new and nervous. Del was surprised that he was accompanied by

192

Castolan, who had brought a complete medical kit and proceeded to unpack it. "I think your bodyguard may be suffering from stress."

"I think he's better left alone."

Andur gave a shout they could probably hear, unaided, everywhere in the building.

Castolan's chin came up.

Del did his best to look avuncular. "He has his own way of working these things out."

"And his novice?" said Castolan.

"As I mentioned, Ser."

"Is it that I'm a woman? We have male doctors."

Del sighed. "He's being disciplined."

"He's being beaten."

Del had been the object of withering contempt before, but Castolan was by far the youngest successful practitioner. He flushed.

Having made some impression, Castolan's face hardened. She prepared to marshal her arguments.

Fighting mother must have been quite a training, thought Del. "Look," he said, "there isn't anything for you to do here." It was, he saw instantly, exactly the wrong thing to say.

"*You* are scarcely competent to decide that." She was past Del so fast he didn't have time to make up his mind to reach and grab. "Andur!"

Andur filled the door.

Castolan's head came to the middle of his chest.

Andur looked down.

Castolan looked up. "Let me in."

Andur smiled.

"Or I'll come back with guards."

Andur looked over her head at Del. Del read his thought: she was alone. He stepped aside, mock gracious.

Castolan didn't see the mockery, and darted through.

Del followed in time to see her expression change as she confronted Teyr, who backed away with a lithe twist that gave the lie to his earlier limp. She turned around. "What's going on here?"

The three of them waited.

"Let me out."

Andur didn't move.

She was a decided inconvenience as a prisoner, and a danger if they wanted to escape.

Wrists bound behind her back, ankles linked by a short length of twisted cloth, she lay on the floor and watched Andur begin going over his equipment. Teyr, too, began that endless preening care which a professional security person uses to pass time or reduce tension: touching up already keen edges, recalibrating perfectly calibrated weapons.

Castolan's eyes were wide.

With cause, thought Del, sorting through the contents of his belt pouch. Andur and Teyr began to gesture to each other, and since they faced each other and not Del, he couldn't follow the conversation.

He went through everything in his pouch: the battered chronometer, the thick-bladed utility tool with its cross-hatched handle, the elegant engraved gentleman's knife, the scent-flask with its carved stopper. Hanro had given him the flask on some family occasion. He wondered how Riana was.

Del closed the pouch with a tug. He hoped Andur or Teyr came up with some use for her. It was not impossible that the correct decision was for them to kill her here and try to get out on their own. Del began rubbing the pain in his chest.

Wordless discussion concluded, Andur, used to the lack of modesty in both-sex security forces, went to the far wall, unfastened his pants, and emptied his bladder into the urinal.

Castolan, doubled on the floor, shivered.

A thoughtful, rather ugly, expression went across Andur's face.

She was afraid of being raped.

Andur, pants still undone, took her by the upper arm.

Del started to speak and closed his mouth.

It is possible for the inexperienced to imagine a heroic death. The violation of self and the potential for repetition make it much harder to imagine being an heroic rape victim.

That Andur was kind to women, and would, in any case, have scorned to be so negligent of his duty, would not be obvious to Castolan, who appeared to have spent her life insulated from the rough-and-tumble world. A little more experience and she would not have been so foolish as to walk past Andur while admitting she had no back-up.

"Not now, Andur," said Del.

Andur released the arm with a shove, and looked at Del with hot, angry eyes: I'm the tough guy, you're the friend.

Del took a breath and rubbed his chest.

She looked at Del, attention drawn by his moving hand. The taunt, wet cloth across her mouth moved faster.

Del gave her a look of friendly conspiracy. *Trust me. I'll try to get you out of this.*

Andur pulled her upright and said, "When I loosen your gag, you'll tell us how to reach the field. If," his thin-bladed knife pricked beneath her ear, "you're thinking about yelling, remember I can guarantee it will be the last thing you do. Do you understand?"

She nodded frantically.

"Good." He slide the blade up—Del could see the cut well blood—and slashed the cloth.

She thrust out the wad of cloth with her tongue.

Andur said, "Begin."

The service passage was clean and afforded plenty of hiding places in its walls, lumpy with equipment and sensors. It would be difficult to track them here, but easy to locate them, once the idea occurred to someone. Their best hope lay in the fact that, since no alarm had sounded, no one knew they were missing.

Del, in charge of Castolan to free the two fighters, eyed the spreading bruise where his hand was locked on one of her arms behind her back. He pitied her, but not enough to face Andur and Teyr if she should escape from his custody. If she gave the alarm she could have them killed, not necessarily quickly. They had useful information, and no friends. Perhaps, at the end, if they made it to a ship, she could be freed. He clung to that thought, even though a colder and more calculating part of his mind told him she would be lucky if Andur decided to take her with them as a hostage rather than execute her on the spot.

Castolan, mouth refilled with wadded cloth, arms bound tightly together at the elbows, moved quickly and compliantly. *It is possible,* thought Del, maneuvering them around a mass of colored-coded conduits, *that she is thrilled by her venture into the forbidden territory of violence.* She might be thinking of replaying the scene for a circle of half-horrified friends. Whatever she was thinking, Del would bet the experience wasn't real to her. She walked far too steadily.

Up ahead, Andur stopped, slowly crouched down to the floor, extended his legs behind himself, and began crawling on his belly.

Teyr, stunner in hand, flattened himself behind some equipment and watched the tunnel ahead.

Del heard a muffled grunt.

Andur, hand on the hilt of his resheathed knife, came back, fast, expression disgusted.

Teyr's face was eloquently disapproving.

Del moved forward with the woman.

Andur had left the maintenance worker face down as he had fallen, and the blood was pooling his body, so there was little to see as they walked past. But the smell of urine, dung, and blood followed them down the narrow passage: stinking reality.

Del could feel Castolan tremble as he urged her forward. Gone was the eagerness of moments ago. Del wondered if she had gotten the nuance. Andur had not regretted killing—he had been annoyed the man had made the single sound.

The lights died and Del froze, relaxing when a cold wind stirred his clothes. Andur had killed the light while Teyr cracked an outer hatch. The jumpers, small, battered in-system ships, stood in rows on their high skids. Del could see the gleam of the field lights in the sightless eyes of their cockpit viewports.

Andur drifted down the line like a stray shadow.

Teyr motioned Del after Andur, not even glancing at Castolan. Del pushed her forward, listening behind him for any small sound that would tell him Teyr was following. His back felt naked.

Nothing.

He was tempted to stop and look back, just in case there was some problem. Andur's cold, order-giving voice replayed itself. *Never question orders once an operation's begun.* Del speeded up his pace. Teyr would follow as quickly as he could.

Del slid into the dark shadow under the belly of the last jumper, and started violently at Andur's hand on his arm. "Uh!" Momentarily inattentive, his grip on the woman's arm relaxed. He felt Castolan tense and turn to run in the same instant he threw all his weight against her. Arms bound, she fell heavily.

Andur brought her face into the glow of light from the building they had just left by gripping her hair and pulling up.

Del looked away from the terrified eyes.

And saw Teyr slide out of the shadow of the next-but-last jumper and crawl across the half-lit space on his belly. Del could smell dust and sweat as Teyr rose beside him.

Andur moved around behind Castolan. Del saw her jerk, then relax as the knife went home. He swallowed the taste of blood in his own mouth. He'd bitten his lip. Andur dragged the body into the deeper shadows at the field's edge.

Del shivered, leaning into the circle of Teyr's arm around his shoulders. He looked into the calm, calculating face that was examining the building behind them. All quiet. Del turned away. There are only three of us, and there are two dead already.

The more analytical portion of his mind gave a cynical snort. *Two that you've seen. So many more that weren't real to you when you were safe on Varriel's ship.* Del shivered again, unsupported. Teyr was hand-linked with Andur in silent conversation.

It was Teyr, rather than Andur, who began the touchy process of turning on the jumper. Del, fastened to his seat, followed Teyr's skilled interrogation of the controls with bewilderment. There were no vocals, so Andur was at a loss, and neither Del or Teyr could read the symbols on the red-lit screens.

Teyr was the one with experience in flying and in deciphering systems. He justified Andur's decision by quickly bringing the systems live. Del could hear the purr of the life-support coming on, the solid thump as the hatch sealed, the whine of the actuators on stand-by.

Del threw his seat locks. They were moments from takeoff.

Teyr paused, eyes closed, fingers on two sets of controls, as if the well-worn metal surfaces spoke to him. He took a breath, made a choice. There was a slight jerk as the parking restraints came off. He swept a glance over the two of them, gripped a control and powered the craft with one smooth push of his hand.

They were gliding down the main runway in the dark. The field lights came up full, blinding. Del could see Teyr squint in the glare. An angry voice spoke from the earphones bouncing in their clip.

Andur reached forward and popped them free. He stowed them in a bin without getting a flicker of attention from Teyr.

Something hit Del in the gut and he grunted.

Power up.

They were airborne.

The jumper stood on one stubby wing and wheeled around it. Del could see the points of light on the ground circle. It was some consolation to Del that Andur was white-lipped and stiff in his seat. Del closed his eyes. A mistake, and he opened them again, instantly. He swallowed hard.

For all the unfamiliar motion, Del could tell the jumper was under control. Teyr's hands on the controls flexed and stroked with quick deliberation.

It was still a relief when the hard thrust of acceleration pushed him into his seat and they began the steep climb out of the atmosphere.

Andur's hands relaxed. So Del's did, too.

He counted silently. A small ship, lightly laden, but with limited thrust capabilities. *It'll be over at one thousand five hundred. No. Two thousand. No. Two thousand five—* Del slumped forward in the seat that seemed to have fallen away from him.

The dingy, misshaped globe swam beneath them, rimmed with cold, blue sunlight.

Teyr switched seats with Andur and began running a program into the navunit.

"Where are we going?" said Del.

Andur pointed into the holo. Out system.

Del bit back questions. There would be plenty of time for explanations. Right now, what they needed was to get underway.

The seat was hard against his buttocks. The jumper, intended for no more than local transit, was not equipped with bunks or more than the most primitive personal that worked on suction. *A few more shifts of this*, thought Del, *and we'll smell pretty ripe*. He leaned back, trying to ease stiff muscles.

They would be hopping from station to station, all of them automatic, refueling, and then hopping again.

Andur released himself from his seat and stretched and strained against the back. "Long pull here. You should get some exercise."

Del dragged his unwilling body from the seat and patiently put it through its paces.

It would be at least another two shifts before they would reach their destination and leave the jumper. If Andur and Teyr had calculated correctly, then there might be other survivors of Varriel's ship there.

Del curled up and contemplated his kneecaps for five slow counts. He almost hoped there would be no one. Surely there was somewhere two men and a—Teyr's long legs went by—three men could disappear and become just another three units in the labor pool.

Del relaxed and rolled forward again. Hold it. One. Two—

Body busy with the repetitions, Del frowned and thought back, worrying away at the memories that continued to replay in his head.

He did not want responsibility for Castolan. He couldn't complain to Andur. He understood the brutal logic. He had spent a lifetime paying people like Andur to make that kind of decision for him, and those who delegate power do not delegate responsibility. His silence had been consent.

Del released the exercise straps and began rolling them to put away. He would have given a good deal not to have seen that terrified face slacken into death. He had deserved her contempt, but he couldn't, even now, see the solution that would have avoided—

The navigation beacon they were approaching challenged them. Teyr said a word or two that might had been unintelligible sounds, and weren't, then answered in slow, correct phrases. The response was unintelligible. Del sighed with relief. There were Varr there.

The mining outpost was quite tidy by the time they arrived and docked: no bodies pooled in blood, all the signs of forced entry repaired. The air held only the subtle stench of recycling, and the automatic equipment hummed as vigorously for its new masters as it had for the old.

And there was instant relief in seeing familiar faces. Del felt for a blurred instant that he was leaving harsh, clear reality for the soft-focus of a dream that never quite turned into a nightmare. The uniformed, uniform bodies of the fesyl passed and repassed them in the corridors.

Del tried to hold, then to regain, the other focus and was finally conscious only that it had slipped away. Everything around him had turned into normal routine.

They were to see Bondre, then Varriel, and in the meantime they would be assigned quarters. This, with the gene-sculpted Varr faces, the faintly feral smells, the rigid routine, this was reality.

Del accepted the deferential gesture of the two Varr at Varriel's door, made his own as he entered the presence.

Varriel, hair thin and white, hands shaking where they gripped his chair arms, looked at Del's expression, which was not, perhaps, as impassive as either of them would have wished, and dismissed his attendants.

"You see how it is," said Varriel.

Del said nothing.

I knew Varriel was dying as soon as I saw him. He was eaten hollow, a shell held upright by will alone.

I had thought I had come back because I had no choice. The fear I felt looking at Varriel's ravaged body reminded me how much I had invested in his dreams. I, too, wanted the Varr to survive. That smooth young face, surprised by death on a dusty landing field, was part of the price I had become willing to pay.

I pulled a chair forward, steeled myself to ignore the subtle stench that perfume did not conceal. "What have you planned?" I asked.

The yellowed hands reached for a portable com. "After my death,"
he said—

The body on the improvised bier looked as if it had been dead a long time. Emaciated, with taunt, yellow skin, Varriel's corpse had none of his vital presence left: a tired old man whose life, prolonged beyond the norm, had failed.

Del looked at the hands, marked with scars and twisted by swollen joints. Varriel had worked with his hands. Del rubbed his own, smooth and carefully tended even in the crisis conditions aboard the ship, and felt vaguely ashamed. He shrugged and speeded up his inspection. In death, the odors of Varriel's illness had become pronounced. It would be a relief to be rid of the corpse.

Everything was in order. Del left the room, nodding to the guard on the door. "They can begin."

There would be no ceremony. There was no place where everyone could assemble and little time to spend devising rituals the Varr did not have. They disposed of their own dead with practical speed, and it was perhaps most fitting that Varriel receive no more than his creations. He would be cremated, and the fine ash scattered at some future, more convenient, time and place.

They were on their way back to Belsyrtis.

Del thought he should feel more about that than he did. He was going home, to the comforts of his house, his family, his friends, his peers, and he felt nothing but apprehension.

Belsyrtis was securely in the hands of the Varr, and in that it was lucky. It might have been transferred to G-R, the Varr's nominal employer, and current rival.

How nominal that had been had become painfully clear, for, although G-R had the power and organization to seize the major ports along the star routes, it had been unable to govern them. Chaos reigned farther in, and there was serious economic disruption everywhere that was in contact at all. Belsyrtis was fortunate in its relative isolation. There might be an acute shortage of luxuries, but no one would starve.

Del spoke up the latest data.

He was consciously resuming the routine he had followed for so many years. When he disembarked in Belsyrtis he would gain a considerable advantage if his former colleagues saw him as one of them: a reasonable man. Every dispute they could skip, every piece of common ground they could take for granted, was a step on the way to the solution the Varr desperately needed. A power base of their own.

Belsyrtis, sophisticated enough to deal with the political forces further in, isolated enough to be independent, and perhaps most important, intimately familiar to Del, had been Varriel's choice.

Now all Del had to do was make that choice desirable, or at least palatable, to the government of Belsyrtis.

He thought he stood a chance.

Del read all the news for Belsyrtis, going over even the most trivial stories in detail. He wanted to avoid every occasion that might remind the governing council how distant he had become from their own interests. The latest vidshows, the price of fugun leaves, the outbreak of malten fever in the crowded slums around the port: the stuff of everyday life, the things he would have known almost by osmosis if he had been living in the city.

As for the other half of the equation, the things Del knew his former colleagues did not, he had less hope of hiding those changes in himself.

In fact, he thought, punching off the com, *I suppose I began to change the day I had to confront the matter of the* Aeguit. *That*—he automatically looked at the life-systems telltale as he opened and closed the door between two ship's sections—*that was when I had to deal with harsher, less abstract realities than ever came to the negotiating tables in Belsyrtis.*

Del signaled his presence at the door, and heard the click of the release.

Carefully dressed to make as little as possible of his differences with humanity, Bondre turned around and raised his eyebrows. Del walked around scrutinizing the effect. "It looks right, but I'd rather you had more experience."

Bondre shrugged.

"I know," said Del. They had to send someone the governing council would see as a real representative. He himself wouldn't do. He had his own role to play.

Bondre is the one with the most experience, and, Del thought, *and probably the best instincts as well. But his silence is a real disadvantage.*

Del gestured approval.

Bondre sat down, tired, and rubbed his thumb tip over his close-clipped nails.

It will do no good to tell Bondre that I'm tired, too, thought Del. They needed to make this work. There was no concealing the danger in their position.

Del would be taking Bondre, nominally in charge, Teyr, theoretically as translator, and Andur, as head of security for this mission. And enough of the fesyl to make a strong presence.

He went to pour himself a drink, then dumped the cup out, untouched, knowing he needed all his overstrained wits about him. He jumped as the door opened without announcement and Teyr and Andur came in, grim-faced and serious.

"I'll go over everything, one more time," said Del, "for luck."

Andur nodded and began stroking the hilt of his knife.

Teyr leaned against the wall, tall as Bondre now.

"Once we have landed at the field," Del consulted his chrono and slipped it back into his pouch, "in about a quarter shift, we will be met by the following people—"

Del had not anticipated how depressing it would be to see his own friends, lean and anxious, greeting him as the representative of a recently hostile power.

Jasil Carnath was the only one who greeted him with warmth, and even his eyes jerked to the patch of makeup concealing the black and white mark over Del's eyebrow. And there was, unexpectedly, Beyba, whose cold, angry face blighted Del's eager recognition.

Still, there was always the bitter tang of fuel and the salt-rot of the sea. Del felt something tight inside loosen. This was, after all, home. The city looked rich, opulent, after the scrabbling frontier outposts of the fringe. Del lifted his eyes to its high towers, its flying buildings, and admired them.

They walked in along the meticulously clean paving to the main port building—walking in itself a sign that things were going poorly—he saw none of the ground-effect vehicles used to shuttle important guests. In other days, this would have been a calculated affront, but the size of the delegation greeting them said, not now.

Deltander broke from his musing to find Beyba close on his left. Not looking, not particularly interested, but there. Del carefully refrained from meeting his eyes.

Beyba said nothing.

They were old friends, and Beyba's silence hurt. Del dismissed the matter. He was here to work, and Beyba was not a friend, but a problem. He knew all of them except Bondre well enough to suspect how desperate the Varr were, especially if Del gave him anything to go on.

Del deliberately withdrew behind his wall of guards.

The preliminaries over, Del ran through his notes one more time. He decided to be frank. It was a good offer, the best Belsyrtis was likely to get.

"It is a pleasure to be home again. I have been many places and seen many things, some of which I would rather have remained ignorant of for all my life. I cannot convey to you how strange it seems to be sitting on this side of the table, rather than that—"

That got a nervous laugh.

"—but I believe what I have to offer is as much to your benefit as ours. You will pardon me for offering a summary of political events leading to the current disruption. When I was last here such information was unavailable, and what data I have received from Belsyrtis has not indicated to what degree that situation has changed—"

There was a shift in posture among the delegation.

He had been right, then, they still did not know much, if anything, about the deeper causes of their problems.

"With the collapse of the Tentroban consortium, and the death of one of the three rulers of Innisfa, there ensued a struggle for control of some of the trade routes among the inner cluster core which had been considered proprietary, due, in part, to the expense of shipping on them.

"Certain technical developments in transportation mechanisms made these more economically viable, and competition became keen. Geffund-Raq, faced with the necessity of raising and maintaining a security corps of enormous size and discipline to defend its long-standing interest, applied to an entrepreneur named Litjin Varriel for assistance. Varriel was known to be in need of capital to continue the development of humaniform clones—"

Del was looking at a wall of faces unconscious of their appearance: they were that attentive.

"I know we find the idea of mimicking humans distasteful, but this feeling is by no means as universal as we might once have supposed, and further in modified humans are commonly created and employed for some types of jobs.

"But creating humaniform workers was not where Varriel's interest lay. He was engaged in the difficult task of actually making a synthetic being much like a human. By almost any standard, he succeeded."

Del put down the old-fashioned script notes his had chosen to use for security and portability.

"How do you know that he succeeded?"

It would be Jasil who asks, thought Del. "Because he encoded his signature into the gene sequences of a being capable of producing viable offspring when crossed with human beings."

"Nothing to say he didn't just append his 'signature.'"

"I'm not an expert," said Del, "and I can't answer your point with technical expertise, but I have seen the testimony. Varriel's accomplishment was thoroughly challenged and then accepted."

Jasil sat back.

Del tapped his notes together.

"Now. I'd like to emphasize that Varriel's creation is represented here by Teyr, who many of you know, and his clone-brother, Bondre. The others standing behind me," Del watched eyes shift across the savage, furry faces, "are not artificial creations. They are modified humans,"—there was a general uneasy shifting—"as can easily be demonstrated by genetic sampling."

It was not welcome news.

There was a slither of rich fabric as the ladies and gentlemen of the delegation looked at one another with dismay. They would far rather have been related to the two gene-sculptured clones. Del caught the tiny, appreciative smile on Jasil's face.

One possible ally, thought Del. *I hope so, for all of us.*

"I know," Del continued, "that you have been hearing rumors of identical, ferocious mercenaries destroying isolated outposts and seizing ships. Insofar as I am aware, nothing of the kind is going on." Del looked into their skeptical faces.

There would have been claims from companies willing to take a fast insured credit exchange when the rumors of raids became widespread. There would be people who now would have to swear those rumors were true or face criminal charges.

The delegation was attentive to Del's every word.

"There have been incidents, largely organized by competing companies, many of which have a size and power you and I are accustomed to think of as properly belonging to governments rather then private enterprises. Many of those companies employ fesyl like these behind me. They may, of course, differ considerably in appearance according to the human stock from which they were originally drawn, and none of them are the products of cloning. Cloning is an expensive and tedious process, and not an economically viable way of producing troops, or, indeed, large numbers of anything else."

Del gathered his notes and tapped the bottom of the pile on the table, waiting.

Jasil's lips moved silently: do you want a question?

Del made no sign, waited.

It was Endrew Imme who raised the question; she said, "So what did Varriel create—these—for?" She looked around, gathering allies, "Toys?"

Del laid his notes down. "I think, originally, he started out to see if the thing could be done, but early on, his notion was to vary the perception of beings so similar to humans that we could communicate fully with the idea of creating some," he lifted his hands, "expansion of our realm of awareness."

He dropped his hands. "Varriel is very concerned with the necessity for increasing the means of communication among human beings. Currently we are resolving very important disputes by the most primitive of means—force. He hoped to create a being capable of seeing and implementing other kinds of solutions."

"They can't speak," said a voice from the back.

"They," Del stopped as Bondre shifted in his seat.

"I," the voice had a harsh slowness, "can speak. Although so poorly it would—distract—your attention from our proposals."

"Del?" said Jasil.

"He had some of them inhibited," said Del. "They have sophisticated techniques for these things further in." *Not to say unpleasant*, thought Del. Varriel was, by his standards, humane: he could have made the inhibition permanent.

"Ah," said Jasil, curiosity unsatisfied, but willing to let the point go for now.

Del squared his notes and watched the slow shift of postures to include Bondre in their center of attention. The delegation hadn't, until now, really considered Bondre.

Del waited for the question: they had to be thinking it, who would speak?

It was Jasil who cautiously asked, overcoming a lifetime's conditioning against asking questions you don't already know the answer to, "Why wouldn't these near-humans just seize power for themselves? Or is that what they're doing?"

There. "The Varr are all male, and, although they can cross with humans, the offspring are not fertile and the complex of traits Varriel created is not only recessive, but actually destroyed in combination with normal human germ plasma. Varr can only be reproduced through expensive and tedious artificial means that require a stable, technologically advanced culture to support them. Their own survival is bound into maintaining that necessary level of technology."

Del looked up, alert. Varriel had assured him these facts were critical and fairly true. Any suggestion that the Varr might take over, or displace true humans, and the pressure to destroy them would be enormous.

He studied the people across from him. People he had known if not all of his life then all of theirs. There were frightened faces and faces gone thoughtful, crafty. Those were the people accustomed to seek any advantage, particularly in a crisis. The Varr represented a potential tool.

"Why should we believe this?" asked the voice from the back.

The delegation's members all wanted the answer to that one.

"I don't ask you to," said Del. "If you agree to our proposal then events will prove the truth. And there are less than fifty Varr left." (In point of fact, they had found twenty-three, but Del saw no reason to say so.) "There's no chance in the long term they could overwhelm us."

Del let the final word sit in the air.

The delegates looked at one another.

Del put the comdeck with the actual terms of the proposed agreement on the table. "We'll withdraw to let you consider the matter." He stood, Bondre stood, and everyone drew together as the Varr delegation walked out to its retiring room.

Where nothing important was said.

Although convention prescribed that a diplomatic retiring room was inviolate: no listening, no peeping, Del was not foolish enough to strain his former colleagues' ethics. There was too much a stake to trust their honesty.

Del wasn't even surprised that the decision was a swift one.

Several orbiting ships full of troops that might be human technically, that certainly were efficient, and could be either defenders or attackers of Belsyrtis made a potent, if unmentioned, argument. It was a nice solid alliance in a time when Belsyrtis needed all the committed defense forces it could get.

Del made his thanks brief and to the point and was on his way.

It was also prudent not to strain their hospitality. There would be time enough for civilities when they had grown used to the idea of what they had done.

Del could see the splotches of color on the ground that must be people waiting for his skimmer to land. He looked at Teyr and got a taunt smile. *A bit of an ordeal, this.* He would have preferred to just walk into his house, get used to the sensation of ground beneath his feet, to the servants behind every door, to just being in an open, safe environment.

But Hanro would be there.

And his family, three children now.

And Del's old friends among the servants, eager to welcome him back.

Del arranged his face suitably. They could be back aboard the ship in three weeks if things went well.

There was the slightest jar on landing. *That's another thing that's different*, thought Del.

Hanro chattered incessantly, mostly, to disguise his interest in one question: was his older brother back to stay?

Del was politely uninformative, admired the two new children, congratulated Riana on her willowy grace, and on her awkward boyfriend, who had the most unsavory complexion Del had ever seen.

But Hanro had reason to present the gangly youth with such enthusiasm. He was male, of suitable age, unattached, and well off, but not so well off as to be in a position to argue with Hanro.

Del managed not to touch cheeks.

And to remove Teyr as quickly as possible, having seen that Riana, in a misguided burst of good taste, was interested in becoming better acquainted with him.

Del's house looked improbably small, clean, and full of people. All of who needed to be greeted with a word, a glance, a promise of future attention. It was hard to muster the required degree of enthusiasm.

I got through it reasonably well, thought Del. *There were no disappointed faces*. He sat, robes unfastened, gathering energy to dress for dinner. Which was supposed to be light and private and wouldn't be if the staff could help it.

He heard the chink of glass from Teyr's direction. "Pour me one, too."

Teyr put the cup in his hand. Del drank half of it, feeling the warmth spread through his chest. It had been a tough afternoon. But successful. And with care, it would be a while—Del hoped a considerable while—before the Varr proved him wrong.

Varriel may have built in safeguards. However, Bondre did a major portion of Varriel's actual work in later years and I would not bet against Bondre's skills. All it would take was peace and quiet and credits. I'm pretty sure I just achieved that for him.

The Varr would figure out how to reproduce themselves.

Del studied Teyr, outlined against the twilight of the balcony window. Varriel's single-sex clones were not limited by Varriel's creation. They would pursue their own interests with intelligence and vigor. *No, humanity's real safeguards are more subtle, embedded in what, for want of a better word*—Del sipped—*might be called the Varr's humanity*—

Del had moved back into quarters with the rest of the Varr delegation—supposedly to make it easier to conduct negotiations—by the time Beyba came calling, unannounced, and unapologetic. Plainly he expected a few reconciling words, an admission Del had worried, some sign Del regretted leaving him in the middle of the embattled field at Lybayos.

But something had torn between them when Del followed Teyr. They had each been right, or lucky, but that instant when they had abandoned each other to go separate ways would stand between them forever.

Del probed his feelings. It hurt a little. He had not appreciated what Beyba had done for him when Beyba was close. But Del's allegiance had shifted to Teyr, and, by extension, his kind.

Beyba shook the ice in his cup. "Not much to say." He put the cup down with a click. "We used not to mind that."

Del gave a rueful frown.

Beyba stood. "You know where to find me." And he was gone.

Del thought the script was probably for him to call Beyba back, say something. Nothing came to mind. Just relief they wouldn't be enemies and a mental note not to make any of his little revealing gestures during negotiations. Beyba knew too well, for example, what Del's rubbing his chest meant, and that was not a thing to give away in a tight place.

Gone, gestured Teyr as he came in.

Yes, signed Del.

Teyr frowned.

Bondre back, asked Del.

Teyr's expression went from social worry to real concern. No.

No?

And it is late, said Teyr's hands.

Who was with him?

Teyr counted off the guards. Five of them, and Bondre was a skillful enough commander that he shouldn't have done anything stupid. The rougher quarters near the port were dangerous. The rumors about the Varr were unquenchable, spread as much from delighted horror as from fear. But they worked on certain sorts of minds. There had been incidents: Tomase beaten before the port guards moved to protect him; Raquel spat upon in the port magistrate's office.

Afraid of being condemned by association, Riana's pimple-faced friend had retreated to his family's estates up the coast. *Which*, Del thought sourly, *is less of loss than Hanro thinks, but it's not diplomatic to point that out*. Del shook his mind from the well-worn track: Bondre was late and that might be serious.

"Get Andur," Del told Teyr. "We'll walk to meet him." They had half-a-dozen guards of their own, with the five with Bondre they should meet with no trouble. A little name-calling, perhaps. Privilege of the unenfranchised.

The street was empty for so fine a spring evening, and Andur kept looking back, up, restlessly moving around the group.

Teyr had caught Andur's fever and moved up so close to Del he could feel his body heat.

"Should we go back, Andur?"

He considered it seriously. "We're nearer the port offices."

Del sniffed the wind. "Burning."

"Yes." Andur looked up, around. "Stay here."

He worked a boot-toe into the stonework of the nearest building and began climbing. At the top he hung and peered for what seemed like an endless time and was probably only a few seconds. He came down the building at a speed at frightened Del. "Let's get going. Back to the plaza."

They didn't quite run, but their steady jog trot ate up the distance.

There was a far-off, muffled roar. "Faster," said Andur grimly. The sound came again. Del fumbled at the sash at his waist, pulled one arm, then the other, free and dropped the encumbering robe. Andur circled back to pick up the mound of cloth, and passed Del again, stuffing the robe out of sight in a doorway.

Del was terrified by the simple precaution.

He ran.

Then he identified the sound: the hungry roar of a mob.

The Varr delegation was housed in one of the small buildings pressed together at one side of the plaza. They were the traditional choice of those delegations that could squeeze into such tight quarters, because the security provided by the thick stone walls and separate entrances was so superior to being housed in the big warren of the general trade delegation's building.

Varr House had heavy gates, added at Del's insistence the day they moved in. When they clanged to behind him, Del found he was shaking all over. He began circling the entrance paving, cooling down, listening to the sound move closer.

Andur crouched at the gates, peering through their pierced design. "Here they come."

"This way?'

"This way," said Andur. "Everybody in."

Through the remotes on the facade they could see the mob boil into the plaza. Overawed by the vast open space, they came around the edges, all except for a few bold souls who gathered in the center, piling together what looked like bits of rubbish: signs, ornamentation from buildings, the carved wooden trim from official doorways. Dragged through the crowd Del could see one, two, three struggling figures.

With sick certainty Del identified Bondre's green and gold robe. The other two were in brown: some of Bondre's guards. The rest must be dead and lucky at that. Bondre was either already stunned or too wise to resist, but the other two fought savagely to free themselves. The mob surged over them.

Del turned to Andur, urgently, "I think—"

Eyes narrowed, Andur was running the whet along his blade.   It would be close work. As a diplomatic mission, they were allowed only stunners. The most they would do was numb a few in the forefront to be crushed under the feet of the others.

"Teyr, you take Del and go to the lowest level. Del, use the command system to report this to the Port guard. Don't be too pressing and don't say where you are."

On the screen, Bondre screamed in unheard agony as they stripped back the muscles of his forearms. Del looked away. He knew every step of the archaic procedure: someone out there was familiar with the old histories.

Don't watch, said a shrill voice in his head, don't watch—

Teyr stared at the screen, fascinated. Del had to pull at him to get his attention from the screen. "Don't watch," he said, voice shaking. It would be like watching oneself die, Bondre and Teyr were so much alike. "Teyr?" said Del, "help me."

Del found he really needed that strong arm down the stairs.

Hands wrist-deep in the icy water, Del leaned over the basin and looked into his own face. Better. He didn't look so green.

He pulled his hands out of the water and shook them, concentrating on the shower of drops, the sweet scent of the soap, the roughness of the towel, anything but Bondre's present agony.

Surely Bondre was too deep in shock to feel most of it.

Del had to go face them.

He knew he wasn't much of a success at the concealing his feelings by the sharp glance he got from Andur, who glanced at Teyr, busy bringing up the external remotes on the back-up surveillance system. Andur came and gripped Del's shoulders, hard. It hurt. "We'll need water, the medical kits, food, if there is any—" He looked at Teyr and said, "Leave that."

Teyr stopped, hands resting on the console.

"It won't help him and we have things to do."

Teyr flicked a glance at Del, a fractional inattention before he rose and began gathering the things Andur had specified.

Del stopped his own motion toward the console. He, too, wanted to be a witness. Somehow they owed Bondre that. But there wasn't time.

Andur opened the heavy door down to the storage vaults in a gust of dank air. It was damp and close down there. But it could be defended for a long time and might even be proof against the mob's firing the building.

Andur reached for the tapestries masking the walls and pulled them down. Del mutely began to help. They were going to need bedding if they were lucky. The minutely embroidered cloth bundled in his arms, Del started down the stairs, already afraid of the upper stories where the bedrooms were.

He wondered if he would ever go back up.

Even in the vault, he could hear the roar of the mob like waves breaking on a distant shore.

He settled himself against a wall, waiting for Andur and Teyr, wondering if the fesyl would join them: he bet not. There were ways over the roofs, and it was possible that mob could be deceived into believing they had escaped into the complex of delegation buildings.

Andur ushered down Teyr, whose hands were vigorously protesting.

Andur silently began explaining Teyr was to guard Del.

It didn't sit well. Teyr was fully capable of fighting with the men. Indeed, as far as the fesyl were concerned, they would follow Teyr in preference to Andur.

I'm staying, said Andur's hands, and you're staying, and—

There was the sound of something splintering above.

Andur turned and used his whole weight to pull the door to the vaults closed, wedging the iron come-alongs used to pull boxes and cases into the opening mechanism.

Del ran a hand over them. "Pull them out: if they jam we don't have any way to cut them. I may be able to throw the lock from in here with an override."

Andur began pulling. "Fast, Asen," he said. "Code it."

Del didn't even bother to nod. He, too, could hear the rising sound. *Concentrate*, he told himself. *First the initiation sequence—* His fingers rapped out a practiced rhythm.

Above him, the roar swelled and swelled.

It has been silent for a long time, long enough that I had almost allowed myself hope. Now I can hear the groaning of the security doors above us being forced and a rising tide of voices. Andur has backed himself against the door-wall, out of sight from the entrance, knife across Teyr's throat. At the hands of the mob a Varr's death will be as agonizing as rage and fear can make it. Eyes almost closed, listening, Teyr leans against Andur, neck against the blade—

Paper slipping from his hands, stylus clattering on the floor, Deltander rose and stood, palms pressed against the damp wall at his back. He looked at Andur, posed for action, and at Teyr, who was listening, lips parted, to the muffled sounds beyond the door.

There was an instant of profound silence outside, and the rapid clicks of the door-ward's safety releasing. *I should have let Andur jam it*, thought Del. *They've got someone who knows the system.*

The door grated back, framing a chaos of grinning faces, waving arms, weapons at every angle. Rigid with fear, Del felt the clammy touch of his robe's hem on his ankles, scented the rank sweat of the mob, and thought, desperate, *Don't look at Andur, don't look at Teyr. Hold their attention, give Andur time.*

He stepped forward, hands spread before him as if asking quiet before he spoke.

Nearly unrecognizable with burns and soot Ibeigne swayed in the doorway and fell forward into the room, hands pawing after him—

214

Andur's arm went tense.

Teyr surged out of his grasp, blood welling from the nick on his throat.

—fingers gripped Ibeigne's robe and pulled him to his feet. Yelling, he vanished into the surge of the crowd.

Helpless, Deltander watched Teyr boosted onto the shoulders of the horde, felt the floor drop from under his own feet as he, too, was lifted. He bit his lips to keep from crying out. *Fear will excite them. Keep still. Maybe they'll take us to someone in authority—*

He began to recognize the faces around him.

Face distorted with yelling, pretty Ettay who had worked in Bondre's offices. What's-his-name, the clerk who kept track of household expenses. Bruma, the hydroponics worker. Harl's assistant. Pente? Pante?

Rough bodies jostling and clinging to Del.

Six or seven fesyl security guards out of uniform, one of when reached up and gripped Deltander's limp and startled hand, hard.

"What's happening?" asked Del, bewildered. His question went unheard in the enormous noise.

The mob swept up the stair, level-to-level, past fire-scarred walls and heavy doors jammed crooked in their tracks, through the main entry where festoons of shattered com equipment hung from the ceiling. They pressed through the gate, its sculptured metal leaves hanging at crazy angles, and out into the open. The air was bitter with the stench of burning.

What he saw was so unexpected that Deltander twisted around to check the facade of the building behind him: they should be facing the governmental plaza. There were no buildings in sight. Where a thriving city had stood a smoking waste stretched to the horizon.

The roar of the crowd was deafening.

Andur's triumphant yell cut across even the jubilation of the Varr partisans. Teyr half on his shoulder, Andur challenged the very sun in the blue, smoke-streaked sky. Looking at him, Del's eyes watered from the smoke and brightness.

Teyr lifted Andur's knife, red-edged with his own blood, high in the air. The horde made a feral sound.

Deltander shuddered. *What's happening*, he wondered, looking at Andur's savage glee. *What's happening, Andur?*

215

But Andur was straining to look back and up. At Teyr, black hair flying into wings and feathers in the wind that also whipped Andur with his Kel manhood braid. As the close-packed bodies beneath him carried him closer, Del could see grey at Andur's temples, deep lines radiating from the corners of his eyes.

Laughing with the man who shared Teyr's heavy weight, Andur reached up, making a game of getting back his knife. He got it, and said something to Teyr, who gripped his carriers' shoulders.

Andur released his hold, caught his plait, pulled it sideways, and sawed at it with the blade. One stroke. Two. The rope of hair parted.

Andur threw it to the crowd.

He pledged it, thought Del. *He pledged it if we got out safe.*

There was a circle of striving bodies and Del saw the long strands pulled apart by eager hands. Then it was gone.

Andur tossed his head as he sheathed his knife and the final twists sprang free. He and Teyr looked up as one to watch the thunder coming down the sky.

Del shaded his eyes and looked up, too.

Then everyone was pointing, waving, and the mass of people began running again. Del held on to the hard muscles beneath him, fearful of falling beneath pounding feet.

There were lighters landing on the fuming plain, black and white logos vivid in the sun. Del could see Ibeigne, riding the crest of the mob, hear the hunting cry of this human pack as they started for their ships.

Deltander felt very cold. *It's the wind*, he told himself. *It takes the warmth out of the sunshine.* Caught in a tide of bodies, he was carried after the rest.

www.ingramcontent.com/pod-product-compliance
Lightning Source LLC
Chambersburg PA
CBHW030307180626
46810CB00003B/960